THE ALPHABET SLEUTHS

Also by Laura Jensen Walker

The Bookish Baker Mysteries

MURDER MOST SWEET
DEADLY DELIGHTS

The Faith Chapel Mysteries

HOPE, FAITH & A CORPSE

The Nightingale Mysteries

DEATH OF A FLYING NIGHTINGALE

The Getaway Girls Series

DARING CHLOE
TURNING THE PAIGE
BECCA BY THE BOOK

The Phoebe Grant Series

DREAMING IN BLACK AND WHITE
DREAMING IN TECHNICOLOR

Novels

MISS INVISIBLE
RECONSTRUCTING NATALIE

THE ALPHABET SLEUTHS

Laura Jensen Walker

First world edition published in Great Britain and the USA in 2026
by Severn House, an imprint of Canongate Books Ltd,
14 High Street, Edinburgh EH1 1TE.

severnhouse.com

Cover and jacket design by © Jet Purdie

British Library Cataloguing-in-Publication Data
A CIP catalogue record for this title is available from the British Library.

ISBN-13: 978-1-4483-1729-5 (cased)
ISBN-13: 978-1-4483-1896-4 (paper)
ISBN-13: 978-1-4483-1730-1 (e-book)

All Severn House titles are printed on acid-free paper.

Typeset by Palimpsest Book Production Ltd., Falkirk, Stirlingshire, Scotland.
Printed and bound in Great Britain by TJ Books, Padstow, Cornwall.

The manufacturer's authorised representative in the EU for product safety is Authorised Rep Compliance Ltd, 71 Lower Baggot Street, Dublin D02 P593 Ireland (arccompliance.com)

Praise for Laura Jensen Walker

"Well-crafted and suspenseful . . . a celebration of the power and wisdom of women of a 'certain age'"
Amy Patricia Meade, author of the Evelyn Galloway Mysteries

"You'll both laugh and feel your heart race while you turn pages as fast as you can"
Maddie Day, author of the Cozy Capers Book Group Mysteries

"Charming. Put the kettle on, cozy fans, and settle down for a treat"
Catriona McPherson, Anthony Award-winning author, on *Hope, Faith & a Corpse*

"The author's humor engages, the twists and turns in the mystery intrigue, and the resolution will both surprise and satisfy any reader who loves a good cozy"
Edith Maxwell, Agatha Award-winning author, on *Hope, Faith & a Corpse*

"Pleasing . . . [Hope is] witty, clever, and kind"
Publishers Weekly on *Hope, Faith & a Corpse*

"Even the suspects are likable in this warmhearted, humorous addition to the pantheon of clerical sleuths"
Kirkus Reviews on *Hope, Faith & a Corpse*

"Entertaining . . . Lively characters complement the twisty plot"
Publishers Weekly on *Deadly Delights*

About the author

Bestselling, award-winning author **Laura Jensen Walker** is the Agatha- and Lefty-nominated author of more than twenty books, including the cozy mysteries *Murder Most Sweet*, *Deadly Delights,* and *Hope, Faith & a Corpse*, and historical mystery *Death of a Flying Nightingale*.

A rabid Anglophile since being stationed at an RAF base with the USAF in her twenties, Laura lives in Northern California with her Renaissance-man husband and two rescue terriers, where she drinks tea and dreams of England.

laurajensenwalker.com

For Sandy Munro
And in loving memory of Sharon Hetland, Lonnie Hull DuPont, and Lisa Jensen Cook.
Thank you for the joy and laughter you brought to my life.
And all the love.
Every woman needs Alphabet Girls like you.

Age cannot wither her, nor custom stale her infinite variety.

—Shakespeare

Age is an issue of mind over matter. If you don't mind, it doesn't matter.

—Mark Twain

ONE

Claire Reynolds hadn't planned to kill a man that day, but stuff happens.

The older you get, the more you realize sometimes things happen that are out of your control, and you just have to make the best of it. Claire was ready to make the best of her life. The most of her life. At sixty-nine, she was changing it up. Saying no. And loving it. For more than sixty years, she had done what everyone else wanted. Her parents. Her husband. Her kids.

No more.

First, she packed away her laptop. Claire refused to spend her golden years staring at a computer screen. She had better things to do with her time.

Like building houses with Habitat for Humanity.

Rescuing a shelter dog.

Learning to rollerblade.

Next, she sold the too-big, too-beige house in the fifty-five-plus golf course community her husband had insisted they buy. Then she took the vacation she'd been dreaming of for years. Alone. To her favorite place on earth: England. When the kids were growing up, vacations had meant Disneyland, "the happiest place on earth."

Claire would be happy if she never saw a pair of Mickey Mouse ears again.

After walking in the footsteps of her BritBox and literary heroes on that sceptered isle, Claire decided to take a page from Jane Austen's book. There's a lot to be said for living a quiet life surrounded by books, art, music, and flowers. With an occasional adventure thrown in.

Lockdown helped.

At the start of the pandemic, for the safety of their residents, the management of Cedar Glen Retirement Community in Santa Bonita, California, instituted a "No Outside Visitors" policy. Claire was content alone in her condo with her books and her dog, but her next-door neighbor Atsuko said it wasn't good for their mental health to be so isolated.

"Ahtz-ko Kimura," as she'd introduced herself, and Claire formed a pod with the neighbors flanking them: Barbara Wright and Daphne Cole. Botoxed Barbara with her long legs and gravity-defying breasts dubbed Atsuko, Barbara, Claire, and Daphne *the Alphabet Girls*. It took time for the women to bond, but watching out for each other during those difficult days helped them forge a deep friendship.

Atsuko met Claire at the clubhouse on Thursday for coffee—tea in Claire's case—on a crisp fall morning, five years after the modern-day plague upended the world. The clubhouse was a popular gathering place for Cedar Glen's seniors, with its seventy-inch flat-screen TV, Tuesday night bingo, and six-days-a-week breakfast buffet. Inside, Atsuko found her friend reheating a cup of tea in the microwave. Claire had returned from England a tea snob, drinking only black English tea and *never* Lipton.

Nibbling a croissant, Claire asked Atsuko, "Is your granddaughter still in Uganda?"

"Yes, her field assignment ends next month. Then she'll come home for a visit." Atsuko gave Claire a wry smile. "My daughter is pressuring her to stay and get a job nearby, but Tomiko's determined to go where there's the greatest need." She stirred her coffee. "For which I applaud her. As one of the Doctors without Borders, my granddaughter is a smart woman perfectly capable of making her own choices. It's not for me to hold her back."

"Spoken like a wise grandmother."

"There has to be some benefit to getting old."

"There is. The benefit of not giving a damn." Daphne, balancing coffee and croissant precariously in one hand, joined them.

Jumping up, Claire relieved her fellow Alphabet Girl of her

hot coffee, as Daphne eased herself into a chair. "Why didn't you ask for help, silly?"

Daphne scowled at the sling supporting her right arm. "I'm sick of asking for help, and I'm sick of this thing."

"Your shoulder surgery was only a week and a half ago," Atsuko said. "You need to take it easy. There's no shame in asking for help. That's what friends are for."

"Don't go all Dionne Warwick on me."

"Ooh, I love that song." Botoxed Barbara sang a snatch of the '80s tune as she joined the girls, setting her smoothie on the table.

Daphne grimaced at the green concoction. "I don't know how you can drink that stuff."

"Kale's good for you. It's full of antioxidants and helps the body flush out toxins."

"And tastes like crap." Daphne bit into her croissant, crumbs flaking onto her Hawaiian shirt. "I'll stick with chocolate." She closed her eyes. "M'mm, heaven."

Barbara's eyes flicked to the former cop's muffin top poking above her sweatpants. Giving her snug yoga pants a reassuring pat, she reminded the girls, "Don't forget; we vote for book club selections tonight."

Daphne groaned. "Please tell me you're not bringing another celebrity 'you too can be fabulous at any age' book."

Barbara bristled. "What's wrong with wanting to be fabulous at our age?"

"And what age is that, exactly?" Claire tilted her pixie head at Barbara, shooting her an innocent look.

"It's not polite to ask a woman her age."

"Politeness is overrated." Atsuko smoothed her silver bob. "I don't care who knows I'm seventy-five."

"I'm happy to have made it to my sixties." A shadow crossed Daphne's freckled face. "I didn't think I'd live to see fifty, much less sixty-two."

Daphne rarely talked about her time as a cop, apart from joking about the stupid criminals she'd encountered during her career. Claire had glimpsed the scars, though, and knew her friend had been through the wars.

Barbara leaned toward Claire, blue eyes alight. "I've had the best idea for your seventieth birthday next month. Let's go skydiving!"

"No thanks," Claire said. "I prefer staying *inside* the plane."

"Exactly," Daphne, who'd been a sergeant in the Air Force back in the day, agreed. "The pilots I worked with always said, 'Why would I want to jump out of a perfectly good airplane?'"

"For the rush of it," the B member of their group said.

"I get enough of a rush finding my way out of IKEA." Atsuko lifted her coffee mug to her lips.

"Aw, c'mon girls," Barbara wheedled. "Where's your sense of excitement?"

"I'm excited by Taco Tuesday," Daphne said, "or when I find socks that match."

"OK, scratch skydiving, then. We can go ziplining instead."

"Now *that's* a possibility. Ziplining looks like fun." Glimpsing her nonagenarian friend at the coffee bar, Claire gave Evelyn a half wave.

Seeing her wave, Lenny Fink, Cedar Glen's most flirtatious resident, sidled over with Vince Merlucci, his partner-in-crime. "Good morning, ladies." Lifting his hat, Lenny revealed his bad gray rug. "Claire, that blouse really brings out your eyes. Maybe your eyes and mine can meet at Red Lobster tonight." Pulling a piece of paper from the pocket of his '70s polyester leisure suit, he added, "I have a two-for-one coupon." Eighty-year-old Lenny still fancied himself a ladies' man. He was unwilling to accept that times had changed, and so had women.

And fashion.

Vince, who in his '60s bowling shirt looked like an older, more dissolute version of Charlie Sheen, ogled Barbara. Smoothing his bottle-black combover with an age-spotted hand, he said, "I have a coupon too, gorgeous. Whaddya say we make it a foursome?"

Daphne waggled her eyebrows at Barbara. "Yeah, gorgeous, whaddya say?"

Barbara shot Daphne a quelling glance before turning to Vince and Lenny. "Sorry, y'all," she said, her Texas drawl resurfacing. "I already have plans. So does Claire. Tonight's book club."

* * *

Daphne took a tramadol to ease the pain in her shoulder as she settled into her recliner with a Lee Child novel. She loved Jack Reacher. Jack was the *man*—making short shrift of any bad guy who crossed his path and always coming out on top.

Too bad real life wasn't like fiction.

Fifteen years as a cop had shown Daphne that all too often it was the bad guys who came out on top, and sometimes those bad guys were in law enforcement. Shaking her graying ponytail at the unwelcome memories, she drained her Coke.

Claire pushed herself up from the garden kneeling pad to admire the results of the red geraniums nestled in among the lavender and coreopsis ringing her patio. She'd hit some tree roots and had to use the shovel to break through the roots and turn the soil. Now, shovel on her shoulder and gallon pot of geraniums in hand, she headed next door.

She had been teaching her neighbor how to plant flowers, but Daphne's recent shoulder surgery had intruded. Claire decided to surprise her and finish the planting. Finding Daphne's patio gate ajar, and with her hands full, she nudged open the gate with her foot. Since her surgery, Daphne napped a lot, and Claire didn't want to wake her. Having been through a few major surgeries herself, she knew sleep was an important part of the healing process.

Intent on her mission, Claire moved on soundless rubber-soled garden clogs across the patio, setting down the pot of geraniums. *Now, where's the best place to plant these?* She glanced about the space littered with sports equipment and overflowing bags of Coke cans for recycling. Hearing an odd noise, she turned.

Claire gasped when she saw a bulky figure in a hooded sweatshirt inside, pinning Daphne to her recliner. The man's hands were around Daphne's throat, and she was making choking sounds. *Oh my God.* Grasping her shovel with both hands, Claire charged through the open sliding glass door and hit the intruder on the back of the head.

Hard.

He fell to the floor, unconscious.

Coughing, Daphne grasped at her throat.

"Oh my God, Daphne, are you OK?"

She nodded, eyes streaming. "Water," she wheezed.

Claire rushed to the kitchen. Handing the glass of water to Daphne, she saw the handprints on her friend's throat and felt sick. Grateful to see the figure on the floor still unconscious, she asked, "Did he break in?"

Massaging her throat, Daphne said, "I left the patio door open to get some air. I dozed off and woke up to him choking me." She eyed the blood seeping onto the blue area rug. Pushing herself out of the recliner with her unencumbered arm, she winced as she bent down beside her attacker. Placing her fingers on the man's thick neck, Daphne expelled a sigh.

"He's dead."

"*Dead?*" Claire staggered, feeling faint. "Oh my God. I *killed* someone?" Stomach roiling, she pulled out her phone with a shaking hand.

"Stop," Daphne ordered. "Don't call the cops."

TWO

Barbara pulled on her Spanx. Hard as she'd tried—daily jogging, doing sit-ups, increasing her gym workouts—she couldn't get rid of the tummy pooch that showed up at sixty. Spanx was the only thing that gave Barbara the flat stomach she'd had all her life. Sixty was well in her rear-view mirror now, but apart from the DMV and her doctor, no one knew her age.

And Barbara was determined to keep it that way.

"It's our secret," she said to the vintage doll occupying pride of place on her dresser. Glancing at Barbie, she observed wryly, "No tummy pooch on *you*." Then she headed out on her daily run.

Earbuds in, Barbara jogged along Cedar Glen's shady pathways, singing along to Beyonce's "Put a Ring on It." Multiple men had put a ring on her back in the day, but after her third divorce, Barbara decided she wasn't cut out for marriage. Hailing from the land of big hair and beauty pageants, she wed the high school football hero after graduation. Three weeks after divorcing her football crush, who turned out *not* to be a hero, she eloped to Mexico on the back of a bad boy's Harley.

Marriage number two ended the day Barbara walked in on her husband in bed with a barmaid who'd overdone the peroxide. She miscarried the next day.

Barbara shook off the unwelcome memories as "Shake it Off" filled her ears. She loved Taylor Swift. So did Daphne. Her retired cop pal had started creating a playlist of Taylor's latest songs until she had to stop when she messed up her shoulder. Barbara had offered to finish the playlist for Daphne, but kept getting sidetracked.

No time like the present. Pivoting, Barbara jogged toward Daphne's condo, enjoying the cool September breeze after the scorching heat of August. On the way, she ran into Atsuko, a Tupperware container in her hands. "What do you have there, Atsuko?"

"Mochi for Daphne."

"I love mochi."

"If you're nice, I might give you some."

"I'm always nice."

Atsuko lifted an eyebrow.

"Well, most of the time."

An unsteady Claire sat on the couch in Daphne's living room.

"Take deep breaths," Daphne instructed. "Nice and easy. That's it."

Unable to look at the dead man, Claire fixed brown eyes on her friend. "Why can't I call the police?"

"I know that guy."

"You *know* him? How?"

"I arrested him years ago. He'd killed someone, and I was first on the scene. Thanks to my testimony, Benny—that's his name, Benny Popov—went to prison. He told me when he got out, he'd kill me." Daphne lifted her shoulders in a shrug. "I didn't know he'd been released."

"He came here to make good on his promise?"

"Evidently."

"And if I hadn't shown up, he'd have killed you?"

"You got it." Daphne patted Claire's hand. "Thanks for saving my life. I owe you."

"You'd do the same for me." Claire's eyes flicked to the figure on the floor. She still couldn't believe she'd killed a man and that he was lying only a few feet away. Daphne seemed to take it all in stride, but then she'd probably seen a lot of dead bodies in her former profession.

A green bottle fly buzzed overhead. Zooming to the body, it landed in the blood.

Claire gagged, ran to the kitchen, and threw up in the sink. When she returned to the living room, Daphne handed her a mint. Keeping her eyes averted from the dead man, Claire said, "Now, tell me why we can't inform the authorities this Benny person was in the process of strangling you, and I stopped him." She swallowed hard. "Permanently."

"It's complicated. And dangerous. The less you know, the better."

A light tap sounded at the front door. "Daphne," Barbara trilled as she and Atsuko entered, "we come bearing gifts." Seeing the body and blood on the floor, she screamed.

Atsuko approached at a clip, mochi in hand. "Is it a workman? Did he fall? Have you called 911?" She pulled out her phone.

"Put that away," Daphne said. "It's not a workman, and he's dead."

Atsuko blanched. "Dead?"

"Yes, and I killed him," Claire said, trying to make peace with the fact. Knowing the man had been a convicted murderer in the process of killing her friend helped.

"*What?*" Barbara gaped at Claire.

"I walked in on him strangling Daphne and hit him in the head with my shovel."

"Claire saved my life," Daphne said.

"Oh my God." Barbara's eyes were huge above taut cheeks.

"And for some reason, we can't call the police," Claire said. "Daphne says it would be dangerous."

A loud knock sounded.

"Daphne?" Condo manager Connie called from the other side of the front door—the door that, thankfully, Atsuko had closed behind her. "Are you OK? Someone said they heard a scream."

"I'm fine," Daphne yelled. "We were just playing a game."

A game? Atsuko mouthed.

Yanking the Dodgers blanket from the back of the couch, Claire dropped it over the dead man. She hustled to the entryway, stopping before the unlocked door. "Everything's OK, Connie," she said, raising her voice. "We were playing charades, and Barbara got carried away. You know how competitive she is."

Barbara blew Claire a kiss.

"Well, please keep it down in future, ladies. One of the residents passing by thought someone was being murdered."

Claire gave a weak laugh. "Only at charades. Atsuko and I killed Barbara and Daphne."

"I want a rematch," Daphne bellowed.

After getting rid of the condo manager, Claire opened the fridge and grabbed a six-pack of Mike's Hard Lemonade. Opening a bottle, she took a long drink before returning to the others.

Barbara held out her hand. "I'll take one of those."

"Me, too," Daphne said.

Atsuko shook her head. "You're not supposed to mix alcohol and painkillers, Daph. I don't want you passing out on us. I'll have yours." Taking a swig, she pinned the D member of the group with her dark brown eyes. "Pray enlighten us as to why we can't inform the police that Claire killed this man in self-defense to save your life."

"I can't get into the details. It would put you in danger. I realize what I'm asking is out of the ordinary"—Daphne fiddled with her ponytail—"and I hate that you've been pulled into something I can't explain. But there are other forces at work here—ugly forces—and if the police get involved, it's not only me who is at risk—it's all of you. The less you know, the better. You'll just have to trust me."

The Alphabet Girls exchanged glances. Slowly, as one, they nodded their assent.

Claire stole a peek at the blanket-covered mound. "What about *him*?"

"Won't his family miss him?" Atsuko asked. As the reigning matriarch of her family, third-generation Japanese American Atsuko took pains not to interfere in her children's or grandchildren's lives. But if one of them were to disappear, she would move heaven and earth to find them.

"He didn't have a family," Daphne said. "Other than a wife who divorced him years ago when he went to prison for murder."

Barbara gave her an appraising look. "Cagney," she said, using the nickname she'd assigned her pal from her favorite '80s TV show, "am I right in thinking you're the cop who put him away?"

"Yup. Something that didn't make me very popular with his buddies." She reverted to cop speak. "The deceased has some nasty friends. Ones I don't want you to meet. That's why we have to get rid of the body before someone comes looking for him." Daphne furrowed her forehead. "I just need to figure out where and how."

"We wrap him in the rug and blanket—they're both ruined anyway—and dump him in the middle of nowhere," Barbara said matter-of-factly. "The desert's always a good place, or a lake. A quarry or construction site could also work."

The girls gaped at her.

Barbara shrugged. "I watched *The Sopranos*, and my second husband was in the Mexican Mafia." Which was why, after the initial shock, Barbara had recovered enough not to be bothered by the dead man on the ground. This wasn't the first corpse she had encountered.

Daphne took charge. "We'll have to wait until tonight when everyone's asleep before we can move him. We'll take him to that construction site downtown where they're putting up a new office building. Some of the crew were at McDonald's last night. I heard them say they're pouring the foundation tomorrow morning."

"Perfect," Barbara said. "Concrete hides a multitude of sins."

"You don't think they'll notice a body dropped in the hole before they pour the cement?" Claire asked.

"No, because we'll have dug down a few feet and buried him." Daphne scowled at her sling. "Correction. *You'll* have dug down a few feet. I won't be much help."

"You can be the lookout," Atsuko said.

"What will we wear?" Barbara eyed her Barbie-pink yoga pants, admiring her perfect thighs. "All black, I assume. I think I'll wear my black turtleneck and leggings." She frowned. "I'll have to buy a black beanie to cover my hair, though. You girls will need to get some too. Should we wear masks? I have a gorgeous Venetian mask from a costume party I went to a few years ago."

"The idea is to be invisible, B," Daphne said. "Not stand out."

Atsuko made a face. "Women over sixty are always invisible."

"Not when there's four of them all dressed in black, wearing matching beanies and outlandish masks," Claire said.

"Exactly." Daphne adjusted her sling. "Just wear dark clothes and rubber-soled shoes."

Atsuko wrinkled her nose at the blanket-draped mound. Having worked in her uncle's mortuary a summer when she was in college, dead bodies didn't faze her. But messes did. "I have some industrial-strength trash bags we can use so we won't drip blood all over the floor." Atsuko kept an immaculate house, the total antithesis of Daphne's condo full of bobble-heads, assorted sports paraphernalia, and empty takeout containers.

"Good idea." Daphne cast a sorrowful glance at the Dodgers blanket. "That was my favorite blanket. I got it after Gibson's historic homer off Eckersley in the bottom of the ninth in game one of the '88 Series."

Claire's eyes glazed over the way they did whenever anyone talked sports. "Sorry, Daph. I thought Connie was coming in, and I grabbed the first thing I could see to hide him."

"You didn't think she would notice a large mound on the floor?" Barbara said.

Claire cut her eyes to a messy pile of clothes in the corner. "Connie would just think it's more of Daphne's laundry."

"Are you saying I'm a slob, Claire?" Daphne asked.

"If the Hawaiian shirt fits."

Inside the entryway of her home, Atsuko slipped off her ballet flats. Padding to the kitchen in bare feet, she filled the teakettle and pulled out the box of green tea from the cupboard. While she waited for the water to boil, she placed the small ceramic container and fragrant sandalwood on the teak coffee table in front of her IKEA slipcovered sofa.

Atsuko needed to prepare herself for what was to come. She had never buried a body before. Not illegally, at least. What if they were caught? What kind of repercussions would there be? Would her children ever forgive her if she was sent to prison? She picked up the wood-framed photo from the table, taken over a decade ago before Kenichi had died and when she still lived in Hawaii. Atsuko's fingers traced her husband's face. They had had a good life together. A good marriage. One of equality, love, and respect.

Unlike Claire's.

After her husband died, Atsuko moved to Santa Bonita to be closer to her children and grandchildren in Northern California.

The kettle whistled, and she made herself a cup of tea. Carrying the cup to the living room, she lit the incense burner. Then Atsuko closed her eyes and began to meditate.

Next door, Claire made a cup of tea as well, removing the gold-rimmed teacup with pink roses from the corner cupboard. She had happened upon the vintage Royal Albert in a Cotswolds antique shop on vacation and been smitten. Pink roses and pink peonies were Claire's favorite flowers. She thought of how much she would miss her china if she was sent to prison for murder.

It wasn't murder, she reminded herself; it was self-defense.

Claire added milk and sugar to her Yorkshire Gold. Today, though, she added an extra sugar. The Brits had taught her that a nice hot cup of sugary tea could fix anything. Father Brown's housekeeper always brought the priest and his troubled parishioners in the Cotswolds a cup of tea. So did the housekeeper of that good-looking vicar on *Grantchester*. Up in the remote North, though, the frumpy DCI with the green hat and trench coat, who always called everyone "pet," had someone else bring a cuppa when she delivered bad news to a murder victim's family.

Claire hoped the tea would work its magic on this accidental murderer as well.

As she sipped from the delicate china cup, Elinor jumped onto the couch, nestling in beside her and giving her hand a reassuring lick. The spaniel-terrier rescue mix always seemed to know when she needed comfort.

Claire drew great comfort from her home. Her sanctuary.

Stepping into her condo was like stepping into a cozy English cottage. A warm hug.

Picking up *All Creatures Great and Small* from the coffee table, Claire snuggled in to try to read again the soothing stories of the Yorkshire country vet to calm her nerves. In a matter of hours, she would be burying someone she had killed. *She had killed.* How was that even possible? The hand holding the book shook. How in heaven's name were the Alphabet Girls ever going to get away with what they were about to do?

What if it all went wrong and they wound up in jail?

Daphne's eyes kept drifting to the back of the brown leather couch. She shuddered, remembering Benny's face looming over her. His dark, beady eyes burning into hers, filled with hate, his thin mouth twisted into a sick grin as he strangled her. The sour smell of his sweat and the beef jerky on his breath. She had thought for sure she was a goner.

And she would have been if not for Claire. Daphne crossed herself.

The girls had wrapped her Dodgers blanket around the dead Benny, rolled him into the stained rug, tied the rug with twine, and placed the corpse inside the two giant Hefty bags Atsuko had provided. Before they did, though, Atsuko removed keys, wallet, and phone from the dead man's pocket and gave them to Daphne. After tying the plastic bags shut, the Alphabet Girls dragged the dead man behind the couch, waiting until dark to take out the trash.

Looking down at the bare floor, Daphne offered up a silent thanks to the Cedar Glen Management for replacing the wall-to-wall carpet in all the condos the month before with luxury vinyl plank flooring. The water-resistant, pet-resistant, impervious-to-stains vinyl that resembled wood was easy to clean.

After depositing Benny behind the couch, Atsuko scrubbed the floor with a vinegar and water mixture, removing every trace of blood and grime. Barbara suggested bleach, but Claire and Atsuko said bleach would ruin the wood-like flooring.

They should know. Those two were the queens of clean.

Daphne scrolled through Benny's burner phone. A familiar number came up on the screen. It had been a long time since she had seen that number, but she recognized it straightaway. Going to the kitchen, she pulled out a hammer from the junk drawer and smashed the phone to bits.

THREE

Ninety-four-year-old Evelyn Blair, Cedar Glen's resident curmudgeon, shook her fist at the gardeners. "Turn off those damn leaf blowers! A person can't think with all that racket."

Claire agreed with Evelyn on the subject of leaf blowers—that's how they'd first met.

Five or six years ago—pre-pandemic—as Evelyn approached the clubhouse one morning, she noticed an attractive woman who appeared to be in her mid-sixties sitting on one of the benches, reading. Or, rather, trying to read.

The paperback sat face down on the silver-haired stranger's lap, and the woman had her hands clapped over her ears. Catching sight of Evelyn, she smiled and lowered her hands. "You'd think with all the technology of today, the least they could do is make quiet leaf blowers. Hi, I'm Claire. I just moved in."

"Evelyn." The noise receded as the gardeners moved away, and she sat down on the bench beside Cedar Glen's newest resident.

"I've always been hypersensitive to noise," Claire said. "I can't stand blaring TV commercials, loud music, or revving motorcycles. It's not an age thing either; I've been this way my whole life. In high school, while most of my classmates were rocking out to Led Zeppelin and Queen, I was enjoying the Carpenters and Peter, Paul, and Mary."

"I love Peter, Paul, and Mary," Evelyn said. "I saw them in concert in the sixties." As the two women talked, they discovered they both loved books—mysteries in particular.

Now, today, gripping her walker, Evelyn shuffled away from the gardeners, muttering, "Whatever happened to good old-fashioned rakes? Everyone's so lazy these days. Everything has to be motorized or computerized. No wonder the world's gotten so soft."

* * *

Barbara jogged to the gated parking lot, the dead man's keys in her fist. Checking to be sure no one saw her, she wove among the parked cars, pushing the fob button. Daphne had tasked her with finding Benny's car.

"I doubt he'll park it inside the gate—too conspicuous—but you never know. Benny was never the sharpest tool in the shed," Daphne said before sending Barbara on her mission.

Reaching the front row of cars, Barbara noticed Connie coming out of the office. When the condo manager stopped to talk to one of the residents, Barbara shoved the keyring into her bra. Then she did a high lunge and tree pose.

"Hi, Barbara," Connie said, drawing near. "What's up?"

"Just doing a couple of stretches."

"I thought you always did your yoga at home or in the clubhouse."

"Usually, but I've been jogging, and my muscles felt a little tight, so I stopped to loosen up. You should join my yoga class sometime. It does wonders." Barbara winked. "It's good for your sex life too. Makes you nice and limber."

Blushing the way she did whenever any of the Cedar Glen seniors brought up sex, Connie peeked at her Apple Watch. "Sorry, I have to run, or I'll be late picking up my daughter."

Barbara jogged in place until Connie's RAV-4 pulled out of the complex. Then, fishing the keyring out of her bra, she continued her search. Realizing the dead man's car was not in the parking lot, she headed toward the street when something caught her eye.

Mark Scott.

Barbara watched as the new handyman squatted on his haunches in black bicycle shorts, tinkering with the chain on his ten-speed. Admiring the view of the muscled calves, lean, cyclist's body, and well-defined pecs, "The Girl from Ipanema" played in her head.

No man boobs there.

Not an ounce of fat anywhere that she could see. *He can leave his shoes under my bed any time*, Barbara thought, and not for the first time. Ever since the sixty-six-year-old retired teacher-cum-handyman, who still had all his hair, had moved in six months ago, Barbara had set her nightcap for him.

She wasn't the only one.

Most of the single women at Cedar Glen fluttered around the widower who looked like Denzel Washington, but Mark Scott had proven immune to their charms.

Smoothing down her form-fitting leggings and sucking in her tiny pooch, Barbara approached the widower. "Hello, Mark," she said in a breathy voice reminiscent of Marilyn Monroe. "Going for a ride?" She stopped herself from adding the sexy follow-up on the tip of her tongue, but the X-rated proposition flashed neon in her head.

And other places.

Straightening, Mark stood up. "I like to get in a nightly ride before dinner."

"Perhaps I could join you one of these nights."

"I like to ride alone. No offense. Clears my head."

"I understand. Jogging does that for me." Barbara flexed her toned calf. "Maybe we can have dinner sometime instead. I make a great shrimp Cobb salad."

"I'm afraid I wouldn't be very good company."

"Barbara," a familiar voice called out. "Daphne's looking for you."

Barbara turned to see Claire in a navy-blue button-down and jeans, standing at the edge of the parking lot, her silver pixie backlit by the setting sun. "I'll be right there." Turning back to Mark, she found him astride his ten-speed, putting on his bicycle helmet. Barbara gave the handsome handyman a bright smile. "Have a good ride."

Claire joined Barbara as Mark cycled away. "Did you find the car?"

"Not yet. I was about to check the street but got distracted."

"I saw."

Five minutes after midnight, the Alphabet Girls headed to the construction site downtown with a dead body and three shovels hidden beneath a tarp in the back of Atsuko's SUV. Daphne rode shotgun while Atsuko drove, and Claire and Barbara sat in the back seat—all four in dark clothes. A black baseball cap covered Barbara's layered blonde bob.

As they approached the office building under construction downtown, Daphne adjusted her glasses and scowled. She slapped her hand on the dashboard. "Crap. I should have realized there'd be CCTV cameras."

Claire, sitting behind her, peered out the side window. "Where?"

"Don't look. Turn your head as if you're talking to Barbara," Daphne ordered.

Earlier, Barbara had finally located Benny's rental car, a silver Ford Focus, parked down the street. At Daphne's instruction to look like frumpy old ladies no one would pay any attention to, Claire and Atsuko put on shapeless, neutral-colored clothing. Their mission, which they'd chosen to accept, was to drive the Ford to a strip mall on the edge of town far from Cedar Glen.

"There's a bar there called the Muddy Pig Saloon where Benny used to hang out back in the day," Daphne told them. "It would make sense that Benny would go there after he got out of the joint, so his car being there wouldn't be unusual."

Barbara pouted. "Why can't I go?"

"You don't blend in, Blondie. You could never pass for a frumpy old lady." Daphne glanced at Claire and Atsuko. "No offense."

"None taken," Claire said. "I like being invisible. Miss Marple's invisible. People always underestimate her."

Claire parked the Ford Focus in the far corner of the Muddy Pig parking lot, and Atsuko scanned the area before they exited the car. "All clear."

Flexing her fingers in her church-lady gloves, Claire said, "Let's do this." The white gloves had been her idea. Daphne had insisted they wear gloves so as not to leave behind fingerprints, grabbing some blue latex ones left over from the early days of the pandemic.

Claire sent a dubious look at the latex. "I thought the point was to be invisible. That blue will make us stick out like a sore thumb. I have a better idea." She left, returning moments later with two pairs of vintage white gloves with pearl button clasps at the wrist.

Barbara released a fond smile. "I used to have a pair just like that."

"When? The sixties?" Daphne grunted. "Women haven't worn gloves since the Dark Ages."

"Tell that to Amal Clooney and Blake Lively," Barbara said. "It was only a few years ago when Amal wore white opera gloves to the Golden Globes to complement her stunning black Dior gown, and Blake wore them to the Met Gala with that gorgeous copper Versace dress whose color changed to Statue-of-Liberty blue when the train was unfurled." Barbara puffed out a blissful sigh. "Breathtaking."

"This isn't the Met Gala," Daphne said. "The point is *not* to stand out. Remember?"

"We won't stand out," Claire reassured her. "We'll just look like prim and proper little old church ladies. No one will give us a second glance."

Grandmothers Claire and Atsuko exited the dead man's car and strolled away from the Muddy Pig, hunching their backs and lowering their silver heads to complete their old-lady disguise. After turning the corner, they clambered into Barbara's waiting Camry.

To celebrate the success of their mission, they went to the Dairy Queen Drive-Thru where Claire and Atsuko had chocolate-dipped cones and Barbara had a diet Sprite.

Atsuko drove away from the construction site. "Anyone want to tell me where I'm going?"

"I'm trying to think," Daphne said.

Barbara smirked in the back seat. "A scary prospect."

"What about that old quarry outside of town on the way to Walnut Grove?" Claire suggested. "It's been closed for years."

Daphne considered. "That might work, although I'm pretty sure there's a chain-link fence around the quarry." Her eyes flicked to her sling. "I scaled plenty of those fences back in my cop days, but there's no way I could climb one now." Turning in her seat, she fastened her eyes on nearly-seventy-year-old

Claire and seventy-something-or-other Barbara. "I think our fence-climbing days are behind us, ladies."

"We don't have to *climb* the fence; we just go through it." Claire held up a pair of wire cutters. She believed in being prepared at all times. She kept tissues, wet wipes, hand sanitizer, a Swiss Army knife—complete with scissors, screwdriver, pliers, nail clippers, tweezer, corkscrew, and toothpick—lozenges, breath mints, protein bars, emergency chocolate, bottled water, first-aid kit, ibuprofen, two pens, a small notebook, and the latest novel she was reading in her tote bag. And for this excursion, Claire had the foresight to include two pairs of wire cutters, a hammer, a roll of duct tape, and bleach wipes.

"You got a chainsaw in there too?" Daphne asked.

"That would make too much noise."

FOUR

At the end of the little-used dirt road, Atsuko's headlights spotlighted the "Keep Out, No Trespassing" sign in front of the abandoned quarry. She cut the engine, and Daphne did a sweep of the area, giving Barbara and Claire the go-ahead.

The two women slipped out of the SUV and strode to a section of the fence not visible from the road. Claire flicked on the heavy-duty flashlight, and Barbara began to cut.

"Damn." Barbara rocked back on her heels. "This chain link's too thick. I can't cut through it."

"Hang on." Mindful of her sling, Daphne squatted down beside them. She shone the flashlight at the bottom of the fence. "Atsuko, do you have a jack?"

"Is the Pope Catholic?"

"Whatcha thinking, Cagney?" Barbara asked.

Daphne pointed. "See those wire clips there? They attach the fence to the tension wire at the bottom. If we unscrew them and cut the tension wire, we might be able to jack up the bottom of the fence and slide beneath it."

"Worth a try." Pulling out her Swiss Army knife, Claire began unscrewing the metal clips with the small screwdriver.

Barbara knelt and cut the tension wire at the bottom. "I feel like Sydney Bristow from *Alias*."

As Atsuko returned with the car jack, Claire eyed it, saying, "Before we try to jack up the fence, shouldn't we bring the body over so we can shove it underneath?"

Daphne gave her a thumbs-up. "Good point."

After a quick consultation, it was agreed Atsuko and Claire would take one side of the dead man, while Barbara took the other.

"I'll help you, B," Daphne offered.

"Not on your life, Cagney. The last thing we need is you

reinjuring yourself and having to take you to the ER in the middle of the night dressed like this."

The three women lifted the corpse. "Oof," Barbara said, "I don't remember him being this heavy when we moved him earlier."

"Maybe that's why they call it dead weight," Atsuko said.

Claire exhaled. "I wanted some adventure in my life, but this isn't exactly what I had in mind."

Daphne beckoned from the fence with her good arm. "Hurry up."

The girls shuffled Daphne's way, straining under the weight.

Claire's hands grew sweaty, and she felt her sciatica start to flare up. *Not now*, she thought.

They continued trudging forward, with Barbara giggling as the earworm of the marching guards from *The Wizard of Oz* filled her head. *Oh-re-oh, ri-oh-oh. Oh-re-oh . . .* Distracted, she stumbled and lost her hold, cursing as she went down.

The unwieldy corpse slipped from Claire and Atsuko's hands, landing on Barbara. Atsuko swore—something she seldom did, having been raised by an etiquette-conscious mother who didn't allow bad language.

"Get him *off* me," a panicked Barbara yelled.

They rolled the dead man onto the ground, and Barbara scrambled to her feet, swiping at her front. "Eww!"

"What's the big deal?" Daphne asked. "He was double-wrapped in plastic. It's when a body's exposed to the elements, ripe and crawling with maggots, that it's gross."

"Are you *trying* to get me to hurl?" Barbara said. "Because I'd be happy to vomit all over you."

Claire held up her hands in a placating gesture. "Ladies, now is not the time." She glanced at her phone. "It's after one a.m. Chop, chop. I need to get back to Elinor. She's not used to my being out this late." Yawning, she added, "Neither am I."

Grunting, they all resumed their positions, following Daphne's flashlight beam to the fence.

After setting down the dead man, Atsuko positioned the jack beneath the bottom of the chain link and began cranking it with her foot. The fence fell off the jack. Repositioning the jack, she tried again. Once again, the chain link slipped off. "Third time's the charm," Atsuko said, angling the jack. This time, a corner of the fence raised up.

Barbara lifted the section beside it, and next to her, Claire did the same until they had a three-foot section of chain link lifted off the ground.

Protecting her bad shoulder, Daphne eased herself to the ground and wriggled backwards beneath the fence. Barbara went next, and the girls did a combination of pushing and pulling the dead man from their respective sides of the fence.

At last, the corpse made it through to the other side. Holding up her section of fence with one hand, Claire crawled through the opening, her back twinging as she did. Dropping the chain link, she managed to pull her feet out of the way just in time. As she did, however, the fence fell off the jack, leaving Atsuko trapped on the other side. "Sorry, Atsuko."

"No problem." Atsuko clambered over the fence, dropping down beside the girls with a grin and a flourish. "My mother always called me her little monkey."

Daphne moved to the quarry edge and shone her flashlight into the massive hole. "Whoo, that's a long way down. No one will find him down there." Bending and using her left hand, she began to undo one end of the trash bag.

"What are you doing?" Atsuko asked.

"We need to add some rocks."

"Rocks?" Claire said.

"So he won't float to the surface." Barbara knelt and picked up some good-sized stones.

Atsuko and Claire followed suit, passing rocks to Daphne who shoved them inside the plastic bag with her good hand. Once she'd judged they had enough, Daphne had Claire pull the ties shut.

"Wait," Claire said. "Shouldn't we say a prayer or something? You're the one who knew him, Daphne. Is there anything you'd like to say?"

"Apart from 'Thanks for croaking, Benny, before you could kill me'?" Daphne's eyes slid to the corpse. "I heard something once to the effect of if there's a Hell, it will be a packed-like-sardines adaptation of Phoenix. Enjoy Phoenix, Benny-boy."

They shoved the bulky rectangle forward, pitching it over the edge. Claire and Atsuko turned their heads. "I can't watch," Claire said.

Barbara had no such compunction.

Daphne high-fived Claire with her left hand, and Atsuko let out a whoop. "We did it!"

"Um, Cagney, you might want to see this." Barbara aimed her flashlight into the quarry.

Peering over the edge, Daphne dropped an f-bomb.

"Exactly," Barbara said. The corpse had snagged on a large rock, leaving Benny perched on a ledge, half on, half off, and visible from the top of the quarry. "You didn't see that sticking out before we launched your buddy here over the side, Cagney?" she asked.

Daphne hung her head. "No."

Claire studied the former cop. "Wait, those are your old glasses, aren't they?"

"WTAF, Daphne." Atsuko never said f-bombs, but she wasn't averse to using the texting acronym.

Barbara glowered at Daphne. "Now what are we supposed to do?"

"First, we all need to calm down," Claire said, "and come up with a solution." She shone her flashlight around. "There." She pointed to another pile of rocks a few feet away. "We can drop some of those at the hanging-off part of the body and topple it over the ledge." She marveled at how easily the word *body* came out of her mouth. In less than twenty-four hours, Claire had gone from being a law-abiding citizen who didn't even jaywalk to someone now disposing of a body illegally.

The body of a man she had killed.

Daphne strode to the rock pile.

"Not you," Claire said. "You'll mess up your shoulder."

"I can still lift with one hand. Besides, I'm the one who fu—" Daphne glanced at Atsuko. "Who screwed up. It's on me to fix this."

"We'll *all* fix it," Atsuko said. "All for one and one for all."

The four women bent as one to pick up a stone. When Claire bent over, though, pain shot through her lower back. Letting out an involuntary yelp, she straightened, grabbing at her back.

"Is it your sciatica?" Atsuko asked.

Through gritted teeth, Claire said, "I'll be fine. Don't worry about me."

"We've already got one injured woman; we don't need another," Barbara said. "We've got this, Claire." She carried a heavy rock to the quarry edge. "You man the flashlight."

Wincing, Claire popped an ibuprofen and made her way to the edge of the quarry, directing the flashlight beam to the small ledge.

Hoisting her heavy rock, Barbara heaved it toward the body, landing the stone atop the plastic-wrapped figure. Only not the part dangling over the ledge. She slapped her thigh with her baseball cap in disgust. "Great. I've just added more weight to the other end."

Daphne stepped up. Encumbered by her sling, her stone was lighter and smaller than Barbara's, but her aim was better. The rock landed on the dangling part, moving it a smidge.

"Yay, Daphne," Claire cheered.

"My turn." Atsuko lifted her rock and threw it as hard as she could. It went wide. She lifted her shoulders. "You can tell I've never played baseball."

Trudging back to the pile, the girls picked up more rocks, grunting under the weight, and tried again. And again. To no avail. The plastic-encased corpse remained stuck on the ledge.

Exhausted, the women sank to the ground. All except Claire who remained standing, hands pressed against her lower back, waiting for the ibuprofen to kick in.

Daphne expelled a sigh. "I guess that's it." *Just a matter of time now before Benny's body is found.* Once that happened, she knew the local crime family he'd worked for would come gunning for her. They'd have no idea Claire had, in fact, killed Benny, and Daphne was determined to keep it that way.

"This isn't 'it,' Cagney," Barbara said, using air quotes. "There's another option. One of us climbs down and pushes the body off the ledge."

Daphne snorted. "You're crazy. We're not Tom Cruise, and we're too old."

"I. Hate. That. Word. I am *not* old. I also hate being told I can't do something. That only makes me want to do it all the more." Jumping up, Barbara started doing stretches. "I'm strong and in good shape. It will be no problem for me to climb down and push him off."

"It's too dangerous," Claire said. "What if you slip and fall? Then we'd have two bodies. Not a good look." She teased Barbara to tamp down the rising terror she felt at the thought of her friend falling.

"OK, B," Daphne said, "maybe you *can* somehow or other climb down there and push Benny off the ledge, but how will you get back up? That's a steep-ass rock face."

"You guys will tie a rope around me and pull me back up."

Claire slapped her forehead. "Rope. That's the one thing I didn't put in my tote." She turned hopeful eyes to Atsuko. "Do you have any rope in your SUV?"

"Just a beach towel."

"There you go," Barbara said. "We can use the beach towel in place of rope."

Daphne grunted. "It won't be long enough. Face it, we're screwed."

"Barbara"—Claire adopted the voice of reason tone she'd used on her kids—"even if we did have something long enough to pull you back up, Atsuko and I wouldn't be strong enough to do so. Not with my bad back and her tiny frame."

"You're forgetting me," Daphne said.

"You're injured. You've only got one working arm."

Atsuko stood. "I may be tiny, and I'm no Tom Cruise, but I used to climb mountains in Hawaii with my husband." She turned to Barbara. "You *are* strong and fit, B, but you're also the tallest, which would make pulling you up harder." Atsuko straightened her shoulders, a determined glint in her eye. "*I'm* the one to go. I'm the lightest and the most experienced. We can fashion a harness out of my sweater." She pulled off her cardigan to demonstrate. "Now, we just need something to make a rope."

Maybe, just maybe, this might work, Daphne thought, her spirits rising. "Bring us that beach towel, Atsuko. We can cut it into strips and tie them together."

Claire pulled out her Swiss Army knife and readied the small scissors. She made four small cuts in the towel and rent it into long strips.

Barbara and Atsuko then tied the four strips together and lowered the makeshift rope over the edge.

Daphne cursed. "We're still about fifteen feet too short."

Backing away from the edge, Barbara removed her Spandex hoodie. "Take off your shirts and jackets, girls," she said. "We'll tie them together—that should give us the extra length we need."

"Take off our *shirts*?" Claire clutched her navy button-down. Apart from her doctor and Elinor, no one saw her without a shirt anymore.

"We're all girls here," Barbara said. "No one's got anything we haven't seen before." She pulled her turtleneck over her head in one fluid motion, revealing a lacy black bra covering perfect, perky breasts.

Daphne whistled. "I'll bet *those* cost a pretty penny."

"They're worth every cent."

Daphne began unbuttoning her plaid flannel. "I'll need help getting this off."

"You got it, Cagney." Barbara helped ease her friend out of her flannel shirt.

Daphne shot a rueful look at her sports bra. Shrugging her freckled shoulders, she said, "As you can see, these are my bargain-basement boobs in all their sagging glory."

"Gravity marches on for all of us." Smiling, Atsuko slipped her long-sleeved t-shirt over her head, revealing a red-and-white-checked gingham bra over small, no-longer-perky breasts.

"*Cute* bra," Barbara said.

Mustering up her courage, Claire unbuttoned her blouse with trembling fingers.

"You have tatts!" Barbara said as Claire shed her shirt. "They're gorgeous."

"Beautiful," Atsuko breathed.

Claire's bra-less chest was a work of art. A pink rose tattoo filled the spot where her left breast had formerly resided, while a pretty pink peony occupied the empty space on the right. Between her favorite flowers, a flame-red-and-gold Phoenix rose from the ashes in the center of her chest. Claire lifted her chin. "After I healed from my double mastectomy and finished chemo, I decided I wanted something beautiful in place of the breasts intent on killing me."

"And you said you weren't strong." Daphne's eyes were bright. "In my book, you're the strongest of us all."

FIVE

The four women tied their shirts and jackets together, testing the knots to ensure they were tight before adding them to the beach-towel rope. Barbara took one end, and Claire and Atsuko the other, pulling as hard as they could to make sure the clothing rope wouldn't come undone.

Barbara high-fived Daphne's good hand. "We really MacGyvered that puppy."

"We sure did, B."

Holding tight to one end, Atsuko and Claire lowered the other end of the rope to the body on the ledge.

Peering down, Daphne groaned. "Crap. Looks like we're still about three feet short."

"Are you *kidding* me?" Barbara cursed. As the girls pulled the line of cloth back up, she said, "We'll use my pants to make up the difference. They're stretchy and should give us at least another three feet." Rolling her black leggings down over slim hips, Barbara pulled them off to reveal her secret: Spandex boy shorts.

"What kind of underwear is that?" Daphne asked.

"It's called Spanx. It holds everything in."

"You don't *have* anything to hold in." Daphne grabbed her muffin top. "Not like me."

Claire hugged her arms over her bare chest, shivering in the cool night air. "Girls, can we get a move on, please? It's getting cold out here."

Barbara added her pants to the rope, pulling on the knot to be sure it wouldn't come undone. Lowering the longer make-shift rope down the rock wall, she released a sigh of relief when the leggings brushed the top of the trash bag.

Daphne pumped her fist. "Now, *that's* what I'm talkin' about."

Barbara pulled the rope back up, and Atsuko affixed one

end to her sweater harness, making sure it was secure. "OK, girls, let's do this," Atsuko said. "Claire, I need you to watch as I descend, lowering the rope a little at a time. Barbara, your job is to hold on tight to the other end and not let go. Got it?"

"Got it."

"If I tug on the rope, or yell, you need to pull me up. Fast." Atsuko gave them a thumbs-up. "Let's go."

Barbara, who in another time and another life had been raised Baptist, hadn't prayed in a long time. Now, she offered up a silent prayer for Atsuko's safety.

Lapsed Catholic Daphne crossed herself.

And Claire, who'd shed her evangelical roots along with her breasts, said an inner mantra: *Please keep her safe, please keep her safe.*

Atsuko free-soloed down the side of the quarry, finding a piece of jutting rock for a foothold.

Claire and Daphne kept their eyes glued on her, with Claire holding tight to the rope and watching as Atsuko made her careful descent, the moon highlighting her red-and-white checked bra.

What in the name of all that's holy ever possessed me to do this? Daphne wondered. *Here I am, trying to protect the girls, and now a seventy-five-year-old woman is rappelling down a frickin' rock wall in her underwear in the middle of the night. I should have put the word out I'd made Benny take a dirt nap and that would have been the end of it. The girls would never have been involved.* Resolute, she came to a decision. *If we make it out of this insanity in one piece tonight, from here on out, the Alphabet Girls will be the ABCs.*

Atsuko had forgotten how demanding and exhausting mountaineering could be. Although she walked five miles a day, did water aerobics twice a week, and practiced Tai Chi, rappelling down a rock wall was on a whole other workout plane. As well as exercising the upper and lower body, mountain climbing engaged the core muscles in ways she hadn't felt in years. She sent a plea upward: *Kenichi, my love, send me your calm and some good-luck vibes.* As Atsuko continued rappelling down the quarry wall, a wave of well-being washed over her, and she found her footing. When at last she reached the ledge, she collapsed on the Hefty corpse and gave thanks.

Up above, the women whooped and gave each other a group hug, being careful of Daphne's shoulder. All three watched as tiny Atsuko pushed the heavy rocks off the top of the black plastic one by one. They continued watching as she crouched and tried to push the body off the ledge.

The heavy body weighed down with stones so it wouldn't float.

"We did *not* think this through," Barbara said. "Remember how the three of us struggled carrying him from the car?"

"And that was *before* we added the rocks," Claire said.

"How in the world is Atsuko going to push that heavy-ass bag off the ledge?" Barbara slammed her hand on the ground. "I *knew* I should have been the one to go down there."

Daphne castigated herself. *No wonder you had to take early retirement.* The oft-repeated refrain her Southern-fried mother always said to her growing up filled Daphne's head: *You don't have the sense God gave a goose.*

Meanwhile, Atsuko sent another request heavenward. *I've reached the end of my rope, Kenichi, and can't go on. I need your help.* Spent, she bowed her head. An owl hooted and a supernatural calm descended. Raising her head, Atsuko adjusted her position to sit behind the body. Placing her feet on the unwieldy corpse, she pushed with all her might, which reminded her of the birth of her first child.

"Push," the midwife had said. "That's it; keep going. I see the head. Almost there. One last big push now." And just like that, her daughter was born.

Atsuko gave a last big push, and the body toppled off the ledge.

The other three Alphabet Girls watching from above shone the large flashlight on the hurtling Hefty bag until it disappeared, the water at the bottom of the quarry closing over it.

Claire collapsed in relief. "Thank God. Now no one, besides us, will ever know I killed a man. We can return to normal life and move on as if this never happened." She felt a tug on the rope.

"Pull her up, girls. Fast," Daphne urged.

Standing as one and digging their rubber-soled heels into the ground, the Alphabet Girls pulled.

"C'mon, Claire, put your back into it. You can do it," Barbara rah-rahed. There was a reason she'd been head cheerleader in high school.

Atsuko had intended to climb back up the quarry wall, but no longer had the energy to do so.

Bit by bit, foot by foot, the makeshift rope fell at the women's feet as they pulled Atsuko up. At last, they pulled her over the top.

All four collapsed in a heap.

"This is like when Inigo Montoya pulled Westley up to the top of the cliff in *The Princess Bride*," Barbara said. Jumping to her feet, she danced about, singing, "We Are the Champions."

"This champion needs to go to bed," a weary Atsuko said. "Let's get out of here."

Undoing the makeshift rope, the women put their tops back on and grabbed their gear. Heading back to the car, they held up the chain link for each other. They had just shut the doors of Atsuko's SUV when they heard the sound of a vehicle approaching.

"Oh my God, someone's coming!" Claire said, glimpsing headlights. "What if it's the cops? What do we do?"

Barbara scooted next to her in the back seat and put her arm around Claire. "Kiss," she commanded.

Claire eased herself into the hot tub, aiming the pounding water at her aching back. As the jets massaged her sciatica, she leaned back and closed her eyes, reliving the evening's adventure. Thankfully, it had not been cops arriving at the deserted quarry, but a teen couple seeking a private spot. When their headlights spotlighted the four seniors fake-making-out in the SUV, the young couple whooped and shouted, "Go, Grandma!"

Claire's hot tub had come with the condo—installed on the enclosed patio off the master bedroom. Initially, Claire had no intention of keeping the spa; she considered hot tubs the province of California girls, partying young people, and couples with romance on their minds.

Until the day her sciatica started acting up.

When she went to the doctor in excruciating pain, he prescribed anti-inflammatories and asked Claire if she had a Jacuzzi tub, saying they were great for loosening muscles and relieving pressure on the sciatic nerve. Regarding the hot tub with new eyes, Claire donned her navy one-piece, slipped into the water, turned on the jets, and fell in love.

She soon developed a spa routine. Three or four times a week, Claire would slip onto the private patio, drink in hand, and relax in the hot tub, leaning back and enjoying the view. There were no condos across from Claire, only an ancient weeping willow and the moon and stars. After a few weeks of this, though, she grew tired of having to peel off a wet swimsuit every time she got out of the spa.

One night, while enjoying a margarita beneath a starlit sky, Claire had a decadent thought. *What if I went into the spa au naturel?*

Naked.

Did she dare? The patio of her garden condo was private and secluded, accessible through her bedroom and an outdoor gate she always kept locked from the inside. The only way anyone could catch sight of her in her birthday suit would be if they stood on a ladder and peered over the wooden fence.

Late one night, Claire decided to be brave and take the plunge. Positioning herself on the side of the tub, she slipped off her robe, turned on the jets, and slid beneath the bubbles. Bliss. Claire had never felt so free. She wondered if the previous owner had also gone in the hot tub in the altogether. Once upon a time, the idea of a nude man in the same spa, sitting on the same seat she now occupied, would have horrified her. Claire reassured herself that draining and scrubbing the spa in concert with the regular influx of chlorine had removed all traces of anyone who had come before.

She flashed back to her teenage years, growing up in a house with one bathroom. Her best friend had warned Claire never to take a shower after her seventeen-year-old brother or she would wind up pregnant.

Sex education had come a long way since then.

Atsuko closed the door behind her and stepped out of her dusty shoes. Going to the bedroom, she stripped down and pulled on her kimono robe. Then she made herself a cup of chamomile tea, hoping it would help her sleep after the stimulating night she'd had. Had she really rappelled down a steep quarry wall with a rope made from clothes? Pushed a body off a rock ledge? Had the girls pull her back up, using that same makeshift rope—a rope that could have come loose at any moment? Atsuko remembered how her legs had shook like a jackhammer breaking concrete on the ledge, unable to go on until Kenichi sent her the owl, his favorite bird.

Domo arigato, my love.

She had to face the fact that her mountaineering days were behind her. Although . . . it would still be fun to go to one of those indoor rock-climbing walls with her granddaughter when Tomiko came to visit.

In her bedroom, Barbara pulled on the autographed Eagles t-shirt from the LA concert she'd gone to in the '70s. The one where she'd met Don Henley backstage. Barbara had moved to the Golden State after the demise of her second marriage and become a California girl—bronzed, blonde, and beautiful. She spent her days at the beach, and her nights as a cocktail waitress. Discovered by a photographer bopping along to the Beach Boys in her hot-pink bikini, Barbara became the forty-year-old photographer's model, muse, and, eventually, wife.

The concert t-shirt was wearing thin in spots and showing its age, but it was her favorite sleepwear. Grabbing her Barbie, Barbara snuggled into bed, clutching the doll. "You won't believe the night I had tonight." She thought over all that had happened in the past twenty-four hours. *What a rush! Reminds me of my days in Mexico.*

Who knew quiet Claire had it in her to whack someone, Barbara mused. *And that she had the balls to get that gorgeous tatt? Claire's badass. I wonder why she didn't get reconstruction, though. I can't imagine not having breasts . . .*

Daphne kicked off her shoes, washed down a pain pill with warm Coke, and fell on the bed in her clothes, the events of the day unspooling in her head, ending with four shirtless seniors disposing of a dead body.

All at her direction.

On the drive home, the Alphabet Girls had made a pact never to say a word to anyone about what they'd done. Claire, using one of the British expressions she loved, said, "Right then, that's done and dusted. Let's move on."

That was Daphne's plan. To move on and not expose her friends to any further danger. "Time to get the hell outta Dodge," she mumbled before falling asleep. "Tomorrow."

SIX

"Good morning," Claire sang to her plants as she watered them. Such a cheerful song from *Singin' in the Rain*. She loved musicals, but they didn't love her.

Elinor tilted her caramel head, gave Claire a mournful look, and ran back inside.

Next door, Atsuko opened her patio door and called out, "What *is* that dreadful noise?"

"Very funny." The girls were always teasing Claire about her singing, but she didn't care. Talking to plants was good for them, so singing had to be even better.

"Want to come over for breakfast?" Atsuko asked. "Omelets and fruit?"

"Let me walk Elinor first. I'll bring blueberry muffins."

"Shall we invite Daphne and Barbara?"

Claire glanced at her smartphone, checking the time. "They won't surface before ten." *Not after last night.* Unlike the B and D members of the Alphabet Girls, she had always been a morning person. Every day without fail, Claire's internal alarm clock woke her at five thirty a.m. Except for today. Since it had been almost three a.m. before Claire got to bed, she felt entitled to sleep in until nine.

Elinor scampered ahead of Claire to her favorite spot, the base of a weeping willow tree. Cedar Glen allowed dogs and cats under thirty pounds, and had designated a small park at one end of the complex for residents to bring their four-footed friends, complete with trash can and poop bag dispenser. Dogs must remain on a leash in the grassy area that boasted a small pond near the ancient willow, but were allowed off leash in the fenced-in dog run.

Claire always walked a leashed Elinor three times around the perimeter of the park before releasing her to run free in the dog run. There were just a handful of dogs in the retirement community, and most were older and friends of Elinor's, so she never felt any concern letting her into the enclosure. Today, though, as they headed to the dog run, a terrier bounded up, leash trailing and barking like mad.

"No, Brontë, no," a male voice called.

Claire scooped up a trembling Elinor and held her to her chest as the terrier at her feet continued to bark. "You're OK, sweetheart," she reassured Elinor. "I've got you."

"Sorry." Handyman Mark Scott rushed over and picked up the pup, who yipped in his arms and tried to wriggle free. "I just got her. She's not used to other dogs yet."

Beneath the scruff, Claire could see the dog only had one eye. Her heart went out to the tiny terrier.

Mark turned the tan-and-white pup to face him and said in a stern voice, "No barking, Brontë."

She ignored him and continued to yip, straining toward Elinor.

"I'm trying to train her," Mark said, "but I have a feeling obedience classes are in our future."

"Did you get her through a rescue group?"

"The pound. She was on a kill list, and I wasn't about to let that happen." He stroked the pup's wiry head. "Was I, Brontë? No one's putting *you* to sleep. You just need some love and socialization."

The terrier licked his nose.

"That's a good sign," Claire said. "Do you have any idea how she lost her eye?"

Mark's mouth tightened. "The pound said the woman who dropped her off told them she was attacked by another dog and hasn't been the same since. She also said she hadn't signed up for a deformed dog—she wanted a *pretty* puppy she could dress up."

Claire's eyes blazed. "People like that don't deserve to have dogs." She hugged Elinor close before letting her down, making sure she held tight to the leash. "This is Elinor, by the way." Slowly, she extended the back of her hand to the one-eyed terrier. "Poor baby. You're a beautiful girl, aren't you?" she cooed.

Brontë licked her hand.

"She likes you." Mark stroked his pup's back as she continued to lick Claire.

"It's obvious she's scared of other dogs, and no wonder." Claire ruffled the fur at the back of the terrier's neck, getting a wagging tail in response. "Good *girl*," she said. "You're a good girl, aren't you, Brontë? You're just scared." She rubbed the dog's neck as Mark continued to stroke Brontë's back. "Did she come with that name?"

"Her previous owner called her Blondie, but I thought she needed a new name for her new life. The names sound enough alike that I figured it wouldn't be hard for her to adjust to the change. Isn't that right, Brontë?" Mark kissed the top of his new dog's head. Gazing down at Elinor, he asked, "By chance, is your pup also named after a literary character?"

"Yes. Elinor Dashwood in *Sense and Sensibility*, my favorite Austen heroine."

On her way to Atsuko's, Claire ran into resident curmudgeon Evelyn shuffling down the walk, a glossy hardcover on the seat of her walker. Noticing the author's name, Claire said, "Ooh, is that the latest Duncan Kincaid and Gemma James mystery?"

Evelyn nodded. "I'm going to the clubhouse to read it over breakfast." She smiled at her fellow bibliophile. "Want to borrow it when I'm done?"

"Yes, please, and I'll give you the latest mystery from that hilarious Scottish author I was telling you about."

After settling Elinor in with her favorite chew toy at Atsuko's, Claire joined her friend at the breakfast table. She sipped her tea, recounting what happened at the dog park.

"That Mark sure is a handsome guy, isn't he?" Atsuko said.

"I hadn't noticed."

"You'd have to be dead not to notice."

"That part of me *is* dead, Atsuko. At this time of life, I have no interest in men. Mark did have a darling dog, though. Poor little thing." Claire took a bite of her cheese and herb omelet. "By the way, how are you feeling after last night's adventure?"

"Sore. I used muscles I haven't used in years. How about you? How's your sciatica?"

"Much better, thanks to the hot tub. It's a miracle worker."

"I love my Jacuzzi," Atsuko said. "These old bones of mine love it too."

"Good thing Barbara's not here. You know how she hates the word 'old.'"

Atsuko rolled her eyes. "I have never met a woman more obsessed with trying to stay young."

"How old do you think Barbara is?"

"Older than you and me."

"Do you really think so?"

"I do, although I'd never say that to her." Atsuko said in a conspiratorial tone, "Remember the first time we saw her vintage Barbie? Barbara said she'd asked her mom for a Barbie doll when they first came out, letting it slip that she was in fifth grade at the time." She smirked. "I researched it and found out Barbie debuted in 1959. Since fifth graders are usually ten or eleven, I did the math. According to my calculations, Barbara is either seventy-six or seventy-seventy years old." Atsuko leaned back in her chair and smiled. "Either way, she's at least a year older than me."

"That would make Barbara the oldest Alphabet Girl."

"Uh-huh."

"No wonder she refuses to reveal her age."

"Barbara's too obsessed with numbers, and America's too obsessed with staying young," Atsuko said. "In Japanese culture, elders are respected and revered. I see no reason to hide my age." She bit into her muffin. "I'm proud to be seventy-five. I've earned every one of these wrinkles."

"You're a wise woman." Claire inclined her head to the Buddha on the baker's rack. "Does some of that wisdom come from being Buddhist?"

"I'm not Buddhist, though I follow some of Buddhism's tenets, like mindfulness and meditation, praying and chanting. I believe in God." Atsuko winked. "I also believe in Dolly Parton."

"Who doesn't believe in Dolly? That woman is a national treasure."

"And she's older than us and still going strong."

"Dolly rocks."

Barbara hit "9 to 5" on her playlist to kickstart her Friday morning. Blending her kale smoothie, she added a second spoonful of protein powder. After yesterday, she needed the extra protein. She chugged down the smoothie, pulled out her yoga mat, and scrolled through her playlist looking for just the right song. As Enya's "Orinoco Flow" began to play, Barbara assumed the tree pose position.

She decided she'd take some sage over to Daphne's to cleanse her condo of the bad juju from yesterday once she finished her yoga routine.

Daphne poured some Cap'n Crunch in a bowl and planned her next move. Slipping off her sling, she moved her arm to the side, testing it. Her shoulder screamed in protest, and she squeezed her eyes shut against the pain. She'd have to drive with the sling on. It would be tricky, but manageable. The doctor's office had told Daphne she couldn't drive for three to four weeks, but then they hadn't just gotten rid of a dead body.

A woman's gotta do what a woman's gotta do.

Scarfing down the last chocolate doughnut, she mulled over what reason she could give the girls for her absence. *I could say I'm going to see my sister*, Daphne mused. A recollection surfaced. *You already told them there's bad blood between you and your sister and you haven't seen her in years.*

Then I'll tell them I'm going to see my niece. Daphne thought for a moment. *I'll say her husband is deployed and she's nervous about being alone—wants me to come and keep her company.* She expanded on the falsehood. *I'll say this pretend niece promised to make all my favorite family recipes. The girls know how much I love my grandma's meatloaf and pot roast.*

Finishing her Cap'n Crunch, Daphne rinsed the bowl in the sink and went to her bedroom. Pulling out her suitcase, she threw in sweats, flannel shirts, and underwear. She grabbed soap, shampoo, and toothpaste from the bathroom, grateful she didn't use all the fancy creams and beauty aids that cluttered Barbara's vanity.

Daphne closed the suitcase and set it down next to the couch. Moving to the kitchen, she filled a grocery bag with peanut butter, the remaining half loaf of bread, potato chips, Oreos, and Cap'n Crunch. She had planned to pack her favorite Welch's grape jelly until the empty jar reminded her she hadn't gone grocery shopping yesterday.

Guess you had other things on your mind, huh, Daph? She decided she'd buy perishables once she got to her final destination. She could also get a Whopper from Burger King when she got tired of PB&J. Finished with her packing, Daphne opened her laptop to write to the girls, deciding it would be easier to leave a note than face a barrage of questions. She had just finished pecking out "Hey, Alphabet Girls" with her left hand when a knock sounded.

So much for a clean getaway.

Expecting to see Claire or Barbara, Daphne opened the door and came face to face with her former partner. Her heart did its usual flip-flop at the sight of the cop who'd once been her good friend. She pushed down the fluttering. "Rick. What are you doing here?"

"Nice to see you too." Rick's hazel eyes flicked to Daphne's sling. "What'd you do, Ace? Trip and fall chasing a perp down an alley? Oh, that's right, you don't do those kinds of things anymore—you're livin' the life of leisure now. Did you hurt yourself playing pickleball with the other old coots?"

"Tore my bicep at the gym and had surgery. Not that it's any of your business." Daphne's brown eyes took in Rick's khakis and black polo shirt with the Santa Bonita Police insignia. Her gut twisted. "I heard you'd made detective. Congratulations." Her voice belied her words.

"You'd be a detective too if you'd stuck around."

"Too high a price to pay for that particular honor."

A muscle worked in Rick's jaw.

Daphne knew that muscle well. It always moved when her former patrol partner was trying to keep his temper in check.

"Can I come in? I've got something to tell you."

"We have nothing to talk about. Those days are long past."

"Two minutes. You'll want to hear this."

Daphne considered, seeing in her mind's eye the body on the living-room floor. *Had all hints of Benny been removed?* The stained area rug had gone and so had every trace of blood—Atsuko had seen to that. Daphne had stopped Atsuko from cleaning the rest of her condo, though, feigning weariness. The pieces of the burner phone Daphne smashed had been thrown into three different dumpsters around town by the Alphabet Girls. There had been nothing in Benny's wallet except a driver's license and a twenty-dollar bill. Daphne had kept the twenty, tossed the wallet, and burned the license.

Confident nothing inside would indicate the dead man had ever been there, Daphne expelled a sigh and led her former partner inside. "Make it quick. I've got somewhere to be."

As Rick followed her, Daphne said over her shoulder, "How's Linda?"

"I wouldn't know. We're divorced."

"And Samantha?"

"She left as soon as she turned eighteen. Moved to Seattle with her boyfriend. Sami texted a few weeks ago to tell me she's pregnant."

Daphne whirled around. "You're going to be a *grandfather*?"

"I am."

Daphne heard the pride in Rick's voice and saw it in his eyes. "Congratulations." This time, she meant it. Rick had always loved kids.

"Thanks." The detective's hazel eyes took in the piles of laundry, empty pizza boxes, and spilled Cap'n Crunch on the table. "I see some things never change. You're still a slob."

"Guilty as charged."

Rick had an odd expression on his face. "Daph, it's about Benny."

Her mouth went dry. "Benny?"

"Benny Popov. The guy you sent to the joint."

How did he find out? Did someone see us loading Benny's body into the SUV? Daphne affected a casual tone. "What about him?"

"He was released yesterday; let out on *good behavior.*" Daphne could hear the disgust in Rick's voice. "I didn't find out until an hour ago. I wanted to let you know so you can keep an eye out. He may come looking for you to try to make good on his threat."

Daphne schooled her features so the relief didn't show. She flapped her unencumbered hand. "Benny's not going to come after me. That was years ago. If he did, he'd wind up back in the joint, and Benny won't want that, not after getting an early release. He'll be keeping his nose clean." She thought of the body at the bottom of the quarry. *Well, maybe not so clean . . .*

Rick regarded her with wary eyes. "That's what Dmitri thinks."

Daphne got a sour taste in her mouth. "You'd know all about what Dmitri Glazatovsky thinks, wouldn't you? Being in his pocket and all."

"I told you then and I'm telling you now, Daph: I'm not in anyone's pocket."

"Keep telling yourself that. Maybe one day you'll believe it."

"Still holier-than-thou, aren't you? And just where did your self-righteousness get you? Early retirement from a job you loved." Rick shook his gray-flecked head in disgust. "I don't know why I even bothered coming here."

"I don't either. In fact, now that you've delivered your message, feel free to leave."

"Gladly." The detective turned, noticing the suitcase. "Going somewhere?"

"My sister's," Daphne replied on autopilot, forgetting the imaginary niece story she'd cooked up for the girls. Having Rick show up unannounced after all this time and everything that had passed between them had thrown her off her game.

"Your *sister*? The one who cut you out of her life? The one you haven't spoken to in years?"

The man's an elephant. "People change."

"Do they, Daph? Do they really?"

She scowled, pushing up her glasses. "*Some* people do."

"Daphne." Barbara's voice filtered through the open window. "You up yet? I've got a present for you."

"I'm outta here." Rick strode to the entryway. "Sorry to have wasted your time." He flung open the door, banging it against the wall in his haste.

Hand poised to knock, Barbara stood on the doorstep in leggings and a crop top that showed off her tanned abs. "Well, hell-o," she said, taking in every inch of the lean, six-foot-plus man who looked like a cross between Liam Neeson and Harrison Ford. "I hope I'm not interrupting anything."

"Nope. We're finished here." Rick stalked off without giving Barbara a second glance. Something she wasn't used to.

Barbara's blue eyes followed Daphne's visitor as he stomped to the parking lot. She turned to her friend. "You've been holding out on us, Cagney. *Who* is that gorgeous long, tall drink of water with the great pecs?"

"My ex-partner, Rick." Yanking Barbara inside, Daphne shut the door behind them and closed the window. "*Detective* Bartlett," she hissed. "He came to tell me Benny was released from prison."

Barbara paled and dropped the stick of sage she'd been holding. "Seriously?" She swiveled her blonde layered head, examining the great room with panicked eyes and stopping at Daphne's recliner and the empty spot where the rug used to be. "You let a *cop* in here? Have you lost your mind?"

"Chill. I knew we'd gotten rid of every trace of the deceased," Daphne said, reverting to cop speak. "Rick insisted on coming in—said he had something important to tell me. I had no idea he was going to warn me about Benny. Don't worry; I handled it. No big deal."

"If it's no big deal, why did your ex-partner storm out of here looking like Sonny Corleone on his way to beat up his sister's husband?"

"Rick and I have a way of pushing each other's buttons. Now, what's this about a present?"

"That man can push my buttons anytime." Barbara bent and picked up the sage she'd dropped. That's when she saw the suitcase.

SEVEN

The Alphabet Girls met in Claire's living room that afternoon minus Daphne, who had flown the coop.

"Tell us again," Claire said to Barbara, shifting to get comfortable. She really needed to get a new couch, one with better back support. "Where did Daphne say she was going?"

"To stay with her niece in Nevada—her husband is in the Army and just deployed to Korea. Apparently, her niece is nervous being alone in the house, so Daphne's going to stay with her for a few weeks, during which time she'll be eating, in Cagney's words, 'plenty of home-cooked meals.'" Barbara wrinkled her nose. "Sounds like a lot of carbs to me." She held out a key to Claire. "Daphne asked if you'd water her plants while she's gone."

Pocketing the key, Claire asked, "What's her niece's name?"

Barbara scrunched up her face. "You know? She never said."

"I didn't even know Daphne had a niece," Atsuko said. "Did you, Claire?"

"Not that I ever heard her mention."

"She's probably Daphne's sister's daughter," Barbara said.

Atsuko inclined her head. "The sister Daphne has no relationship with. The one she said she hasn't spoken to in years. That seems strange."

"Not to me," Barbara said. "My sister and I once had a knock-down, drag-out, and she didn't speak to me for two years. In that time, my niece Jennie—her daughter—and I never stopped seeing each other."

"I've heard you mention Jennie," Atsuko said, "but I've never heard Daphne say a word about a niece."

Barbara munched on a celery stick. "You know how tight-lipped Cagney is. She likes to keep things close to the vest. Like that good-looking cop partner of hers." She sent the girls a sly gaze. "I'll bet there's a story there."

Claire crunched on a mini carrot. "Tell us about this partner."

"He reminded me of Harrison Ford. Tall. Rugged. Great body."

"I meant tell us about his interaction with Daphne," Claire said. "Why did he come to see her?"

"I already told you. Cagney said he wanted to let her know about Benny Popov being released from prison. Rick—that's her ex-partner's name—came to warn her so she could be on her guard." Barbara giggled. "Not knowing, of course, that Claire here had already dispatched Benny-boy to the great beyond. Pretty ironic if you think about it."

Atsuko frowned. "This doesn't feel right." She dipped a carrot in the bowl of hummus on Claire's coffee table. "Something's going on."

"I agree. It seems odd that Daphne's former partner shows up out of the blue—the day *after* this Benny's demise, not that many hours after we dumped him in the quarry." Claire scratched her head. "Then, right after her partner's visit, Daphne takes off for parts unknown."

"But we know where she went," Barbara protested. "To visit her niece in Nevada."

"Did Daphne take an Uber to the airport?" Atsuko asked.

"No, she drove."

"And you *let* her?" Claire's eyebrows lifted. "She's still recovering from major shoulder surgery. She's not supposed to drive for another two or three weeks."

Barbara bristled. "I didn't *let* Daphne do anything. She's a sixty-two-year-old woman, for God's sake. She can do what she wants. *You* try to stop Cagney from doing something once her mind's made up."

Atsuko's forehead puckered. "But why would she drive to the airport instead of taking an Uber or asking one of us to drive her? It doesn't make sense. Do you know how much the parking garage at the airport charges? It would be astronomical to leave a car there for a few weeks. Daphne doesn't have that kind of money."

The pieces started falling into place.

"I don't think Daphne went to the airport at all," Claire said thoughtfully. "And I don't think there's a niece who needs her help either." She regarded Atsuko and Barbara. "I think Daphne left town because of *us*. To distance herself from us, to protect us."

"Protect us from what?" Barbara asked. "The bad guy's gone to a place no one will ever find. No one besides us knows what happened to him, and no one except us ever will. There's no problem. It's taken care of. 'Done and dusted.' Isn't that what you said last night, Claire?"

"That was before the cop showed up. Was he in uniform?"

Barbara shook her head. "Khakis and a black polo shirt. Cagney said he's a detective." Her eyes widened at the implication.

Atsuko placed a finger to the side of her nose, contemplating. "I think Claire's right. I think Daphne left to protect us. Remember when we asked why we couldn't call the police after Claire killed the guy in self-defense? Daphne said she couldn't get into the details; it would put us in danger."

Barbara gave a slow nod. "Cagney said, 'The less you know, the better.'" She stared at her friends. "Usually, the reason you don't get the police involved is when they're already involved . . . *with* the criminals." She leaned in. "I told you my ex was in the Mexican Mafia. Johnny was low on the totem pole in the family business—small potatoes," she said. "But one of his jobs was paying the local policia to turn a blind eye to the illegal activities his family engaged in: robbery, assault, drug running, even murder." She lifted her shoulders. "There's always been crooked cops in bed with criminals. I doubt the Santa Bonita Police Force is the exception."

"I wonder if that's why Daphne retired early," Atsuko mused. "Knowing her, she would never get involved in that kind of thing."

"Maybe that's also why Cagney's never talked about her ex-partner to us." Barbara's mouth turned down. "It could be the gorgeous detective is one of those crooked cops."

Claire considered. "He knows the murderer Daphne sent to prison has been released—the guy who made threats against her. And so does whatever criminal group the dead man was involved with. When he comes up missing, people will start asking questions, start looking for him. And Daphne's detective friend will pay her another visit, wondering if she had something to do with his absence."

"*That's* why Daphne left town so fast," Atsuko said. "She knew this Rick would be back asking questions before long."

Claire nodded. "And if he saw *us* with Daphne, and realized we were friends, he would question us as well. With Daphne gone, he doesn't know our connection to her."

"Apart from me. He saw me when I showed up at the door. Although"—Barbara pouted—"he didn't seem to register my presence."

"I find that hard to believe," Atsuko said.

"So do I." Barbara smoothed her hair. "I think he and Daphne may have had a fight. He wasn't a happy camper."

"Well, if he does come back and question you," Claire said, "play dumb."

"I'm an expert at that. I've played the dumb-blonde card to great effect over the years." Barbara batted her eyes, resurrecting her Texas twang. "People—men in particular—have always underestimated l'il ol' me because of how I look. Especially when I lay the Southern accent on thick, y'all."

"Men always underestimate women," Claire said. "My husband underestimated me throughout our marriage, and so did the lawyers I worked for—back when secretaries were like office wives. In addition to my clerical duties, I picked up my boss's dry cleaning, bought presents for his wife"—she paused—"and sent flowers to his girlfriend."

"What a charmer," Atsuko said.

"So sexist. My first two husbands expected me to be the perfect little housewife, always smiling and saying, 'Yes, dear.'" Barbara snorted. "My third husband knew I wasn't the housewife type. Phil had other expectations. Like my being available twenty-four/seven for sex and to pose for him and *only* him." Her eyes flickered. "He was the jealous type."

"I was lucky," Atsuko said. "Kenichi always encouraged me to follow my dreams, to do what I wanted. But back to the matter at hand, what are we going to do about Daphne?"

"I don't think there's anything we *can* do." Claire shrugged. "Barbara's right. She's a grown woman."

"A grown woman who concocted a ludicrous getaway story," Atsuko said.

"Granted." Claire took a drink of water. "But Daphne wouldn't have left so fast if she didn't have a good reason. I think we need to respect that and leave her alone."

"*And* keep our eyes and ears open," Barbara added. "If the gorgeous detective comes back asking questions, we call Cagney and let her know."

"We also do some research," Atsuko said. "Find out about the criminal element in Santa Bonita. For instance, do we have anything here like the Mexican Mafia?" She scrunched up her face. "I seem to recall reading something about the Russian Mafia in Northern California when I first arrived and was staying in Sacramento with my daughter."

"I remember that," Barbara said. "The realty world was buzzing about the real-estate fraud a group of Russians had done. A pastor from a big Slavic evangelical church in Sacramento was involved and went to prison."

Claire lifted an eyebrow. "A man of the cloth involved in something shady? Color me shocked."

"If you want to be really shocked, I've got stories about some Texas preachers that will curl your hair," Barbara said.

Atsuko steepled her hands. "Let he who is without sin cast the first stone."

"I've had enough stone throwing to last me a lifetime, thank you very much," Claire said.

EIGHT

Daphne opened the cabin windows. It had been months since she'd been up to the mountain hideaway, and the musty air had the definite smell of mouse. Dropping her suitcase on the floor, she returned to the car for groceries. She kicked the door shut behind her and set the bag on the ancient Formica counter. She'd intended to stop at the small store in town for milk, cheese, eggs, and butter, but after the two-hour drive, her shoulder hurt like a mother.

Daphne grabbed a Flintstones glass from the lone cupboard, filled it with water, and downed a tramadol. Then she made her way to the sagging plaid couch and collapsed, thinking of Rick and their cop days together.

There'd been one particular day when she and Rick had been patrolling the streets of downtown Santa Bonita. They'd been partners for several years by then and had developed an easy rapport, even though Rick was a Giants fan and always teased her about the Dodgers.

Daphne took a drink of her Big Gulp and munched on Doritos as she steered the Ford squad car through the city streets. "Sorry I was late today."

"Would expect nothing less from a Dodgers fan."

"I have to cut out a little early, too."

"Would expect nothing less from a Dodgers fan."

Daphne crunched on a Dorito, sending a side glance to her partner. "How's Samantha handling the separation?" Rick and his wife had been having marital issues for the past several months and were now separated for the second time. The couple had a young daughter, Samantha, whom Rick adored.

"She's handling it OK," Rick said. "Actually, Sami and I are getting along better now that Linda and I aren't living under the same roof. All that tension's not good for a kid."

"I hear ya." Daphne's parents had fought all the time when

she was growing up, divorcing when she was twelve. She'd opted to live with her father, while her sister, a carbon copy of their mom, stayed with her mother. Daphne and her dad were best buddies, going fishing and camping together, and attending baseball games all summer long. She'd inherited her love of the Dodgers from her dad.

He'd been gone five years now, and she missed him every day.

Turning the corner, Daphne spotted a familiar figure exiting the Asian fusion restaurant considered the hottest ticket in town among the fine-dining crowd. Daphne didn't understand "fusion" food, preferring to stick to the basics: burgers, steak, meatloaf, chicken, pizza, tacos, and sweet-and-sour pork with chicken chow mein and egg rolls. She grunted as they passed the Gourmet Dragon. "Look, it's our resident crime lord pal, Dmitri."

Rick and Daphne had arrested seventy-year-old Dmitri Glazatovsky, a recent transplant to Santa Bonita, a few years ago, on suspicion of running a drug-trafficking operation. The evidence had been flimsy, though, and a small-time pusher had taken the fall instead and been sentenced to three years in prison. Dmitri's high-powered lawyer had gotten all charges against his client dropped. Since then, Daphne had kept her eye on the Russian mobster, determined to catch him in illegal activity. In addition to drug trafficking, word on the street was Glazatovsky had his hand in several other criminal enterprises, including fraud, prostitution, and theft.

Maybe even murder, although no one could prove it.

"It really sticks in my craw that that guy gets away with everything," Daphne said.

"He's a slippery one, all right." Rick flipped the lid on his insulated coffee tumbler and took a drink. "Always manages to keep his hands clean."

"Yeah, while his minions do the dirty work." Glancing in her rear-view mirror, Daphne noticed a Lexus deposit the mayor, police commissioner, and her superior officer in front of the restaurant. She dropped her Doritos when she glimpsed Glazatovsky fling his arm around Captain Dunlap's shoulder and the police captain laugh at something he said.

Rick brushed Dorito crumbs from his sleeve. "Jeez, Daph, you're such a slob."

"Rick, do you think the captain is bent?"

"What? No way. Dunlap's a straight arrow. As straight as they come."

"Then why do he and Dmitri look so chummy-chummy? Glazatovsky's rubbing shoulders with the commissioner and the mayor too."

"Probably some PR event. I heard our Russian friend made a big donation to the Boys and Girls Club, trying to get in good with local leaders. But you can bet the captain's keeping a close eye on him. Don't worry, we're going to nail Glazatovsky one of these days."

But they never did.

Four hours later, Daphne woke up starving and furry mouthed in a dark room. For a moment she didn't know where she was. Then she remembered. Turning on the moose lamp beside the '70s couch, she made her way to the bathroom. After rinsing out her mouth and washing her hands, she went to the kitchen for something to eat.

Pulling the half loaf of bread from the bag, Daphne noticed someone had beaten her to it. A mouse—possibly more than one—had chewed through the side of the loaf, burrowing a tunnel to the bottom. Squinting through her glasses, Daphne saw the last slice remained untouched by rodents' teeth. Should she chance it?

"Gross." She could hear Claire's voice in her head.

"Dis*gusting*," Barbara would say, wrinkling her pert nose.

Atsuko would regard the pristine piece of bread with a dubious air. "I'd throw that away if I were you. Too close for comfort."

Daphne dropped the bread in the trash and pulled out the package of Oreos. She cursed. The mice had made inroads there as well. Stomach growling, she removed the jar of Jif and box of Cap'n Crunch, letting out a sigh of relief to see the peanut butter remained untouched. She rattled the box of cereal and listened. No rustling or squeaks. Opening the lid, Daphne peered inside. All clear.

Pouring some cereal into a bowl, she grabbed a spoon and the peanut butter and sat down to dinner. Dipping a spoonful of peanut butter into the Cap'n Crunch, her thoughts returned to her ex-partner. Rick still looked good. Not that different from the last time she had seen him at her retirement send-off nearly two years ago, apart from some gray in his hair. Glancing down at the muffin top poking above her sweatpants, Daphne grimaced. She knew she'd let herself go in retirement.

Depression has a way of doing that.

Why is it men always age so well?

She answered herself. Maybe because Rick goes to the gym five times a week and he's still working. Knowing him, he's still jogging too, like Barbara.

Barbara. Daphne slapped her hand to her forehead. She'd promised B she would text once she got to her niece's. Hours ago now. She pulled out her phone, wondering if she'd get a signal. Reception was often spotty here. That's when she saw three text messages from the girls and a missed call from Barbara.

Atsuko and Claire wrote they were sorry they didn't get to say goodbye to her before she left and hoped Daphne had a nice visit with her niece. (Although Claire's text said "lovely" rather than nice. Ever since she had returned from England, Claire had taken to saying the word "lovely" with regularity.)

B's text message was short and sweet.

BARBARA: Hey boo, hope you made it to Nevada in one piece.

Her voicemail wasn't as polite.

Daphne sent a group text to the girls, supporting her sling with her left hand and tapping out a message with her right.

DAPHNE: Arrived safe and sound. Sorry, been busy catching up. Talk soon.

She ended the text with a sunflower emoji followed by a kissy face emoji. Daphne loved emojis. Then she scrolled the Santa Bonita Police social media pages. She didn't have to scroll long. Jack Dunlap, her former captain, shook hands with Dmitri Glazatovsky in front of the refurbished dog and cat shelter Glazatovsky had funded while Rick beamed in the background.

Daphne slapped the laptop closed. Grabbing the broom and cradling her sling, she swept the floor free of dust and mouse droppings, brushing them out the back door. Then, rooting around in the junk drawer, she found two mousetraps. She set the traps, using peanut butter and Cap'n Crunch for bait, placed them on opposite ends of the cracked kitchen linoleum, and went to bed.

Before drifting off, she wondered how long it would be before Rick and Glazatovsky realized Benny was missing. And how long before Rick returned to Cedar Glen to nose around.

Saturday morning when they met at the clubhouse for breakfast, Atsuko showed Claire a picture of her latest ikebana arrangement on Instagram. Atsuko and Barbara were always posting on Instagram, although Barbara's photos were usually perfectly curated selfies showing off her latest outfit or yoga pose.

In full makeup, of course.

Atsuko had helped Claire sign up for Instagram, but Claire couldn't figure out how to upload photos to the app. Besides, she wasn't into selfies. She preferred spending her time with a good book.

Atsuko filled her tray with yogurt, juice, a banana, and coffee at the breakfast buffet. Claire did the same, although she added half a bagel and had tea rather than coffee. And not from the carafes the clubhouse provided. Claire, the confirmed Anglophile, would only drink tea from water that had been boiled in a proper *kettle*.

Claire had bought an electric kettle for the clubhouse, but George Hansen ruined it by not keeping an eye on his grandson. It wasn't until George smelled burnt plastic that he discovered five-year-old Nicholas had stuffed the kettle full of Legos. Now Claire made her favorite English tea at home with milk and one sugar. She'd carry her mug of Yorkshire Gold to the clubhouse, but by the time she got there, the tea was no longer piping hot.

"There's nothing worse than tepid tea," she declared as she stuck it in the microwave. Claire wasn't shy about expressing her opinion these days. For years, she had kept quiet, acquiescing to others, going along with what they wanted. No more. Life was short. Who knew how much time she had left? Sure, she might live to be a hundred, although she'd rather not.

Next month, she'd turn seventy, and as she reflected upon this milestone birthday, Claire thought of the friends and family she had lost. Her coworker Joni had dropped dead of a heart attack at sixty-five, her childhood pal Liz had died of cancer at sixty-nine, and Irene, an energetic woman she had built houses alongside of at Habitat for Humanity, passed away at seventy-four from Covid. Then there was her husband, Stan, who'd had a stroke on the ninth hole and died at seventy-two, golf club in hand.

Claire didn't fear death; she feared not living the life she wanted.

After her UK vacation, Claire considered moving to England and living there as an expat. She fantasized about living in a stone cottage (thatched roof optional) in the Cotswolds, Cornwall, or Yorkshire, like the ones she lusted after on *Escape to the Country*, but Brexit scuppered those plans when they ended retirement visas. The only way she could live in England now was to marry a Brit, and Claire had no intention of ever marrying again.

Atsuko was always encouraging her to be open to the idea, though. "Don't shut yourself off to marriage, Claire," she said, finishing her bagel. "Just because your husband was a jerk doesn't mean all men are. The universe is full of possibilities. Who knows? The love of your life might be right around the corner, ready to sweep you off your feet."

"Then I'll be sure not to turn the corner."

Claire had married her high school sweetheart as the women's movement was taking off. Raised in a religious household, she had been taught to believe a woman's greatest job was to take care of her husband and children. It wasn't until she joined the workforce in her mid-thirties that she started to see women could have lives of their own. Claire began taking tentative steps toward such a life, but it wasn't until her husband died that she found true independence.

And she wasn't about to give that up for any man.

NINE

Early Saturday evening, Claire pulled the pies out of the oven and set them on the counter to cool. It was her turn to lead book club, and she had less than an hour to get everything ready. They should have met Thursday night, but Benny's unexpected arrival and departure and everything that came afterwards had forced them to postpone. Since Barbara had a date last night, they'd moved their meeting to tonight instead.

As she got things ready, Claire pushed all thoughts of the dead man at the bottom of the quarry out of her head. She preferred to fill her mind with happy thoughts, starting with her grandson Josh, who'd spent the night last night.

Fourteen-year-old Josh liked coming over to his grandma's, although he hadn't in the beginning. During the waning days of the pandemic when his parents got divorced—after his dad ran off with "that blonde bimbo"—his mother declared she needed the occasional girls' night out. When she did, she dropped Josh off at Cedar Glen to stay with her mother.

The first time Josh had to spend the night at Claire's, he hated it and wasn't shy about telling his grandmother how he felt. He couldn't believe Claire had no Xbox or computer, and that she refused to let him spend his time with her "hunched over that phone." She also wouldn't let him watch *Game of Thrones* on streaming.

"Way too violent," she said.

"This is so boring," Josh yelled. "What are we supposed to *do*?"

That's when Claire gave her grandson his first cooking lesson.

Preparing for book club, Claire smiled, recalling her grandson's excitement last night when he'd added his latest culinary creation to his phone.

"That makes eight things I know how to cook now," Josh said.

"Stir fry, salmon, spaghetti, pot roast, chili, tacos, enchiladas, and lasagna."

Josh's mom, Claire's daughter Grace, didn't cook. And Claire wasn't about to let her grandson subsist on rotisserie chicken, pizza, and salad in a bag.

Pulling out her list of book club questions, she read through them again. In honor of tonight's book, Claire had handwritten the questions on vintage stationery from England with a floral border, instead of the customary pad of paper she typically used. Unlike the other girls who typed out their questions and emailed them to one another—with Atsuko printing out a copy for her—Claire wrote her questions on a yellow legal pad with a black Uniball. She loved watching the black ink flow from her pen, forming words on paper. The ink looked even lovelier on the pale pink stationery.

When the girls arrived later, Claire asked Barbara, "How was your date last night?"

"Don't ask. I should have known better than to go out with an insurance salesman. Talk about boring with a capital B."

"How did you meet him anyway?" Atsuko asked.

"My hair stylist set us up. He's one of her clients. She said he was a nice guy, recently divorced, and a good tipper. Drives a Lexus and has a beach house." Barbara released a sigh. "It was the beach house that got my attention. I miss living near the ocean."

"So what was the problem?" Claire asked.

"Besides the boring factor, you mean?" Barbara's mouth twisted. "I can't stand people who drone on and on about their jobs. I mean, unless you're Richard Branson or Evil Knievel, who cares?"

"I hate to break it to you, but Evil Knievel is dead," Atsuko said.

"You know what I mean. Someone exciting. Which would *not* be an insurance salesman."

"Did the guy have any redeeming qualities?" Claire asked.

"He had good hair," Barbara admitted. "I'll give him that. But that was about it."

Atsuko sipped her wine. "What about the beach house?"

"His wife got it in the divorce."

"Let's move on to book club now." Claire handed the girls a piece of homemade pie.

Barbara took a bite and spit it out. "That is absolutely disgusting." She drained her glass of wine and poured another.

Atsuko grimaced. "It's pretty awful, Claire." Lifting a napkin to her mouth, she spit out the bite she'd taken and cleansed her palate with a huge gulp of Moscato.

"I wanted us to understand and experience the kind of World War II food deprivations the members of *The Guernsey Literary and Potato Peel Pie Society* underwent," Claire said.

"I already understood that well enough from the book." Barbara shook her head. "I can't believe you made an actual pie from potato peels. Where did you find a recipe?"

"In the book, based on what Amelia wrote in her letter to Juliet about how the literary society got their name. There wasn't an actual recipe per se, but Amelia said one of the members made a potato peel pie using mashed potatoes for the filling, strained beets for some sweetness, and potato peelings for the crust, so I did my best to replicate it." Claire set her fork down and took a sip of wine. "Forget the pie, though; what did you think of the book?"

Atsuko beamed. "I loved it. Such a beautiful story. Wonderful, richly drawn characters, and, of course, I adored all the literary references."

"I loved it too," Barbara said. "I kept rooting for Juliet and Dawsey to get together and sobbed my eyes out when we learned what happened to Elizabeth."

"So did I," Claire said. "It breaks my heart every time I read it."

"*Every* time?" Barbara regarded her. "How many times have you read it?"

"This makes six." Claire tilted her head. "Or is it seven?"

"Whoa. I've never read any book that many times. Although," Barbara reflected, "I did read *Peyton Place* and *Marjorie Morningstar* twice. Once in high school, and again years later to see if they were as racy as I'd remembered." She grinned. "They weren't."

Three phones pinged at once.

Barbara held up her iPhone. "Well, looky here, a group text from Cagney."

Atsuko and Claire picked up their phones to read the message from the missing Alphabet Girl.

DAPHNE: Thanks for postponing the book club voting until I'm back. When C said this was an epistolary novel, I had no clue what that meant. When I saw it was a bunch of letters, I didn't want to read the book. After the first few pages, though, I was hooked. Did you know there's a movie too? Let's watch. Had pot roast for dinner tonight. Yumm.

Daphne ended her text with a heart and an emoji of licking lips.

BARBARA: You missed Claire's potato peel pie. It was the bomb.

Atsuko followed Barbara's text with three emojis of licking lips.

CLAIRE: If you're nice I'll make a PP pie for you when you get back.

The next morning, Claire daydreamed of England as she took Elinor on her daily walk in the designated pet area. So wrapped up was she in her memories of rolling green hills, ancient stone cottages, and cream teas that she didn't notice the other dog until she heard a frenzied yipping. That's when she saw the one-eyed terrier and its owner approaching.

Elinor hid behind Claire's legs.

"Hello, Brontë. Hello, Mark. How's the training going?"

"Not bad." Mark smiled. "As you can see, Brontë's not straining at the leash anymore."

"That's an improvement." Kneeling to the dog's level, Claire ruffled the back of her neck. "Good girl."

Elinor peeked out from behind Claire's legs, and Brontë growled.

"No, no." Mark knelt down to look his rescue dog in her lone eye. "That's not nice, Brontë. Elinor is our friend."

Claire picked up her dog, soothing Elinor. "It's OK, sweetheart. It will take Brontë time to get used to you, but hopefully, before long, you'll be friends."

"Won't that be nice, Brontë?" Mark said. The pup licked his face. "I'll take that as a yes." Smiling, he stood up. "There's hope."

"There's always hope," Claire said, "*Hope is the thing with feathers that perches on the soul . . .*"

"*And sings the tune without the words, and never stops at all.* Emily Dickinson is a favorite." Mark studied her. "Have you been at Cedar Glen long, Claire?"

"Six years, give or take. I moved in a few months before the pandemic started, soon after my husband died."

"I'm sorry. I didn't realize you were a widow."

"That's OK." Claire refrained from saying she knew Mark was a widower and that all the unattached women in the retirement community were panting after him.

"How long were you married?" Mark asked as Brontë stretched out on the grass.

"Forty-seven years." Claire couldn't stop the grimace from forming. "Unfortunately."

Mark lifted an eyebrow.

"Sorry. Was I too forthright? I believe in calling a spade a spade, and the truth is, I stayed in my marriage far too long. I should have left years ago."

"Why didn't you?" His question was curious, not judgmental.

"Because I was brought up to believe divorce was a sin. Also, I have two children. At the time, I thought—as did society—it would be better for my kids to have a mother *and* a father. I've since realized I was wrong, but that's a whole other story." Claire regarded Mark. "What about you? How long were you married?"

"Not long enough."

She glimpsed the deep wells of sorrow in the widower's eyes.

"Thirty-nine years," he said. "My wife died last year from breast cancer." Closing his eyes, Mark gave his head a brief shake. "Angie was the love of my life."

"I'm so sorry." Claire felt at a loss for words in the face of such love.

"I hate cancer."

"It's a terrible disease, and no respecter of persons." Claire gestured to her flat chest. "I had it a decade ago. The biopsy showed cancer in only one breast, but there were several pre-cancerous lumps in the other one, so I told the surgeon to take both of them. I didn't want to live my life waiting for a time bomb to go off."

"Angie did the same," Mark said. "Breasts don't make a woman."

"It's refreshing to hear a man say that. In my experience, and many of my friends', I'd say you're in the minority."

Mark made a sound of disgust in the back of his throat. "Men are too obsessed with breasts. I blame Hugh Hefner and the whole *Playboy* culture."

His pup pawed at his legs. "Brontë agrees with me. Don't you, girl?"

The one-eyed terrier yipped and wagged her tail.

"Smart dog." Elinor wriggled in Claire's arms. "Sorry, Mark. I need to get this girl into the dog run. Nice talking to you."

"You, too." He smiled and gave her a half wave. "Hopefully, the next time Brontë sees Elinor, she'll be a little friendlier."

Barbara made two kale smoothies while her guest took a shower. Ten minutes later, when Ryan joined her in the kitchen, towel-drying his hair, she regarded the fifty-year-old's flawless physique with appreciation. "I thought you might want this after our workout." She handed him one of the smoothies.

"Thanks, babe," the physical trainer said. He took a long drink. "That *was* quite a workout, wasn't it?" Ryan gave her a seductive smile. "You sure know how to rock a guy's world." He wagged his finger at her. "But don't think today's bedroom gymnastics gets you out of your strength-training session tomorrow. I expect to see you bright and early at the gym."

"Of course. I wouldn't miss it." Barbara placed her arms around Ryan's neck and pulled him into her, giving him a lingering kiss.

Five minutes later, he left. Barbara watched from the sidewalk as Ryan jogged to his car, admiring the trainer's bronzed, muscled calves and perfect glutes.

"Friend of yours?" a familiar female voice said.

Barbara turned to see Connie the condo manager's eyes flick from the departing Ryan to her.

"You could say so. There's nothing like a little afternoon delight to perk up a girl." Barbara gave Connie a wink. "You should try it sometime."

TEN

Two days later in the clubhouse, Atsuko scooted her chair closer to Claire. "Here's what I've discovered." She glanced around to make sure she wouldn't be heard, but the cluster of seniors watching *Grace and Frankie* on the flat screen were too caught up in Frankie's shenanigans to pay the Alphabet Girls any mind. "There *is* a local Russian Mafia connection in Santa Bonita, led by a guy named Dmitri Glazatovsky."

"Glazatovsky?" Claire frowned. "Are you sure? If it's the same guy I'm thinking of, I've seen his picture in the paper. He's a do-gooder. He and some other local entrepreneurs opened a children's playground downtown for at-risk youth a couple of years ago. And not long ago, he made a hefty donation that allowed the old cat and dog shelter to be renovated and refurbished. Thanks to him, the shelter was able to add a dozen more pens, doubling the number of dogs they can take in." Something near and dear to Claire's heart.

"I read that too," Barbara said. "There was some ribbon-cutting ceremony with the mayor and the chief of police, I think."

"Mr. Glazatovsky is quite the philanthropist," Atsuko said, "which makes a good cover for his criminal activities. He was connected to that Russian real-estate fraud in Sacramento years ago and arrested, but released for lack of evidence. After that, he left Sacramento and lived in San Francisco a while. According to an article in the *Santa Bonita Herald*, though, he didn't like the big city and moved here around five years ago with his family." She paused. "What I found even more interesting is that, a few years ago, our Mr. Glazatovsky was arrested on suspicion of drug trafficking. Guess who the arresting officers were?"

"Don't tell me," Barbara said. "Would that be our own Cagney and her partner, the gorgeous Rick?"

"Ding, ding, ding, jackpot," slots-loving Atsuko said.

"Uh-oh," Barbara peered over Claire and Atsuko's silvery heads. "Speak of the devil, guess who just walked in? Connie's with Daphne's former partner, and she's pointed me out to him." Barbara gave a little wave to the duo. "Detective Gorgeous is now heading this way." She sat up straight, sucking in her infinitesimal pooch and smoothing her hair. "If I were you, girls, I'd make like a tree and leave."

Claire stood. Bending forward, she clutched at her back and grimaced. Following her lead, Atsuko put an arm around Claire and guided her to the side door in a fake old-lady shuffle as the two Alphabet Girls made their escape. "This awful sciatica," Claire said in a loud voice as she exited.

Arriving at the table, Rick said, "Hello. Barbara, is it?" He smiled. "We met last week in front of Daphne Cole's place. I'm Detective Bartlett. I'd like to ask you a few questions if I may."

"Certainly, Detective. I'm always happy to help the boys in blue." She gazed up at Rick through lowered lashes, noticing his perfect white teeth and wondering if they were veneers. "Although, as I recall, we didn't actually *meet*." She offered her manicured hand with its turquoise nails to the detective. "I'm Barbara Wright. Formerly Barbara Butler, Alvarez, and Weston." She gave him a dazzling smile. "And your full name is?"

"Rick Bartlett." He shook her hand and sat down. "I understand you're a friend of Daphne's?"

Barbara gave a careless shrug. "More like an acquaintance. Daphne and I don't have much in common, but I always try to be friendly to *every*one." She gave him a meaningful look.

"Do you happen to know where Daphne is?"

"Hmm, let me think. I believe she mentioned she was going to stay with a niece in Nevada." Barbara's face cleared. "That's right, I remember now. The poor girl's husband got deployed to Korea. Can you *imagine*?" She shuddered. "How scary. Korea's always shooting off those nuclear missiles. One of these days, that whole country's going to blow sky high. Personally,

I would avoid that place like the plague. Now, Europe? I'd go back there again in a heartbeat."

She placed her chin in her hand, a dreamy expression on her face. "There's this great topless beach in Sardinia. I was there on a photo shoot with my third husband, Phil. Maybe you saw his pictures of me in *Vanity Fair*?" Barbara batted her lashes. "They were rather scandalous at the time."

"I don't think so."

"I'm happy to show them to you," Barbara purred. "You just say the word."

The detective's face reddened. He tapped the notes icon on his phone. "Did she ever mention a man named Benny Popov to you?"

"Daphne's niece?"

"No, Daphne."

"I don't think so. *Should* she have?" Barbara leaned forward and whispered. "Is he Daphne's boyfriend? She's always pretty close-mouthed about her private life. Although, if I'm being honest, Daphne's pretty close-mouthed about everything." Barbara giggled and gave a playful shake of her head. "She is a law unto herself."

"Truer words were never spoken."

Barbara made her eyes wide. "I hope Daphne's not in some kind of trouble, Detective? You can tell me. I won't breathe a word. Cross my heart." She drew a slow X over her left breast with her finger and licked her lips.

"No, nothing like that." Rick stood abruptly. "Thank you for your time." He pulled a card from his wallet. "If you happen to hear from her, would you please ask her to get in touch with me?"

"Of course." Barbara took the card, her fingers lingering on the detective's hand. "Although I doubt I will. As I said, Daphne and I aren't really close."

Rick flushed and cleared his throat. "Thanks again. I, uh, have to go now. Duty calls." He practically sprinted from the room.

* * *

Claire and Atsuko laughed as the B member of the Alphabet Girls recounted her meeting with the detective. "I think I can safely say Detective Bartlett won't be back," Barbara said. "You should have seen the look on his face when he thought I was coming on to him."

"Cougar," Claire teased.

"There's a lot to be said for younger men. For one thing, they have more energy and stamina than old geezers." Barbara flashed back to her session with her trainer Ryan, her lips curving up at the memory.

Atsuko sent her an innocent look. "Are you saying Lenny and Vince are not your cup of tea?"

"Tea, coffee, whatever. Those two are not my cup of *any*thing."

Claire pulled out her phone. "We need to text Daphne and let her know her old partner was here asking about her and Benny."

"Not so fast." Atsuko tapped her finger to her mouth, considering. "If we do that, I wonder if it might make Daphne go even further underground."

"What do you suggest?"

Barbara piped up. "I think we should tell her in person."

"And how would we do that when we don't even know where she is?" Claire asked.

Barbara waved her iPhone. "*I* do." She smirked. "You know how Daphne's always losing her phone? Well, after like the zillionth time that happened, she and I linked our iPhones so I could always find her phone when it went missing. All I have to do is hit 'Find my iPhone' and it shows us exactly where she is."

Atsuko stared at her. "Why didn't you tell us this before?"

"Because we'd agreed we were going to respect Daphne's wishes and leave her to her own devices. Now that Detective Gorgeous is sniffing around, though, I think we should tell her in person."

"But won't she know to turn off this feature or disable it or whatever?" Claire asked.

Barbara shook her head. "We're talking about Cagney here; she's almost as technologically impaired as you, Claire."

"I resemble that remark."

"So where the heck is she?" Atsuko asked.

"A couple of hours north of here, past Clear Lake."

Claire shook her head in exasperation. "She drove all that way with her bad shoulder. I'm going to kill her when I see her."

"We'll kill her together," Barbara said. "You know what this means, don't you?"

Atsuko and Claire sent her a quizzical glance.

"Road trip, baby."

Two hours later, as the Alphabet Girls loaded their suitcases into Atsuko's SUV, a male voice intruded. "Hi, girls, where ya going?" Lenny Fink asked. "Can I come?"

The ABC women turned around to find the randy octogenarian in a powder-blue leisure suit ogling them from beneath his bad rug.

"Sorry, Lenny," Barbara said. "This is a girls' trip."

"I thought you girls were always a quartet." He squinted at them. "Where's your pal Daphne?"

"Visiting family out of town." Claire checked her tote bag to make sure she had everything they might need. She had picked up the *Sense and Sensibility* tote bag with her life quote—"I will be calm. I will be mistress of myself"—in England.

"Well, with Daphne out of town, you've got room for a fourth, then," Lenny persisted.

"Lenny," Atsuko said in a measured tone, "what part of *girls* did you not understand?"

"Don't be so narrow-minded. These days, anything goes." He smirked. "For all you know, underneath this suit *I* could be a girl."

"Lenny is right, Atsuko," Barbara said. "You need to keep up with the times." She fastened her eyes on the '70s throwback. "What pronouns would you like us to use when we address you, Lenny?"

"Huh?"

Vince strolled up. "Hey, Len, where ya been? I thought you

were coming over to watch *Ocean's Eleven* with Frank and the original Rat Pack." He held up a six-pack. "I got the beer, and Tony's bringin' the subs."

"Don't let us keep you." Claire climbed into the SUV.

"Sorry, ladies," Vince said. "Didn't mean to interrupt." He noticed the suitcases. "Goin' on a trip, huh?"

"That's right." Barbara opened the door behind the driver's seat and hopped in. "Girls' trip to Vegas."

Putting on her seatbelt, Atsuko started the SUV. "Let's get this show on the road, ladies. My slots are calling." She backed out of the parking space, leaving Lenny and Vince in the dust as Barbara waved goodbye.

"Uh-oh," Barbara said an hour later from the back seat. "We've got trouble."

"What is it?" Claire asked.

Barbara held up her phone, and Claire saw the face of the man she'd killed. A face she'd never forget. Beneath the dead man's photo in the online edition of the *Santa Bonita Herald*, the headline read, "Have You Seen This Man?"

"Want to share with the class?" Atsuko turned down the Golden Oldies station.

Barbara read aloud. "Benny Popov, longtime resident of Santa Bonita, recently released from prison, is missing. Mr. Popov's parole officer said he failed to check in, and his employer, local businessman Dmitri Glazatovsky, said Benny never reported to work, to the job waiting for him upon his release. A rental car registered in Mr. Popov's name was found in the parking lot of the Muddy Pig Saloon."

Barbara continued reading. "Jake Hetland, longtime owner of the Muddy Pig, said he has not seen Mr. Popov since before he went to prison, years ago. 'I'm surprised Benny didn't come straight here once he was released,' Hetland said in an interview. 'He always said the first thing he'd do when he got back here was come to the Pig for a Jack and Coke. I told him the drink would be on the house, but he hasn't collected it yet. Benny, if you're reading this, your Jack and Coke is waiting for you,' Hetland said."

Barbara exhaled before finishing the article. "If anyone knows Mr. Popov's whereabouts, call the Santa Bonita Police Department and ask for Detective Bartlett, who is leading the investigation into the disappearance. Mr. Glazatovsky is offering a reward of $10,000 for information. 'Benny is a valuable employee of mine,' Glazatovsky said, 'a good worker who has paid his debt to society. I look forward to welcoming him back to the Glazatovsky Company.'"

Atsuko and Claire cursed.

"That's what I say," Barbara said.

"We need to get Daphne back here before she comes under suspicion," Atsuko said. "Now that it's public knowledge Benny's missing, what do you want to bet fingers will start pointing at the cop who sent him to prison?"

"The cop he threatened with death upon his release," Claire said.

"The retired cop who skipped town the day after Benny got out of prison," Barbara said. "Atsuko, put pedal to the metal."

ELEVEN

Daphne was bored. Usually, she came up to the cabin to fish, but not this time. Not with her arm in a sling. She'd gone to the store and bought provisions, went through the Burger King drive-thru a couple of times, and trapped and killed seven mice. She'd also finished the Lee Child novel she'd been reading when she arrived, and read two of her dad's Louis L'Amour paperbacks from the bookcase she'd helped build when she was twelve.

No TV watching, though; her father had always refused to have a boob tube in his rustic retreat. "We come up here to get *away* from civilization, not to watch *Judge Judy*," he used to say.

Daphne honored her dad's memory by not bringing up a TV. Before this, though, whenever she had come to the cabin—always alone—she'd fished and hiked, enjoying the wildlife and the scenery, the quiet of nature all around her. Daphne enjoyed the solitude. The peace. The cabin had always been a refuge for her, a welcome respite from the druggies, wife beaters, and assorted lowlifes she encountered day in and day out in her work as one of Santa Bonita's finest.

She didn't become a cop until her forties. Before that, Daphne served in the Air Force, retiring after twenty years. Her dad had always encouraged her to get a government job, so she'd have a pension. After two decades of pencil pushing in an office, though, she had a midlife crisis and changed careers. Daphne wanted to do something that mattered.

Something that made a difference in the world.

The youngest member of the Alphabet Girls had loved being a cop. Helping people, putting the bad guys away, and keeping the streets of Santa Bonita safe for its citizens. In the beginning, due to her age and her sex, Daphne had had to work harder than the other cops to prove herself. Her first partner had been a Neanderthal in his sixties who didn't think women belonged in law enforcement, apart from working in the office or dispatch. Once Rick Bartlett—six years Daphne's junior and married to a feminist—became her partner, though, it was smooth sailing.

Working with Rick always made Daphne think of that line in *Forrest Gump* about going together like peas and carrots. When she joined the police force, she had a long-range game plan: to serve twenty years and retire as a detective. Ha! What's that saying? *If you want to make God laugh, tell her your plans.*

After her unplanned early retirement, Daphne retreated to the cabin for a month. She fished, hiked, hunted, licked her wounds, went through several cases of beer, and read through her dad's entire Louis L'Amour collection.

This time, though, her injury hampered her from enjoying the great outdoors. Daphne had figured she would stream her favorite shows on her laptop, but with Wi-Fi so spotty in the woods, that wasn't happening. Just as the latest *Law and Order: SVU* episode reached a critical point, she lost reception. Again.

Daphne swore. She couldn't play *World of Warcraft*, *PGA Tour*, or any of her other video games either. She was now rethinking her decision to leave town. Maybe she should head back in another day or two, although the idea of driving did not appeal. Removing her arm from the sling, she tried to move it and winced. Better than Friday after the drive up, but still painful. Once she started PT, Daphne knew she'd regain her strength and full use of her arm, but it would take some time.

After scarfing down a PB&J and half a bag of Doritos, she dozed on the couch. She was dreaming of driving along the coast in a convertible with Brad Pitt when the sound of car tires crunching on pine needles awakened her. Picking up the SIG P365 she kept close, Daphne transferred the gun to her right hand and held up her slinged wrist with her left hand. After years of carrying, it had felt like a part of her was missing, not having a weapon when she retired. She got a concealed weapons permit and bought the SIG, going to the range regularly to stay proficient.

Peeking through the faded curtains, Daphne saw Atsuko's SUV. She strode to the door, SIG in hand, and yanked it open as the three Alphabet Girls exited the vehicle. "What are you guys doing here? And more importantly, how did you find me?"

"Nice to see you too," Claire said.

Barbara pinned blue eyes on Daphne. "Simmer down, Cagney. And could you put that gun away, please? You're making me nervous. Although I do like that robin's egg blue—I never knew guns came in different colors. As for how we found you"—Barbara wiggled her iPhone—"your phone is linked with mine, remember?"

Daphne groaned.

From the adjacent woods, a skunk appeared and started to amble their way. Claire and Barbara squealed, hotfooting it inside while Atsuko followed at a more sedate pace.

"Hurry up and shut the door," Claire yelled, "before it gets inside."

Daphne chuckled. "A skunk's not going to come inside a house full of people. Besides, it's more afraid of you than you are of it."

"Wanna bet?" Claire was petrified of wild animals apart from the ones at the zoo and on the Disney jungle cruise. Although she did love that Christian the Lion video. She teared up every time she watched the reunion of the two men and their pet lion on YouTube. Her heart swelled along with the music when Christian ran to his former owners and hugged them with his giant paws. Barbara had told her the soundtrack to their sweet reunion, "I Don't Wanna Miss a Thing," was a famous Aerosmith song. Surprised, since she wasn't a fan of hard rock, Claire thought it was still a pretty song.

Barbara, the style queen, took in the '70s paneling, cracked linoleum, sagging couch, dirty dishes, and mousetrap in the kitchen corner. "I love what you've done with the place, Cagney. Very retro."

"You know how I love vintage."

Atsuko startled as she passed a mounted fish on the wall. A fish that moved and began singing "Don't Worry, Be Happy."

"Meet Billy Bass," Daphne said, returning to the couch. She

narrowed her eyes at the Alphabet trio. "Now, will someone answer my question? What are you *doing* here?"

Bypassing the sagging couch, Barbara sat on the wooden chair beside it. She nudged Daphne's foot with her own. "Your gorgeous detective friend paid me a visit. He asked where you were and wanted to know if you'd ever mentioned a guy named Benny Popov."

Daphne put her head in her good hand. "Great."

"Don't worry, I played dumb and got rid of him."

"We have bigger problems, though." Claire handed Daphne her phone, showing her the photo of Benny and the accompanying newspaper article. "I suggest we help you pack and head back to Cedar Glen forthwith."

Barbara tilted her head at Claire. "*Forthwith*?"

"I've been reading Jane Austen."

"And how will we explain our quick return after we were supposed to be on a girls' trip to Vegas?" Barbara asked.

"Vegas?" Daphne lifted her eyebrows.

Atsuko shrugged. "We had to come up with an on-the-spot excuse for Lenny. He waylaid us as we were leaving." On autopilot, she moved to the sink and began washing the dishes, musing as she did so. "Everyone thinks you're in Nevada staying with your niece, Daphne, but they don't know *where* in Nevada. Maybe it's outside of Las Vegas." Atsuko rinsed the plates and set them in the drainer, thinking it through.

Drying her hands, she turned and faced the girls. "I've got it! We'll say we popped in to say hi to Daphne on our way to the casinos and found her in a lot of pain with her shoulder." Atsuko nodded at Claire. "As the only one of us with any medical experience, Claire thought it best we get Daphne back to her doctor straightaway."

Barbara glanced at Claire. "I didn't know you had a medical background."

"Me neither," Daphne said.

Claire grunted. "Not much of one. A lifetime ago, I went through medical assistant training at a local trade school. After receiving my certificate, I got a job in a doctor's office. I loved that job and was good at it." Claire's eyes took on a faraway expression, remembering. "But I was there less than a year. Stan wanted me home with the kids when they were growing up. He didn't like them being in daycare and said it was a mother's job to be with her children."

Barbara snorted. "I can't believe you stayed with that jerk as long as you did. I'd have dumped him years ago."

"I should have." Claire studied her hands, noticing a hangnail. "But being raised in an old-fashioned, traditional family, I had it drilled into me my whole life that divorce was not an option."

One of the many reasons she later left the church.

"Growing up Baptist in Texas, it was drilled into me too," Barbara said. She gave the girls a sly grin. "Meeting my second husband helped drill it right out of me."

"We're getting sidetracked." Atsuko cocked an eyebrow at Daphne. "Don't you think we need to get a move on?"

"Yeah." Daphne expelled a sigh. "It won't look good, my leaving town, especially now it's common knowledge Benny's missing. Rick will find it way too coincidental, I'm sure." Closing the bag of Doritos, she opened her suitcase and started packing. "Let's hit the road."

A grunting sound filtered through the open window.

Claire jumped. "What's that?"

"Bear, probably." Daphne continued packing.

"A *bear*?" Claire yelped. The color drained from her face. Barbara's too.

"Yup. We're in the woods," Daphne said matter-of-factly. "Bears *live* here. This is their natural habitat. Don't worry; I have an electric fence around the property. Had to install it a few years ago after a bear tore apart the cabin searching for food. It's the only thing that keeps them out."

Claire squeaked. "A bear inside *this* cabin? The cabin we're in right now?"

"Chill. It's no big deal. Like I said, there's an electric fence around the property."

Atsuko moved to the window. "Was it a black bear that got inside?" she asked. "A *big* black bear? Like the one staring at me right now?"

"Oh my God." Barbara's eyes darted to the wildlife on the other side of the fence that had the A member of the Alphabet Girls in its sights. "He's huge."

Grabbing food from the fridge, Claire started throwing it into her tote. "We need to get out of here, *now*."

"How?" Atsuko asked. "There's no electric fence around our cars."

Claire stopped her frantic packing, fear etching her features.

"Jeez, Louise." Daphne slammed her suitcase shut. "Bunch of city slickers." Striding to the kitchen, she grabbed an air horn from the top of the fridge and joined Atsuko at the window. "Move," she ordered.

As Atsuko stepped aside, Daphne blasted the horn in the bear's direction. The black bear ran into the woods, disappearing from sight.

"I don't know about the rest of you," Claire said, "but I'm getting out of here now before Smokey the Bear comes back." Grabbing Daphne's Cap'n Crunch from the counter, she scurried to the front door.

"Right behind you." Barbara picked up Daphne's suitcase. "Come on, Cagney, I'll drive."

"Hang on, B. I need to make sure I haven't left any food behind." Daphne opened the fridge and cupboard, and did a quick scan of the rest of the cabin.

"Claire got it all," Atsuko said, striding to the door. "Now, let's go."

"I just need to spring this last mousetrap." Daphne nudged the trap with her booted foot. When it snapped, she grabbed the trap with a paper towel and tossed it into the bag of trash in her hand. "Don't want to leave any bait behind for the critters."

TWELVE

"I have never been so happy to leave a place in my whole life," Claire said to Atsuko as they drove away. Her voice wobbled. "I can't believe we were that close to a bear!" She shook her head. "I have never understood the attraction of roughing it."

"A cabin isn't roughing it, Claire. Packing in twenty miles into deep wilderness with a heavy backpack and sleeping in a leaky tent in the rain is roughing it," Atsuko said. "No bathrooms, and you have to bury your own poop."

Claire wrinkled her nose. "No thank you. That's one good thing I can say about Stan. He liked his creature comforts. The handful of times we took the kids camping, we rented a Winnebago."

"I think that's called glamping."

"Camping, glamping, I don't care what they call it—it is *not* for me."

Atsuko stole a sideways look at her friend. She could see Claire was still shaken by her close encounter with a wild animal. She wondered if it was more than that, though. After all, it had only been a few days since Claire had killed a man. Not something someone gets over easily. Unless they're a sociopath.

"What we need is a little *Wicked*," she said.

"'For Good' never fails to cure what ails me." Leaning her head back on the headrest, Claire closed her eyes, blocking out the events of the past few days and letting the music by Kristin Chenoweth and Idina Menzel take her away. When the song about friendship ended, she turned to Atsuko and said, "Thank you for rewriting my life by being my friend."

Meanwhile, the B and D members of the Alphabet Girls rocked out to "We Are Never Ever Getting Back Together" in Daphne's car.

"Taylor Swift is the bomb," Daphne said. "Best songwriter ever."

"Carole King and Joni Mitchell might disagree."

"Good point. *Tapestry* is an amazing album. I wore that out in college. How about Joni, Carole, and Taylor as the best songwriting trifecta?"

"Now, *that* I can get behind." Turning down the music, Barbara pinned her eyes on her friend. "OK, Cagney, come clean. Were you and the gorgeous detective romantically involved?"

"Absolutely not. Rick was married when we worked together. Also, he's six years younger than me."

"Nothing wrong with a younger man. After divorcing my last husband, a man two decades older than me, I started seeing younger guys. They're more chill. Not mired in all that patriarchal b.s. we were raised with." Barbara tightened her hands on the steering wheel. "I prefer men who don't hold me back and try to put me into a box of society's making." She cut a sideways squint at her friend. "Back to the gorgeous Rick, though. I don't know how you could keep your hands off him, working in such close quarters. I'd have probably jumped his bones in the back seat of the squad car."

"I have a strict rule about married men, B. Besides, Rick and I were buddies. Pals. Nothing more." What Daphne didn't tell Barbara—would never tell *any*one—was there was a time when she and her partner had flirted with becoming more than friends. The memory resurfaced.

Back then, Rick had been separated from Linda. Again. Had been for several months. This time, he wanted to file for divorce. "I'm sick of all the fighting and drama," he'd said as he and Daphne patrolled the streets of Santa Bonita in the Ford sedan. "It's not worth it—it's too hard. Relationships shouldn't be this hard. Look at you and me."

"Huh?" Daphne pushed up her glasses. "Whaddya mean?"

"We get along great. There's no bickering and fighting. No jealousy or drama. No insistence on always being right." He paused. "Apart from your misplaced love of the Dodgers, of course." Rick's white teeth flashed in the dim car lighting.

"We're friends. *Good* friends, Daph. I can count on you. You've got my back, and I've got yours. Plus, you're easy to talk to. Not like Linda. I should have married *you*," he teased. "Where were you twenty years ago?"

"Skiing with Tom Cruise in Aspen," Daphne said. "You're a good-looking guy, Rick, but you're no Tom Cruise."

"Who *is*?" Beating his hands on the dash, Rick hummed a snatch of "Danger Zone" from *Top Gun*. "I am taller than him, though, and like Tom, I do my own stunts. Remember when I jumped off the roof chasing that perp?"

"This is true. And the tall thing *is* a bonus, I have to admit. I don't like towering over the guys I date." Shaking her head, Daphne made a clicking sound at the back of her throat. "When Tom and I were together, I always had to wear flats."

Rick waggled his eyebrows. "You wouldn't have to wear flats with me, baby."

"That clinches it. We *should* have gotten married." Daphne grinned. "Just my luck. Always a day late and a dollar short."

Rick returned her grin. Then something flickered in his eyes. Tilting his head to the side, he gave her an odd look.

"What? Do I have mustard on this mug again?" Daphne's hand went to her face. She stuck her tongue out of the side of her mouth to lick away the errant condiment.

"No." Rick continued to regard her with a strange expression. "I was thinking . . . maybe it doesn't have to be a day late and a dollar short."

The radio crackled to life. "Ten thirty-two, three units needed. Ten sixty-five, armed robbery. SB Bank."

"Christmastime." Rick activated the overhead lights.

Daphne hit the siren and gunned the squad car, speeding to Santa Bonita's main bank downtown. When they arrived, another unit was already exchanging gunfire with the robbers. Rick and Daphne spilled out the sides of the Ford, crouching low, guns drawn.

A bullet whizzed past Daphne's ear. She ducked. The next bullet hit her in the chest, and she went down.

"Daph!" Rick raced to his partner's side as another squad car pulled up, providing cover. He shielded Daphne, cradling her in his arms, all the while shouting, "Officer down, officer down."

Daphne came to in a hospital room, recovering from surgery. Opening her eyes, the first thing she saw was her out-of-focus partner.

"Hey, there," Rick said softly. "You gave me quite a scare, Daph. Don't do that again, OK?"

Through the fog of pain meds, Daphne realized he was holding her hand.

"The doc said you're going to be fine. You were lucky; the bullet missed your vital organs. You'll be good as new in no time, but until then, you're to relax and take it easy. Don't worry," Rick's mouth tightened. "We got the perps, and they're in custody."

Daphne gave him a groggy thumbs-up and fell back asleep.

Rick visited his partner every day in the hospital, bringing flowers, candy, and, one day, a Tommy Lasorda bobblehead.

"You know the way to a girl's heart." Daphne chuckled as she made the legendary Dodgers' manager's head bob.

"That's the plan."

Daphne got an odd feeling—as if a bunch of moths were playing tag in her stomach. When Rick left moments later, she asked herself, *What is* happening *here?*

Before anything could happen, though, Daphne discovered something that proved to be the death knell of any kind of a romantic relationship with Rick. What she discovered also proved to be the death knell of their work partnership and her career with the Santa Bonita Police Force.

Daphne's cell blared out the *Mary Tyler Moore Show* theme song. "Hey, Claire, what's up?"

"Put me on speaker so Barbara can hear."

"What's going on?" B asked.

"Atsuko and I realized we rushed out of the cabin so fast after our Smokey encounter that we didn't confirm the story we're going to tell when we get back."

"Sure we did," Barbara said. "Atsuko said if anyone asks why we came back from Vegas so fast, we say we stopped by to see Daphne at her niece's and found her in a lot of pain. With her medical background, Claire said we should get Cagney back home right away, so her doctor could see her." Examining her nails on the steering wheel, Barbara thought, *Time for a new color.* "Isn't that about the gist of it?"

"Nearly verbatim," Atsuko said. "I'm impressed. I didn't realize you listened so closely to what I had to say, B."

"I always listen." Barbara made a face at the phone, glad Cagney hadn't put them on FaceTime. "You forget that a long time ago in a galaxy far, far away, I used to be an actress. I've always been good at memorizing lines."

"Sorry. I *had* forgotten that."

"That's OK. It was a long time ago. I only did a handful of plays, and my film career was relegated to a background dancer in *How to Stuff a Wild Bikini* with Frankie Avalon and Annette Funicello, three commercials, and a bit part in a Woody Allen film. This was during Woody's Diane Keaton days." Barbara wrinkled her nose as if she'd smelled something bad. "Decades before he married his stepdaughter."

"You've lived quite the glamorous life, B," Claire said. "Is there anything you haven't done?"

"Slept with Al Pacino. Although not for lack of trying. That's a story for another day, though."

"I'll hold you to that," Claire said. "I've loved Al Pacino since *Serpico*."

Atsuko took control of the conversation before the two Alphabet Girls went down one of their movie-loving rabbit trails. "So we're all in agreement on what to say. Anything else?"

Daphne shifted in her seat, pushing her seatbelt away from her sling. "I think it's time I gave Rick a call and set up a meeting. Don't worry; I'll stick to the party line. See ya back at the ranch, girls."

Ending the call, she punched in Rick's number, relieved when it went straight to voicemail. "Hi Rick, it's Daphne. I hear Benny Popov is missing and you want to talk. I'm on my way back from my niece's. Won't get home till late. Need to see my doc in the morning for my shoulder, but after that I'm free all day. Let me know when you want to meet."

Forgetting she'd told Rick she was going to see her sister, Daphne hung up, face flushed. Sweat beaded on her upper lip, and beads of perspiration dotted her forehead. All at once, a wave of heat engulfed her body from the waist up. She could feel the sweat trickling down her back. Squirming in her seat, Daphne reached her good hand beneath her shirt and unhooked her bra. Then she slapped on the AC full blast and pointed the vent at her face. "Damned menopause."

Barbara smirked and belted out Linda Ronstadt's "Heat Wave."

Back at Cedar Glen, Evelyn Blair made her way to the clubhouse for Taco Tuesday. Holding tight to her walker, she shuffled down the sidewalk in her Hush Puppies, hunched over from osteoporosis. She struggled, trying to balance her unwieldy purse and tote bag holding her assorted bingo paraphernalia—daubers, Butterscotch Lifesavers, cash, and two lucky troll charms.

Evelyn had christened the pink-haired troll Lisette, and the orange-haired troll Fleur. As well as being Taco Tuesday, it was also bingo night, and Evelyn never missed bingo. If you'd have told her in her fifties that she'd become one of those bingo-playing old ladies she used to scoff at, she'd never have believed it. But things change, bodies change, and you do the best you can with what you have. She quickened her steps, but in doing so, her tote fell to the ground spilling out the contents. Evelyn cursed.

Lenny Fink and Vince Merlucci hurried over to the elderly woman. "Let me help you there," Lenny said, picking up the tote and putting everything back inside. "Shall I carry that for you?"

Evelyn grunted a curt thanks.

Relieving her of her bag, Lenny turned on the charm, "May I say you're looking especially lovely today, Evelyn?"

"You can say it, but I won't believe it. This old body of mine is sagging and bagging all over the place." Evelyn scowled. "My osteoporosis doesn't help either. That saying *getting old isn't for sissies* is certainly true."

Vince patted Evelyn on the shoulder. "You're as young as you feel."

"Well, I feel old as dirt." She glared at the two men. "How about that?"

Over her bent head, Lenny and Vince rolled their eyes. Lenny was beginning to regret his offer to help the crusty nonagenarian. He cast about for something to engage Evelyn. "Is that why you didn't go to Vegas with the other girls?" he teased.

Evelyn stopped in mid-shuffle. "What in blue blazes are you talking about, Lenny Fink?"

"Atsuko, Barbara, and Claire left on a girls' trip to Vegas earlier today."

Evelyn snorted. "I'd believe that of Atsuko and Barbara. Atsuko loves to gamble, and Barbara would be right at home with all those fancy showgirls. But Claire?" She shook her head. "I don't think so. Claire once told me she hates Las Vegas. She can't stand all the noise and crowds and people throwing good money after bad."

"Is that right?" Lenny's fingers tightened on Evelyn's tote, his eyes narrowing to slits. Those girls had lied to him. Played him for a fool. No one plays Lenny Fink for a fool.

THIRTEEN

Claire collected Elinor from her daughter's house the next morning, enveloping the pup in a huge hug. "Mommy missed you, sweetheart." She snuggled her face into Elinor's fur. When they got back to Cedar Glen, she took her dog on her daily laps around the dog park, grateful to be back in civilization again with animals that were domesticated.

Claire shuddered, remembering. Driving away from the cabin in the woods, she and Atsuko had seen a possum waddling along the side of the road, its offspring hanging on its back.

"Look at those darling baby possums," Atsuko exclaimed. "Aren't they cute?"

Claire turned away from the sight. In her eyes, possums were the antithesis of cute. Scary creatures, always hissing and baring their teeth. They looked like giant rats with their long, skinny tails, and Claire hated rats with a passion. Between the skunk, not-so-Gentle Ben, and now this family of possums, she had seen more than enough animals in the wild to last her a lifetime.

An excited yipping roused her from her reverie. Claire looked up to see Mark and Brontë approach, Brontë panting to see her new friends.

"Hello, Claire. Hello, Elinor," Mark said with a smile.

"Hi, Mark." Claire squatted down to pet the terrier with the tail wagging like a propeller. "Good morning, Brontë, and how are you today?"

But Brontë only had eyes for Elinor.

The two dogs sniffed each other, Elinor a bit warily. Once Brontë licked her on the nose, though, Elinor responded in kind.

Claire smiled at the two dogs. "I think this is going to be

the beginning of a beautiful friendship," she said, echoing Humphrey Bogart from one of her favorite movies.

"I hope so." Mark smiled at her.

Elinor's mom felt a strange fluttering in her chest.

Later that day, Claire rollerbladed over to the bank of mailboxes at the clubhouse. As she sorted through the circulars and envelopes, dropping the junk mail into the recycle box, a familiar voice wafted her way.

"My main man, how's it goin'?" she heard a familiar voice say.

Looking up, she noticed Vince Merlucci talking to a silver-haired man in a bespoke suit outside the Cedars, the combination nursing home and assisted-living facility at Cedar Glen.

Claire recognized the man from newspaper photos: Dmitri Glazatovsky.

Daphne knocked back a pain pill as she settled into her recliner, waiting for Rick to arrive. Tamping down the butterflies swirling in her stomach, she wondered if he was dating anyone since his divorce. *Don't go there, idiot*, she told herself. *Remember, your partner—your* friend*—is the reason you took early retirement.*

Dozing off, she came to with a start half an hour later when the doorbell rang. Opening the door, Daphne saw Rick wasn't alone. An attractive brunette in khakis and a black polo shirt with the same police emblem as Rick's stood beside him.

A detective, Daphne thought. *One who looks like she's in her mid-forties.* A surge of envy shot through her.

Rick piped up. "Daphne Cole, Jessica Miller. Jess is my partner, Daph."

Daphne pushed down the jealousy she felt bubbling up. "Nice to meet you, Detective Miller. Won't you come in?" Her words were stilted. Formal.

Rick gave her a bemused side-eye as she led them into the living room.

"Can I get you something to drink?" Daphne asked. "Water? Iced tea?" *Strychnine?*

"No thanks. We just had lunch, and I have a drink." Rick's

new partner inclined her head to the stainless-steel water bottle in her hand.

Daphne kicked a pile of laundry out of the way and nodded at the leather couch. "Take a seat." She eased herself into the recliner, supporting her sling. "How can I help you?"

Rick cleared his throat. "Daph, as you know, Benny Popov is missing—"

Daphne interrupted him. "Yeah, I saw that in the paper. Nobody's seen him since he got out of the joint, huh?" She shook her head. "That's odd."

"Very odd," Detective Miller said. "Especially since he had a job waiting for him here, *and* an apartment provided by his employer. Don't you find that strange, Daphne—may I call you Daphne?"

"Sure, *Jessica*." She cut the detective a fake smile.

Sensing tension, Rick interjected, "Daph, have you seen Benny since the last time I was here?"

"Neither hide nor hair of him, sorry. But I've been out of town, visiting my niece." *My phantom niece.*

Rick considered her. "I thought you were going to your sister's?"

Daphne gave herself an internal kick. "My niece is my sister's daughter—the three of us all got together."

The detective Rick had called Jess continued her interrogation.

"Several people heard Benny Popov threaten you at his sentencing, Daphne." Jessica flipped open a notebook. "Benny said, and I quote, 'The first thing I'm gonna do when I get out is kill you.'" Her brown eyes met the former cop's. "I won't repeat the name he called you since that's a word I despise. A word men use far too frequently to describe women."

Daphne grimaced. "It's not one of my favorites either."

"We understand Benny doesn't have any family," the detective continued. "Is that your understanding as well?"

"Yep. The only family I knew of back in the day was his wife." Daphne scrunched her forehead, pretending to try to remember. "Sheila, I think her name was. She split and divorced Benny not long after he got sent down."

Jessica eyeballed Daphne's sling. "If you don't mind my asking, what happened to your arm?"

"Tore my bicep at the gym. Had to have surgery."

She winced. "I'll bet that hurt. When was your surgery?"

"Third of September—the day after Labor Day."

Pen poised over her notebook Jess said, "Two weeks ago. A week before Benny was released." She studied Daphne. "A friend of mine had that same surgery last year. She had to keep her sling on for five weeks and not lift anything heavy or do anything strenuous during that time. I assume your recovery is the same?"

"Uh-huh. Doc says my arm will be out of commission for four to six weeks."

Jessica's eyes flicked to Daphne's left hand. "Are you a southpaw by chance?"

"I wish. Then using my laptop wouldn't take so long. The hunt-and-peck method is the best I can do right now. Luckily, I start physical therapy soon."

Detective Miller closed her notebook and stood. "I think that's all we need." She glanced at Rick.

"You go on ahead. I'll meet you at the car in a minute."

"OK." Jessica nodded at Daphne. "Nice to meet you. Keep an eye out for Benny; he may still try to deliver on his promise."

"Duly noted."

After Jessica left, Rick examined his former partner, assessing her.

Daphne did her best to maintain an open, guileless expression.

Rick's gaze shifted to the wall behind her. Scanning the condo, his eyes came to rest upon the bare floor near the recliner.

Daphne's heart scudded in her chest.

Rick lifted his eyes to meet hers. "Any idea what might have happened to Popov, Daph?"

"Not a clue. I haven't seen the guy in years." She shrugged. "Who knows? Maybe he met someone and left town."

"You don't leave Dmitri Glazatovsky."

"You would know."

Rick's jaw worked.

Not wanting a repeat of the other day, Daphne changed the subject. "Your new partner seems nice. You two dating?"

A smile played at Rick's lips. "I don't think her wife would like that."

Claire sent a group text to her Alphabet pals.

CLAIRE: You'll never believe who I just saw! Dmitri Glazatovsky and Vince Merlucci in front of the Cedars, looking awfully chummy.

Atsuko called Claire immediately. "Are you sure it was Dmitri Glazatovsky?"

"Did we see a bear in the woods?"

"I wonder what he was doing here?"

"Maybe he's going to make another charitable donation and upgrade the Cedars or something."

"Maybe . . . Or maybe he was visiting someone there," Atsuko mused. "I have a friend at Cedars who's a nurse's aide. I'll find out."

"But what's Vince's connection to the local crime boss?" Claire asked.

"*That* is the million-dollar question. We'll ask Daphne when she finishes her meeting with the detectives."

While she waited, Claire decided to make chocolate-chip-peanut-butter bars. Her grandson loved her cookie bars. At home, the only cookies his mom made were the slice-and-bake ones, and then, only at Christmas.

Claire loved to bake. When the kids were growing up, she'd baked all the time—cookies were her specialty. Her children were the envy of their classmates when they told them their mom had cookies fresh from the oven waiting for them after school. As a result, soon the Reynolds' home became a magnet for her son and daughter's friends.

As she pulled out the baking ingredients, Claire listened to the soundtrack from *The Greatest Showman*, her current favorite musical. Half an hour later, the doorbell rang, causing Elinor to bark and run to the entryway. Elinor pawed at the door and continued to bark.

Expecting it to be Atsuko or Daphne, Claire scooped up Elinor and opened the door to find Edie and Doris, two of her Cedar Glen neighbors, on her doorstep.

"Hello, Claire," the diminutive Edie said. "Doris and I were wondering if you'd like to join our bunko group. We're down a couple of people since Betty moved to North Carolina, and Helen broke her hip and went to rehab."

"How is Helen?" From her medical training, Claire knew broken hips could often be a death sentence for the elderly. That's why she made sure to take her daily walks and strengthen her aging bones with calcium and Vitamin D.

"She's in fine form. Complaining as always," octogenarian Doris said. Doris always reminded Claire of an overgrown Chihuahua, always yipping and yapping. "So what do you say, Claire"—she clicked her dentures—"you up for joining the Bunko Babes?"

Elinor yipped.

"Stop that, Elinor." Claire gave Edie and Doris a rueful smile. "Sorry. She always barks when someone comes to the door—Elinor's a good guard dog." She ruffled the pup's fur. "As for bunko, it sounds like fun, but I'll need to think about it. I've got so many things going on already—book club, poker night . . ." Her voice trailed off. *Hiding a crime from the police, dumping dead men's cars, disposing of bodies.* "I'll get back to you soon."

After the women left, Claire pulled the cookie bars out of the oven and set them on the counter to cool. Her phone alarm buzzed. *Crap. I forgot about Elinor's vet appointment.* Her eyes skimmed the messy kitchen. She hated to leave it in such a state, but if she didn't leave now, she'd be late. She'd have to clean up when she got back.

An hour later, Claire returned home to chaos.

When she opened the front door, Elinor sprinted to the kitchen, barking in a frenzy. Following Elinor, Claire came to a standstill in the kitchen doorway. Barstools were tipped on their sides, drawers and cupboard doors were flung open, and flour, sugar, and chocolate chips were spread all over the floor. She scooped up Elinor before she could get to the chocolate, holding the trembling pup to her chest.

Claire trembled as well. Someone had broken in and trashed her home in her absence. *But who? And why?* She thought of the man she'd killed. The man buried at the bottom of the quarry in two Hefty trash bags. The murderer who'd been released from prison and worked for local crime boss Dmitri Glazatovsky—the man who'd posted a reward for information on his missing employee. The same crime boss who'd been outside the Cedars only an hour ago talking to Vince.

Could the Russian mobster or some of his minions have found the body and figured out I killed Benny Popov?

That's ridiculous, Claire's rational side interjected. *The quarry was deserted apart from you, the girls, and the dead guy. No one could have seen you get rid of him. Besides, his body is weighted down with stones and sunken beneath a hundred feet of water. It would be impossible for anyone to have found him.*

Claire puffed a gust of air out of her mouth, recognizing the validity of that reasoning and considering other possibilities. Could it be that someone here saw what happened at Daphne's that day and wants to claim the reward? Ten thousand dollars isn't a lot of money, but to someone living on Social Security, it would seem a fortune. *Why trash my kitchen, though?*

Her catastrophic thinking side piped up. *To serve as a warning. Maybe they want you to know* they *know and are intending to blackmail you to keep quiet. Maybe they want more than ten grand. Maybe they think you're loaded.*

Ha! Claire's reasonable side added her two cents. *Or maybe it's just a simple burglary. Kids playing a prank. Is anything missing?*

She skimmed her surroundings. That's when she noticed half the pan of cookie bars gone, along with her CD of *The*

Greatest Showman. Definitely something a kid would do. Especially one who likes musicals. She texted Daphne.

CLAIRE: Someone broke into my house.

Barbara jogged down Cedar Glen's curving pathways, listening to the Beatles. Out of nowhere, a man stepped in front of her, bringing her to an abrupt halt. Barbara's hand flew to her chest. She yanked out her earbuds. "Lenny, you scared me."

"Sorry, I didn't mean to break your stride. You girls have a good time in Las Vegas?" Lenny asked with an innocent air. "That was a quick trip. What happened? You crap out at the tables and lose everything that first day?"

"No, we dropped by to see Daphne. Did you know she was visiting her niece in Nevada?" The lie slid smoothly off Barbara's tongue.

Lenny shook his head.

"Daphne's niece lives outside of Vegas, so we decided to pay her a quick visit on our way to the casinos." The sides of Barbara's mouth turned down, and she adopted a concerned expression. "Unfortunately, Daphne was not in a good way. She was in a lot of pain from her shoulder surgery. Claire said we needed to bring her back home and take her to the doctor."

"I didn't realize Claire was a nurse."

"She's not. I mean, she wasn't. Back in the day, though, she used to be a medical assistant, which means she has more medical background than the rest of us, so we thought we'd better listen to her." Barbara gave a light laugh. "Claire has a way of making people listen to her."

"You don't say." Maybe he had gotten it wrong. Maybe the girls hadn't lied to him after all. He fingered *The Greatest Showman* CD in his pocket. Lenny liked Daphne, a fellow Dodgers fan and vet, although she had served in the Air Force rather than the Navy. "How is Daphne now?" he asked. "What did the doctor say?"

"He said she over-exerted herself too soon after surgery. Ordered her to stay home and not go gallivanting all over the place until she's out of her sling," Barbara lied effortlessly.

"Good for him." Lenny gave the Cedar Glen senior with the

perfect body a speculative glance. "Shame you had to miss your trip to Vegas, though. I know how much you were looking forward to it."

"Easy come, easy go." Barbara winked. "Vegas will always be there. We'll go another time." She started to put her earbuds back in, but Lenny stopped her.

"Do you think Daphne will listen to her doctor?"

"We'll make sure she does." Recalling that the octogenarian with the bad rug had been in the Navy, Barbara gave Lenny a mock salute. "Don't you worry; the Alphabet Girls are on duty. We'll make her toe the line."

"Good to know."

Barbara gave a little wave and jogged off.

Lenny watched her go. Even as he admired the sight of Barbara's retreating figure, he thought to himself, *Those girls are up to something.*

FOURTEEN

"What's new at Cedar Glen?" Kenzo asked as he FaceTimed with his mother and sister.

"Nothing much," Atsuko flapped her hand at her son. "Same old, same old." If they only knew.

"Can we talk about Thanksgiving?" Hana asked.

"Thanksgiving? That's still two months away," Kenzo said.

"I know, but we need to make a plan." Hana was all about plans. "Since Tomiko will be home, I'd like to have Thanksgiving at our house this year," she said. "Drew will make the turkey—he's dying to try out his new smoker."

"Works for me," Kenzo said.

Hana continued. "I'll make mashed potatoes, gravy, stuffing, cranberry relish, and baked yams. Mom, will you do the pies?"

"Of course." Atsuko wondered if it would cause a riot if she made something other than her usual.

"Yum." Kenzo licked his lips. "It's not turkey day without Mom's pies. I look forward to your pumpkin pie all year long, Mom."

I guess pumpkin's still on the table.

"Tomiko *loves* your pecan pie," Hana said. "So does Drew. I love both. That's why I always take a sliver of each."

Guess I can't take pecan off the table either, Atsuko thought. She decided instead of removing her usual pies, this year she'd add something new to the mix. *Maybe chocolate mousse?*

"I'll bring my standard rolls," Kenzo said.

"Not this year, little brother," Hana said. "You need to actually *cook* something for a change—it's not fair that Mom and I always have to make everything."

Atsuko watched her daughter push her hair behind her ears.

"I'm putting you in charge of green vegetables this year," Hana told Kenzo. "I don't care if you bring green beans, Brussels sprouts, peas, or whatever—that's your choice. Just as long as it's green, a vegetable, and made by your own two little hands." Her dark eyes upon her sibling were fixed. Unwavering. "Think you can handle that?"

"No prob."

"Do you want to invite one of your girlfriends to join us, Mom?" Hana asked. "Claire's your closest friend, right?"

"Yes, but Claire usually has Thanksgiving with her family. I'll ask her, though. Otherwise, I'll see if Barbara or Daphne would like to come."

"Bring them both. We've got plenty of room."

Daphne answered Claire's text, telling her not to touch anything and saying she'd be right over. Daphne whistled at the kitchen carnage when she arrived. "What a mess."

"It's driving me crazy," Claire, still holding Elinor, said. "I'm dying to clean it up."

"Not yet. We need to report this and get the cops over here. You haven't touched anything, right?"

"Nope."

"Anything missing besides the cookies and the CD?"

"I have no idea. You told me not to touch anything." Claire's voice quavered. "I was wondering if maybe Glazatovsky or one of his henchmen could have done this. Maybe they found out about Benny, and this was their way of telling us they know."

Daphne peered at Claire over her glasses. "By stealing a CD and cookies? Nah. Looks more like teens to me. I'll call it in."

Claire waited until Daphne finished reporting the break-in. "Did you get my text?"

"Yeah, that's why I'm here. You said someone broke in."

"Not that text. The group text I sent you and the girls earlier, saying I saw Dmitri Glazatovsky over at the Cedars talking to Vince Merlucci."

"What?" Daphne stared at Claire. "What was Glazatovsky doing here—and talking to Vince, no less?"

"That's what I'd like to know."

They were interrupted by the arrival of a young police officer who questioned Claire about the break-in. Daphne held on to

Elinor as the cop led Claire through the house to see if anything else was missing.

"Who's a good doggie?" Daphne cooed to the little dog with the big eyes.

Elinor wagged her tail.

After rejoining Daphne in the kitchen, Claire asked the police officer, "Are you going to dust for fingerprints now?"

"No, ma'am."

"Why not?"

The rookie cop swiveled his eyes to Daphne.

"In a minor vandalism case like this, Claire, we—I mean the police—don't usually dust for prints. There's not the time or manpower for that," Daphne said. "If it was a burglary involving major theft, like cars or electronics, that would be a different story. But for a few cookies and a CD, it's not worth the trouble. Most likely, it was kids."

"But how did they get in?"

Daphne walked over to the kitchen patio door, sliding it open. "Here would be my guess."

Claire's face pinked. "Oh. I was in such a hurry to get to the vet's, I forgot to lock the patio door." She gave the policeman an apologetic look. "Sorry to waste your time, Officer. I have no one to blame but myself. I'm just glad they didn't take anything valuable." Claire grabbed the broom and started sweeping up the mess as the cop left. "I hate to think of a stranger in my home. Even if it was only kids pulling a prank, having fun messing up an old lady's house, it's disconcerting." Her hands on the broom shook.

"I know. I'm sorry." Daphne gave her a side hug, her sling preventing a full frontal.

"Can you do me a favor, please?" Claire bit her lip. "Would you let the girls know, but tell them I'd rather not talk about it? Not yet, at least. I'd like to simply forget this and move on."

"You got it. And Claire?" Daphne met her friend's eyes. "Anytime you want to talk, I'm here."

FIFTEEN

Over wine and cheese that night at her condo, Atsuko informed her fellow Alphabet Girls that Dmitri Glazatovsky came once or twice a month to the Cedars to visit an elderly resident in the nursing home. "Jill, my friend who works there, said Dmitri's the only one who visits Olga Ivanova," Atsuko said. "He brings her flowers and chocolate every time he comes—apparently, Olga has a sweet tooth. She doesn't have any family nearby, and her dead husband used to work for Dmitri."

"OK, that explains Glazatovsky's presence here," Daphne said, "but what the hell is Vince's connection to our local Russian crime lord?"

"Maybe he once worked for Dmitri as well," Claire speculated.

Barbara took a sip of her wine. "I always thought Vince had a touch of the mobster about him."

"I'll check with some of my sources." Daphne popped open a Sprite. "See what I can find out."

"Meanwhile, how'd it go with Detective Gorgeous today?" Barbara asked with a smirk.

As she drank her Sprite under Atsuko's watchful eye, Daphne kept stealing longing peeks at the girls' wine glasses. "Fine. All's well."

"What kind of questions did he ask?" Atsuko stroked Elinor, who had snuggled up beside her after Claire arrived with her dog hugged to her chest.

"You mean what kind of questions did *she* ask. Rick brought his partner, Detective Miller. The *young* Jessica Miller."

But Daphne wasn't bitter. Not at all.

Barbara regarded her pal. "Is this new partner hot, Cagney?"

Daphne shrugged. "Attractive. Slender. Rick said she's gay." She refused to examine why that pleased her so much.

"So what kinds of questions did Detective Miller pose?" Claire asked.

"She asked if I thought it was strange Benny Popov hadn't been seen since his release from prison. She also asked if he had any family." Daphne eyed her sling. "And then she asked a bunch of questions about my injury and my surgery, whether I was left-handed, blah, blah, blah. I think she was trying to figure out if I might have been able to put down Benny."

"Put down?" Atsuko asked.

"Kill him."

Claire dropped a cracker into her wine glass. "You're kidding."

Daphne sucked air through her teeth. "Nope."

"Did she actually come out and accuse you of killing him?" Atsuko asked.

"Nah, she was fishing. Don't worry, I think she concluded I was too incapacitated to do such a thing." Daphne didn't tell the girls how Rick had remained behind and scanned her place from top to bottom, knowing that detail would freak them out. "I don't think they'll be back."

"Good." Claire poured herself a fresh glass of wine. "Now we can put this whole sorry business behind us."

"It wasn't *all* sorry," Barbara said. "I don't know about you, but I had a blast playing Sydney Bristow the other night. It's good to shake things up now and then."

"I found rappelling down the side of the quarry in the dark equal parts fun and terrifying." Atsuko speared a cube of cheese. "It wasn't as much fun going back up, though. From now on, I'm sticking to those rock-climbing walls."

"Tell me where and when and I'm there," Barbara said.

Daphne swigged her Sprite. "Me too."

Den mother Atsuko cut her a look.

"Once I finish PT, of course."

Claire picked up the gift bag she'd set on Atsuko's counter and handed it to Daphne.

"What's this? It's not my birthday."

"Open it and you'll see."

Daphne plucked out the tissue paper with her left hand but struggled to get the gift out.

"Let me help, Cagney," Barbara offered. Aware of the contents, she turned the bag on its side and held the bottom, while Daphne pulled from the top.

Daphne held up the plush throw, speechless.

"I wanted to replace your couch blanket I ruined," Claire said. "I tried to get an exact replica of the one you had, but this was the closest I could find."

Daphne got something in her eye. Bending her head, she pretended to check out the sports team emblem. "Thanks, Claire. It will be nice to have Dodger blue back in my living room again."

Atsuko cleared away the plates and glasses after the girls left, putting them in the sink full of soapy water. She enjoyed washing dishes by hand—she found it a meditative act that gave her time to think. Rinsing the soap off the hors d'oeuvres plates, Atsuko reflected on what Jill, her nurse's aide friend at the Cedars had told her about Dmitri Glazatovsky's visits to Olga.

Visiting the widow of one of his former employees, a lonely old woman in a nursing home, sounded innocuous enough, but was it? Or did the Russian mobster have another reason for coming regularly to the Cedar Glen Retirement Community? And if so, how was Vince involved?

Atsuko recalled from her research that Glazatovsky had been involved in the real-estate fraud in Sacramento as well as suspected drug trafficking here in Santa Bonita—both charges he'd managed to beat and walk away from scot-free. *Could it be Dmitri was still involved with drug trafficking, and some of it was taking place here, with Vince acting as his inside man?*

Placing the wine glasses on the wooden drying rack, Atsuko thought it would be interesting to see what Daphne's sources turned up.

As Barbara did her nightly sit-ups before bed, she too wondered what Vince's connection to Dmitri Glazatovsky could be. Perhaps she should arrange to accidentally run into Vince and see what she could find out . . .

* * *

Evelyn Blair sucked on a Butterscotch Lifesaver, debating whether or not to tell her son what she'd seen. After conducting an internal argument with herself, she decided against it. *Chuck will think I'm imagining things—call me senile and put me in the Cedars. He's been wanting to do that for some time now, ever since I dropped that jar of pickles and got a tiny cut on my leg from the broken glass. You try opening one of those lids. They make them so tight now.*

Don't forget about the kitchen fire, Evelyn's conscience reminded her.

It wasn't an actual fire. I simply forgot about the hard-boiled eggs and burned a pan. Two kitchen accidents don't make me senile—only old and clumsy. I'm still sharp as a tack. Granted, the tack is getting a little rusty. Yours would too if you were almost ninety-five.

Evelyn considered. Perhaps she should say something to Connie about what she'd witnessed? As manager, Connie should know what was going on at Cedar Glen. Thinking it over, she sighed and shook her white head. *No, she'll think you've lost your marbles too and insist you can't live alone any longer. Connie will try to move you next door to assisted living, where you'll have no privacy and all your freedoms will be taken away.*

Not to mention your independence. Just like prison.

No way would she let that happen. Evelyn refused to live in a place where too-cheerful aides came in anytime they wanted, bringing medications and saying, "And how are we today, sweetheart? Do we need help with the toilet?" Speaking to her as if she were a child. The very idea infuriated her. Not to mention the wheelchair brigade that lined the hallways and dropped in for a chat whenever they felt like it.

So much for privacy.

Evelyn cherished her solitude and refused to give it up. She had always been suspicious of people who couldn't be alone. Those who complained they were *bored* and needed to go searching for an activity to do with others.

How could anyone be bored with all the books there were in the world to read?

All the art to admire.

Beautiful music to listen to.

Evelyn contemplated the floor-to-ceiling bookcases she'd had installed in the living room years ago. Looking at her books, her best friends, made her happy. So did the art she had collected over the years.

Her eyes roamed the walls, taking in the Impressionist scene of San Francisco she'd bought at an art show before moving on to the nude Sebastian had painted of her in her prime. *A lifetime ago*. Evelyn gazed at the trio of Van Gogh prints she'd brought home from the Musée D'Orsay. Finally, her eyes came to rest on the street scene of Montmartre and the charcoal sketch beside it. The sketch had been done by a Montmartre street artist on her first trip to Paris. Evelyn's fingers reached up to touch the framed sketch.

So many memories . . .

The only way she would ever leave her condo would be in a pine box.

Unwrapping a Little Debbie Nutty Bar, Evelyn decided to say something to Claire instead. She felt a kinship with the pixie-haired Claire. Even though she was twenty-five years older than the elegant widow, she felt the two of them were birds of a feather: both big readers, haters of noise, and technologically impaired. Evelyn applauded Claire when she got rid of her laptop. She had had no truck with computers. Her Underwood Selectric suited her fine.

So did her landline. Her son had given her a cellphone for emergencies, but Evelyn couldn't be bothered with it. She hated the way everyone walked around these days, heads bent over their phones. They missed a lot glued to their small screens—like the beauty of Cedar Glen. The retirement community where she had lived for more than twenty years had an abundance of trees—maple, oak, willow, sycamore, and dogwood—and a plethora of flowers lining the pathways. Folks missed that when they were focused on their phones.

They also missed the people right in front of them.

At her son Chuck's insistence, Evelyn kept the cell phone in her purse "just in case." She never used it, though, preferring to make calls from her landline. She did so now, dialing Claire's number and sighing when it went straight to voicemail.

"Claire, it's Evelyn. I need to talk to you about something important. Can you swing by when you get a chance? If tonight doesn't work, then how about first thing in the morning? I'm up at the crack of dawn, as you know." She lowered her voice to a stage whisper. "I've discovered some shady goings-on at Cedar Glen, and I'd like your opinion on what I should do. As the old saying goes, two heads are better than one."

Claire had her phone set to mute when she was at Atsuko's so she wouldn't be disturbed. She didn't notice she had a message until undressing for bed that night. Listening to Evelyn's voicemail, she eyed the clock on her nightstand. *Ten forty-five. Too late to call or go over now.* Evelyn was always in bed by nine and didn't appreciate having her "beauty sleep" interrupted, as she'd told her neighbors on more than one occasion.

I'll go over first thing in the morning, Claire decided. Drifting off, she wondered what sort of shady goings-on Evelyn could be talking about.

SIXTEEN

The next morning, Claire called Evelyn at six thirty to tell her she'd be bringing fruit and croissants for breakfast, along with some Yorkshire Gold. She had introduced Evelyn to her favorite English tea, and the nonagenarian was now a devotee as well. After six rings, the answering machine clicked on. Claire left a message, frowning as she did so. Evelyn always answered by the second ring unless she was in the bathroom.

She waited a few minutes and called again, once more getting the answering machine. Sticking her phone and keys in her pocket, Claire picked up the breakfast platter and left. Moments later, she rang Evelyn's doorbell. No answer. She rang again and waited. Still no answer. Claire pulled out the spare key Evelyn had given her for emergencies. Opening the door, she called out, "Evelyn, it's me, Claire."

Silence.

Claire's eyes scanned the living room, noting her friend's beloved books and art. Nothing seemed out of place. Setting the platter on the counter, she continued on, filled with a mounting sense of dread.

"Evelyn," she called as she walked down the hall, "it's Claire. Are you all right?" She stopped in front of the closed bedroom door. *Evelyn never closes her door.* Heart thudding, Claire turned the knob. Inside, she found her friend sprawled on the floor beside her bed, unmoving.

She screamed.

Moments later, Cedar Glen's handyman rushed inside. "Everything all right?" Mark shouted.

"In here," Claire called out in a hollow voice.

Entering the bedroom, Mark found Claire on the floor beside Evelyn, cradling the elderly woman's white head in her lap. "She's gone." A tear slid down Claire's cheek.

"I'm so sorry." Mark laid a gentle hand on her shoulder. "I need to call 911 and Connie, but is there anyone else I should call?"

"Her son needs to be notified, but I'll do that since Evelyn and I were friends." Claire's voice wobbled on the last word. "Can you call Atsuko and have her tell the girls?"

While Mark did that, Claire pulled out her phone and called Chuck Blair with the news. Chuck said he'd be there straightaway. Then she texted Daphne.

CLAIRE: Evelyn left a text saying she needed to talk to me about some shady goings-on. Now she's dead. Seems suspicious. What should I do? Mark's calling 911.

Half an hour later, the condo was crawling with people, including Evelyn's furious son.

"What do you mean this might be a crime scene, and my mother's body can't be moved?" Chuck Blair asked the detective.

"I'm sorry, sir. I understand your anger, but your mother reported some suspicious goings-on to another resident," Rick Bartlett said. "As well, we found the patio door in her bedroom open. Someone may have entered that way."

Claire's eyes widened at hearing that.

"We need to make sure there's been no foul play," Rick added.

"Foul play? That's ridiculous. My mother was ninety-four years old. She had congestive heart failure and the beginnings of dementia. She died of old age."

"That may be, sir, but we need to make sure." Rick nodded to his partner, Jessica.

The female detective ushered the group out. "We'll need everyone to please leave now, so the coroner can do his work."

"I'm not leaving my mother," Chuck said.

"I'm sorry, sir, you have to. We'll come get you when we've finished." Jessica inclined her head at Connie. "Is there somewhere Mr. Blair can wait?"

"Yes, of course." Connie signaled the Cedar Glen handyman with her eyes. "Why don't you come with me, Mr. Blair? I've got some coffee in my office—you can wait there with me until the authorities have finished."

"Right this way," Mark said in a gentle voice.

Viewing Connie and Mark with a vacant expression, Chuck Blair let them lead him away.

After the coroner dismissed the paramedics, he addressed Claire. "I understand you found the deceased—is that correct?"

She nodded.

"Is it also correct that you touched the body?"

"Yes."

The coroner shook his head and expelled a sigh. "Contaminating a possible crime scene."

"I'm sorry. I never thought." *You should have, though*, Claire scolded herself, *after all the British mysteries you've watched.*

"That's all right," Rick said. "Tell us what you did when you arrived, and what you touched."

With Daphne at her side, Claire recounted how Evelyn didn't answer the door, so she let herself in. "I set the breakfast I'd brought on the kitchen counter and started looking for Evelyn. When I reached her bedroom, I knew something was wrong."

"Why was that?" Rick asked.

"Evelyn never shut her bedroom door; she said it made the room too stuffy."

"Then what happened?"

Claire's heart clenched. "I opened the door and saw her lying on the floor next to the bed. I screamed and ran to Evelyn, checking for a pulse, but there was none. Then I lifted her head off the floor and laid it on my lap."

"Why did you do that?" Rick asked

"To provide a cushion for her head. The floor was hard."

"But she was already dead."

"I know." A tear trickled down Claire's cheek.

The coroner sighed and waved them away.

Rick led Claire to the living room to continue his questioning. "Daph, you can go," he said to his former partner.

"If it's OK, I'd like Daphne to stay for moral support," Claire said. "I've never discovered a dead body before." Unbidden, the thought flashed through her head. *Although I have disposed of one. And killed a man too.* She shoved the thought away.

The Alphabet Girls munched on fruit and croissants around Claire's kitchen island. All except for Claire who couldn't eat.

Atsuko made her a cup of tea with two sugars and ordered Claire to drink it. As she did, the Yorkshire Gold did its magic, and Claire regained her sense of equilibrium.

Her friends were full of questions.

"Who would want to kill Evelyn?" Atsuko mused. "Did she have anything valuable? Was she robbed?"

"Did Evelyn give you any clue as to what she'd found out that might have made someone want to silence her?" Barbara asked.

Daphne held up her hand in a stop motion. "Slow down. We don't even know yet whether Evelyn was killed or died of natural causes. We won't know until the coroner releases his findings."

"Will he have to do an autopsy?" Claire asked, feeling sick at the thought.

"If he thinks it's a suspicious death, yes."

Claire thought of Evelyn's son and how he would react if that happened. She'd seen enough autopsies on her BritBox mystery shows to know how grisly they could be. Bowing her head, she telegraphed a mental apology to Chuck Blair.

"How long does it take to get the results from the coroner?" Atsuko asked.

"Usually only a day or two, unless there's a backlog of bodies to process," Daphne said. "Of course, the coroner won't reveal his findings to us since we're not law enforcement."

"Naturally," Atsuko said. "And why would he tell a bunch of old ladies anything?"

Barbara bridled. Pulling out her compact from the cross-body bag slung across her tank top, she examined her face, noticing the crow's feet. *Time for some more Botox.* She snapped the compact shut. "I could always invite the coroner out for a drink," she said. "I'm sure I could get the information out of him."

Daphne grinned. "You probably could, Mata Hari, but

there's no need. If it turns out Evelyn *was* murdered, it's a sure bet Detectives Bartlett and Miller will be back. They'll conduct a full-scale investigation and question everyone who knew Evelyn or had any interactions with her."

Barbara turned to Claire. "Tell us exactly what Evelyn said in her message."

Claire pulled out her phone. "Listen for yourself." She played the voicemail as she'd done for the detective.

"'Shady goings-on.'" Atsuko rested her hand on her chin, considering. "I wonder what Evelyn was talking about."

"Why don't we find out?" Barbara suggested. "We should help the detectives with their investigation."

Daphne snorted. "Yeah, that's not gonna happen. Cops don't take kindly to civilians playing Columbo."

"I see us more like Charlie's Angels." Barbara struck the famous pose from the '70s TV show and shook her hair. "I always wanted to be Farrah Fawcett."

"I preferred Kate Jackson," Atsuko said. "She was the smart one."

"I'm afraid I don't have the appropriate jiggle factor to be an Angel." Claire glanced down at her flat chest. "Miss Marple is more my style."

Daphne squinted down at her muffin top poking over her ubiquitous sweats. "Guess I'd be Vera, then. Anyone have a green hat I can wear?" Her smile faded. "Seriously, though, girls, the police don't appreciate civilians playing detective."

"What they don't know won't hurt them," Barbara said. "We'll conduct our own investigation on the down-low."

"Works for me," Atsuko said. "The Alphabet Girls are on the job. Although"—she paused, considering—"for this, perhaps we should rename ourselves the Alphabet *Sleuths*."

"Count me in," Claire said. "I want to find out what kind of shady dealings Evelyn was talking about, especially if they wound up resulting in her death. Even though she was ninety-four, Evelyn still had a lot of life left in her." Her voice wobbled.

Atsuko patted her hand.

"All right, Cagney," Barbara said, "you're the expert. Where do we start?"

"First, we retrace Evelyn's steps. Find out where she went and what she did in her last days, starting with yesterday when she called Claire," Daphne said. "Then we go backwards from there. We can—"

A knock at the door interrupted them.

"Shh," Barbara said, "act natural. Maybe it's the cops with more questions."

Atsuko slid off her barstool. "I'll go." Striding to the front door, she opened it to find Mark Scott on the doorstep, a concerned expression on his face.

"I came to check on Claire," Mark said, "to see if she's OK."

Atsuko ushered the handyman inside.

Elinor raced over to him, tail wagging, and licked his legs.

Squatting down, Mark rubbed the back of her neck. "Hello, Elinor. Good to see you again."

Barbara sent Claire a knowing smirk.

"Brontë will be ready for another play date soon, pretty girl," Mark cooed in the baby-talking voice dog lovers use. The voice that non-pet-owners roll their eyes at.

"Brontë?" Atsuko asked.

"My rescue terrier. She's skittish around most dogs. I've got her in behavioral training, though, and they've started socializing her. She's already made friends with this sweet girl," he said, stroking Elinor's fur.

"Mark rescued a darling dog from the pound," Claire explained. "She'd been attacked by another dog, poor thing, and lost an eye. Naturally, when Brontë first saw Elinor at the dog park, she was a little aggressive." She smiled at Mark. "I'm glad the training's going well."

Patting Elinor on the head, Mark stood. "What about you, Claire?" He touched her arm and looked into her eyes.

Claire pushed down the flutter in her stomach at the touch of Mark's hand on her skin.

"How are *you*?" the handyman asked. "What an awful shock, finding your friend like that. I'm so sorry. I came to make sure you were all right."

"I'm better now, thanks. My Alphabet Girls have rallied around me."

"Alphabet Girls?"

"I dubbed us that during the pandemic since our names start with A, B, C, and D." Barbara batted her false eyelashes at the gorgeous widower.

"Would you like a croissant, Mark?" Atsuko offered. "We've got plenty."

"Thanks, but I wouldn't want to disturb you during your girl time."

Barbara snorted. "We have girl time all the time. It's a nice change of pace to have a man around."

Mark focused on Claire. "Well, if you don't mind. With everything going on, I missed breakfast this morning."

"Have a seat." Claire stood and pulled another plate from the cupboard. "We've got fruit and croissants."

"No coffee, though." Daphne chuckled. "Claire hates coffee."

"Something we have in common." Mark grinned. "I never developed a taste for coffee. Unlike most people, I'm not crazy about the smell either, which earned me a lot of ribbing in the teachers' lounge."

"What did you teach?" Atsuko asked.

"High school English."

"For how long?"

"Thirty-five years."

Daphne whistled. "You're braver than me. High schoolers are a tough bunch."

"They're not so bad."

"Do you miss teaching?" Atsuko asked.

Mark brushed croissant crumbs off his fingers. And onto his plate, Claire noticed. *Someone raised him right.* Stan had been forever dropping pieces of food on the counter and floor, knowing she would clean up after him.

"I miss the kids," Mark said. "I don't miss the standardized testing that got in the way of teaching, or the amount of time I had to spend on documentation."

"I hear ya on that," Atsuko said.

"So, Mark"—Daphne popped a grape in her mouth—"did you see Evelyn yesterday?"

"Afraid not. The last time I saw her was Tuesday night on her way to bingo."

Atsuko smiled. "Evelyn loved bingo. She never missed a game. She always placed her two trolls on the table next to her daubers—her lucky charms, she called them. Evelyn told me she gave the trolls French names because she loved Paris so much."

Daphne scrunched her forehead. "Didn't she call them Fleur and Laurette?"

"Lisette," Atsuko corrected.

Barbara's mouth twisted. "I don't play bingo." *The quintessential old-lady game.*

"I don't either, usually," Claire said. "Although I did go once with Evelyn."

"I didn't realize so many people enjoyed bingo until I moved here," Mark said. "The clubhouse was really hopping Tuesday night. Standing room only. A couple of the guys gave up their seats for the ladies."

Barbara sipped her orange juice. "I guess chivalry isn't dead after all."

"Not if Vince and Lenny are anything to go by," Mark said. "On the way to bingo, I noticed Evelyn drop her bag. I headed over to help her out, but Lenny beat me to it."

SEVENTEEN

After Mark left, Barbara said, "So, Ladies-Man-Lenny was hitting on Evelyn now? I thought he liked them younger." She teased Claire. "Don't be jealous."

Claire ignored her. "I doubt Lenny was hitting on Evelyn. He was probably doing his good deed for the day."

"Lenny?" Daphne snorted. "He wouldn't know a good deed if it came up and bit him in the ass. Lenny doesn't do anything unless there's something in it for him."

"But what could be in it for him to help Evelyn?" Atsuko asked.

"I don't know." Barbara fluffed her hair. "But I think we should find out. And I think Claire needs to be the one to talk to our resident Romeo since he has the hots for her."

Claire sighed. "Oh, all right, if I must."

The theme music from *All Creatures Great and Small* punctured the air. "That's my daughter; I'll need to take this." Claire picked up her phone. "Hi, sweetheart, how are you?"

"Busy as always," Grace said. "I'm calling about your birthday. How would you like a big party for your seventieth?"

"I wouldn't, actually."

"Oh, come on, Mom. Seventy is a milestone birthday. We want to mark the occasion with something special. And believe it or not, brother Doug's even offered to help foot the bill. He can't come over from Spain, of course—work's too crazy—but he'll Venmo me his portion."

"That's sweet of you, Grace, but you know I'm not a big one for crowds."

"We'll make it a smaller party, then. Fifty or sixty people tops."

Claire shuddered. She couldn't imagine anything worse, other than going out with Lenny. "Honey, I appreciate your wanting to do this, but I'm not a party person."

"You used to be when Dad was alive." Claire heard the pout in her daughter's voice. "We were always having big parties."

"That's because your father loved them. I never did."

"Well, then, what *would* you like to do for your birthday?"

"Go back to England." Claire expelled a wistful breath. She had first fallen in love with the Great Britain she'd seen on TV. The rolling green hills and thatched-roof cottages of Father Brown's Cotswolds, James Herriot's beloved Yorkshire Dales, and Poldark's wild Cornish coast. Her solo trip to the UK had only deepened that love. "I know that's not possible, though," Claire said. "I'm happy simply having a nice birthday dinner with you and my grandson. Afterwards, we could watch episodes of *Escape to the Country*—the next best thing to being in England."

Grace sighed. Her conversations with her mother were often punctuated with sighs. "All right, if that's what you really want."

"It is."

"Well, I've got to go. I've got a Zoom meeting for work."

Barbara shook her head as Claire ended the call. "I can't believe you turned down a big birthday bash. That would have been so much fun."

"Not for me."

Daphne polished off a second croissant. "Yeah, B, haven't you figured out yet that Claire is our resident introvert? Not everyone is a party animal. Different strokes for different folks."

"Exactly." Atsuko regarded Claire. "In addition to your family celebration, I'd like to make you a birthday dinner for your seventieth. Just the four of us. How does that sound?"

"Wonderful. Thanks, Atsuko." Claire smiled at her kindred-spirit friend. Then, turning to the girls, she said briskly, "Right then, that's sorted. Back to business. We've agreed I'll talk to Lenny to try to find out what I can about his interactions with Evelyn. What are the rest of you Alphabet Sleuths going to do?"

"We'll start talking to some of the other residents." Daphne turned to Atsuko. "You always go to bingo—did you notice any out-of-the-ordinary interactions Evelyn had with any of the other bingo players that night?"

"I wasn't there. Remember? That's the night we brought you home from your cabin."

Claire shuddered. "The night of Smokey the Bear."

"Sorry," Daphne said. "Since retiring, I never know what day it is anymore."

"I have the same problem," Atsuko said. "My pill box is the only way I know the day of the week."

Barbara grumbled. "Starting to sound like a bunch of old ladies now, talking about pills and forgetfulness."

"Face it," Atsuko said. "We *are* a bunch of old ladies."

"*You* may be, but I'm not." Bounding off the barstool, Barbara did a side plank pose followed by a king pigeon pose to demonstrate.

"I don't know how you can bend yourself into a pretzel like that, B," Daphne said.

"It's called daily yoga." Barbara wasn't about to tell the girls she thought she might have just pulled a muscle. "Now, I'm going to jog over to the clubhouse to talk to Olivia and see what I can find out. I'll catch y'all later."

Olivia Walsh was the new activities director Connie had hired to replace her predecessor Emma who had decided to go to graduate school.

"Guess that leaves you and me, babe," Daphne said to Atsuko. "How about we tackle Evelyn's neighbors? Do you want the one on the left or the one on the right?"

"I'll take Doris Franklin," Atsuko said. "She likes to gossip, so I may learn something interesting."

"That leaves me with Georgie-Porgie Hansen." Daphne grimaced. "The one who always corners people to talk about his glory days as a stonemason. I can steer the conversation to Evelyn, though, find out if he's noticed anything unusual in the last few days."

Claire slid off her barstool. "Right then, girls, let's do this."

Barbara waited until Olivia had finished demonstrating how to make beaded necklaces to the geriatrics group in the clubhouse. Sucking in her gut, she approached the twenty-something girl with the cut arms and flat stomach. "Hey, Olivia, what's goin' on?"

"Hello, Barbara. Did you want to make a necklace? I've got plenty of beads left."

God, no. Might as well stick a fork in me 'cause I'm done. Barbara didn't say that aloud, though. "No, thanks. I just wanted to come over and say hi, see how you're settling in."

Olivia beamed. "I love it here. Everyone's been so nice and welcoming."

"Glad to hear it. In fact, I hear you had them packed to the gills in here the other night at bingo."

"Yeah, that was insane. I think it's because of the special prizes we had. Everyone wanted to win the Target gift card or the four-pound box of See's Candy."

Barbara whistled. "A *four*-pound box of See's? That would be gold around these parts. Who coughed up the big bucks for that? I can't see tight-fisted Connie shelling out the dough."

Olivia blushed. "I was able to get the manager of the local See's to donate the candy." Olivia left out the part that her mother, the See's manager, had told her old people loved their sweets, and the candy would make her first bingo night a huge success.

"Good for you. I'm impressed. So, who wound up winning the candy?"

Olivia's face fell. "Evelyn Blair. I doubt she got to eat much of it, though, before she . . ." The young activities director cast her eyes at the group intent on their necklace-beading and whispered, "*Died*. Isn't it awful? I've never known anyone who died before. Not that I *knew* Evelyn," she added, "but she seemed so alive at bingo. She was having a great time with her ten cards in front of her and her cute little good-luck trolls."

"Ten cards?" Barbara said. "Sorry, I don't play bingo. What does that mean?"

"It's the number of bingo cards a player has in front of her. Or him," Olivia explained. "Most people play more than one card at a time because it increases their chance of winning. The majority of people play four or five cards, but some, including Evelyn, play the maximum we allow—ten."

"Whoa. You'd have to pay close attention to play all those cards at once."

"Definitely. You really have to concentrate," Olivia said. "Bingo requires good hand-eye coordination too. Some of the players, especially the ones with memory issues or arthritis, struggle with that."

"But not Evelyn?" Barbara probed.

"Not at all. You'd think she would have, though, because of her age, wouldn't you? Goes to show it's not about the numbers."

"That's what I'm sayin'." Barbara's eyes gleamed. *This Olivia chick knows what she's talking about.* Then she thought about Evelyn winning the big prize at bingo. She wondered if that would have been reason enough for someone to want to kill her.

For a box of candy? I doubt it, Farrah. If you want to be a Charlie's Angel, you'll have to think harder.

Barbara tilted her head at Olivia. "Were there any issues when Evelyn won?"

Olivia's eyes widened. "How did you know?"

"Lucky guess. What happened?"

The activity director observed the beading group to make sure they were still occupied with their necklaces. Olivia leaned toward Barbara. "One of the other ladies called bingo at the same time as Evelyn did, so we thought we had a tie. But when I examined her card, I saw a seven had been made into a two with a Sharpie."

Barbara raised her penciled brows. "Did you accuse her of cheating?"

"Oh no. I didn't want to do that in front of everyone. I simply told her she'd made a mistake, and it wasn't a good bingo. When I said it, though, I looked her straight in the eye, making sure she knew that *I* knew she'd changed the number."

Barbara whispered, "So who was the cheater?"

"I'd rather not say," Olivia said primly.

"Good girl. Anything else out of the ordinary happen that night?"

"One table of ladies got drunk." Olivia pursed her lips. "As you know, alcohol is not allowed in the clubhouse since it tends to make our older residents dehydrated. I suspected they may have been pouring vodka into their Sprite, but they all denied it, and I couldn't prove it," Olivia said. "One of the women was so drunk she nearly fell when she got up to go buy another card, but the guy at their table grabbed her and caught her before she could fall."

"A man at a table full of ladies," Barbara mused. "Hmm. Would that man by any chance have been Lenny Fink?"

"How did you guess?" Olivia pulled a face. "That guy gives me the creeps. He's always staring at me. He *accidentally* brushed up against me when he walked past me a couple of times. Once, he even touched my butt." Her eyes flashed. "I told him if he ever laid a hand on me again, I'd report him for sexual harassment. I told Connie too, and she's keeping an eye on him. What a douche. What makes men think they can do crap like that and get away with it?"

"Lenny hasn't figured out it's the twenty-first century and that kind of Neanderthal behavior isn't tolerated anymore."

"Well, he'd better get with the program, because I *will* report him."

"Good for you." Barbara thought back to her youth when this kind of thing—and worse—happened all the time. Men, especially older ones, were always grabbing and touching her as if they were entitled to do so. Back then, though, women didn't make waves; they learned how to deflect men's advances with a joke and a smile.

The old Virginia Slims commercial flashed through Barbara's head.

We really have come a long way, baby.

EIGHTEEN

Atsuko finished her second ikebana arrangement, adding in some marigolds as a final touch. Although she knew her friend's favorite flowers were roses and peonies, Claire had once mentioned that the sight of yellow marigolds in the fall always made her smile. Atsuko had honored Claire's wish of not wanting to talk about the vandalism she'd recently experienced, but she knew it had to have unsettled her.

It would have unsettled Atsuko.

The very idea of someone breaking into her home and causing the destruction—or "malicious mischief," as the police called it—the way they had in Claire's condo would be so upsetting. Such a violation. Atsuko, like Claire, considered her home her sanctuary. A place of peace and comfort. An oasis of calm and beauty. And to have that peace shattered by a stranger was not only disconcerting but also frightening.

She carried the flower arrangement next door and rang Claire's doorbell. Immediately, Elinor began to bark. "It's OK, Elinor," Atsuko called out. "It's only me, your favorite neighbor."

Claire opened the door, carrying her dog, who gave an excited yip at the sight of Atsuko.

Holding the flower arrangement in one hand, Atsuko ruffled the fur beneath Elinor's chin with her other hand. "Hello, sweetheart," she said. "Good girl for barking. You're Mommy's good little watchdog, aren't you?"

When Claire set Elinor down, she scampered over to Atsuko and licked her leg.

Atsuko handed the ikebana arrangement to Claire. "I was experimenting with fall flowers and thought you might like this."

"It's beautiful. Thank you."

"You know, I think you have the right idea, Claire." Atsuko pinned her eyes on her friend. "Elinor is a great watchdog. An effective deterrent against unwanted guests. As a woman living alone, I'm beginning to think maybe *I* should consider getting a rescue dog too."

Daphne sat on the bench outside George Hansen's condo, pretending to scroll through her phone as she waited for the elderly man to come out. She knew George often took a daily constitutional about this time, and if she stayed put, it wouldn't be long before he joined her. Everyone at Cedar Glen—residents and staff alike—knew to avoid this particular bench. If you happened to stop there unawares, George would trap you for an hour or more and bore you with his long-winded stories.

Today, though, Daphne *wanted* to be trapped.

Hearing George's door open, she watched as he set off with his walker. Daphne's eyes dropped back to her phone, feigning interest in the daily crossword.

"Mind if I join you, my dear?" George asked.

"Please do. It will save me hours of frustration trying to do this crossword puzzle. How are you, George? I haven't seen you in a while."

"I was going to say the same thing to you." His faded blue eyes homed in on her sling. "Looks like I'm doing better than you. How's the arm? I heard you had to have surgery for a torn bicep. Did I ever tell you about the time I tore my bicep when we were making that stone archway over at the library?"

"I think you may have, but remind me again. I don't remember the details."

And George was off.

Daphne listened with an attentive air as the retired stonemason regaled her with the minutiae of the type of stone used to build the arch, the origin of the stone, the number of men he had worked with on the project, the specifics of each man, how long it took to build the arch, and all manner of inconsequential detail. As George droned on, Daphne offered up the occasional "Really?" or "Is that right?" affecting an absorbed interest in his lengthy tale.

When he finished at last, Daphne said, "You've got a real eye for detail, George. I'll bet nothing gets past you."

"No sirree, bub."

She extended an open bag of Werther's Originals to the eighty-five-year-old.

"Don't mind if I do." He pulled out two of the wrapped caramels.

Sucking on the hard candy, Daphne said with a casual air, "I imagine you saw all the activity over at Evelyn's this morning."

"I did." George crossed himself. "May she rest in peace. But then again, Evelyn was ninety-four. I'm surprised she lasted this long."

"Why is that?"

"I don't mean to speak ill of the dead," George said, "but to tell you the truth, Evelyn was a crotchety old woman. Full of herself. Would never sit and shoot the breeze with folks. Always squirreled herself away reading and listening to opera and such." He sneered. "I don't hold with that fancy foreign singing. I like good old country and western myself. Give me Johnny Cash or Reba any day." He hummed a snatch of "Folsom Prison Blues."

Daphne tamped down her impatience. "But what has that got to do with your surprise at Evelyn living as long as she did?"

"It's not healthy hiding yourself away with a bunch of dusty old books and such, and not socializing with other people," George said. "Makes you shrivel up and die."

"Evelyn did go out, though. She played bingo at the clubhouse every week."

"Yes, but she spent the whole time she was there bent over those cards of hers, not talking and laughing with other folks like everyone else." George frowned. "During the breaks, she kept her nose stuck in a book, instead of making conversation. Always acted like she was better than everyone else. Evelyn was an odd duck." He sucked on his caramel. "Then there was that set-to she had with Mabel Brown after bingo."

Daphne's ears perked up. *Now we're getting somewhere.* "Set-to? What happened?"

"Mabel tied with Evelyn to win the grand prize—the biggest

box of See's Candy you ever saw." George chuckled. "Mabel loves her chocolate. She was licking her lips in anticipation. She figured since they tied, she and Evelyn would split the box: two pounds for Evelyn, two pounds for Mabel. But then that new activities director said Mabel's card wasn't a valid bingo, so Evelyn was the sole winner."

Daphne frowned. "I don't get it. What's the problem?"

"Afterwards, Mabel followed Evelyn out of the clubhouse. Evelyn had that big box of See's open on the seat of her walker." George nodded to his black metal walker. "She's got the same kind as mine with a seat so you can sit down if you get tired. Anyway, she was eating a piece of candy when Mabel waylaid her. She asked Evelyn if she would split the candy with her since they'd tied." His eyes gleamed. "Guess what happened?"

"I have no idea," Daphne said, ready to throttle George if he didn't get to the point soon.

He chortled. "Old Evelyn looked Mabel right in the eye and said there was no tie. She said Mabel had cheated, trying to win the prize, but it hadn't worked. Evelyn told her if she wanted some See's Candy to go buy her own." He snorted. "Mabel got so mad that she shoved the box of See's off the walker, spilling candy everywhere." George chuckled. "Mabel was on that chocolate like a dog in heat. She started shoving candy in her mouth, her purse, her pockets, wherever. Evelyn gave her this look and said, 'What a pathetic creature you are.'"

"Whoa."

"Mabel got spitting mad. Swore a blue streak and called Evelyn names. Names I'm too much of a gentleman to repeat. Told Evelyn she'd better watch out; she would get her comeuppance one of these days."

"Mabel threatened Evelyn the night before she died?"

"Hold your horses there, Sparky," George said. "Mabel wouldn't hurt a fly. She's all talk and no action. She does have quite a temper, though; I'll give you that."

Enough of a temper to make good on her threat? Daphne wondered.

* * *

Atsuko sat on Doris Franklin's patio, enjoying a glass of iced tea and some Pepperidge Farm Milanos.

"Poor Evelyn," Doris tutted. "Such a shock. One day she was here and the next she wasn't. You never know, do you?"

Shaking her head, Atsuko munched on a Milano. Over the years, she'd learned the value of listening and letting others talk. You can learn a lot that way.

Doris reached for another cookie. "I wonder if that terrible fight she had with Mabel Brown Tuesday night had anything to do with it?"

"Evelyn and Mabel had a fight?"

"It was mostly Mabel fighting; she was yelling at Evelyn to beat the band. Mabel has quite a temper, you know."

"I didn't know."

"Oh, yes," Doris warmed to the topic. "You don't want to get on the wrong side of Mabel. You'll never hear the end of it. The lungs on that woman. She could put a fishwife to shame." She sent Atsuko a curious look. "I'm surprised you didn't hear her yelling. Lots of people did."

"I wasn't here; I was out of town that night."

"Oh, that's right. You, Barbara, and Claire were all off on a girls' trip to Las Vegas, weren't you?" She delivered a sly look to Atsuko. "Pretty quick trip."

"Unfortunately. We needed to get Daphne back home to see her doctor."

"Poor thing." Doris adopted a concerned air. "I hope she's OK."

"She's fine now. She just over-exerted herself a bit too much after surgery." Atsuko leaned in toward the gossipy woman. "You were saying you wondered if Mabel's fight with Evelyn might have had something to do with her death?"

"Well, yes. I mean Evelyn was calm and collected during the entire exchange," Doris said. "Cool as a cucumber, that one. But I don't care how calm and cool you appear on the outside; it's bound to have an effect on the inside when someone's yelling at you and saying awful things," she offered with a sage nod. "Maybe the stress from that nasty fight gave Evelyn a heart attack or stroke."

"I hadn't thought of that."

"Although there were sure a lot of people at her condo after she died," Doris mused. "Paramedics, cops . . . I even saw the coroner's van. That's a lot of folks for a heart attack of a ninety-four-year-old woman."

Atsuko offered a noncommittal *hmm*.

"I heard Claire's the one who found her. Poor thing, that must have been quite a shock. Did Claire say if they told her what Evelyn died of?" Doris probed.

"No one told Claire anything. I don't think they always know the cause of death right away. Sometimes it can take a day or two."

"Uh-huh." Doris's eyes narrowed. "Wait a minute. Doesn't a coroner usually only come out if it's a suspicious death? Are they saying Evelyn's death is suspicious?" Her eyes gleamed at the possibility.

"I have no idea. I wasn't there and I'm not a medical person." Atsuko stood. "Well, I'd better be going. Thanks for the tea and cookies and the conversation."

"Anytime." Doris gave Atsuko a speculative glance. "I wonder if Lenny Fink may have had something to do with it. He's always slinking around at night. In fact"—her head snapped up—"I just remembered . . . I saw Lenny out back behind Evelyn's condo the night before she died. I was closing my living-room drapes, and the motion sensor went off. I could see Lenny clear as day, running away." Her eyes grew large in her round face. "Do you think he murdered Evelyn and that's why he was running away?"

"This is quite the surprise," Lenny said when Claire sought him out in the clubhouse. "To what do I owe this unexpected pleasure? Usually, you don't give me the time of day."

Claire pasted a contrite expression on her face. "I'm sorry, Lenny. No offense." She laid it on thick. "I guess I'm just one of those one-man women. I haven't dated anyone since my husband died, and I have no interest in doing so. I'd rather be alone."

Very alone. Although she was enjoying her new friendship

with Mark. *I wonder if it could ever develop into something more . . . Don't be ridiculous*, she told herself, pushing the thought down.

Lenny's age-spotted hand snaked across the table to pat her hand. "You shouldn't shut yourself away like that, Claire. You're a very attractive woman. I can respect you not wanting to get into a serious relationship again. How long were you married?"

"Forty-seven years."

He whistled. "Forty years longer than me. Lulu and I made it past our seventh anniversary, but then that seven-year itch kicked in." Lenny stroked the top of Claire's hand in a circular motion. "We all have our needs," he said. "Even you."

Claire jerked her hand away.

Lenny's eyes narrowed to slits.

"It's not you . . . it's me." Claire put her face in her hands. "Finding Evelyn was such a terrible shock," she said in a voice that trembled. "She didn't have any health problems that I know of. The last time I saw her, she was fit as a fiddle—her usual spunky self."

"Spunky's one word for it," Lenny grumbled.

"Evelyn *was* a bit of a curmudgeon, wasn't she?" Claire said fondly, tears pricking her eyes. She pulled out her handkerchief. "Sorry."

"That's OK." Lenny refrained from patting her hand this time. "I didn't realize you and the old girl were close."

Careful . . . he may think Evelyn confided in you.

"We weren't really," Claire said. "Not as close as I am with Atsuko. But unlike Atsuko, Evelyn and I both hated computers and loved books. Evelyn is"—she paused—"*was* a big reader like me. We'd swap books occasionally."

Lenny's face cleared. "Sounds like me and Jerry Thomas. Jerry's one of the old-timers at the Cedars. We're always swapping Nelson DeMille and Clive Cussler paperbacks."

"I haven't read those authors."

"That's because they're guy books. Action-packed and full of adventure."

"Well, there you go. If there's no tea parties and it's not set in England, I'm not interested." Claire smiled. Trying to figure out how to steer the conversation back to Evelyn, she added, "I wouldn't be surprised if Evelyn had some of their titles, though. That woman had more books than anyone I know. Did you ever see her wall-to-wall bookcases?"

"They're something else. That's for sure." Lenny got a panicked look in his eyes and a sheen of sweat appeared on his upper lip.

Claire pretended not to notice. "Evelyn said her son installed the bookcases for her years ago. I wish my son would do something like that for me, but he's off living the high life in Spain." She shrugged. "Oh, well. By the way, I understand Evelyn had some difficulties on her way to bingo the other night, and you helped her out." She gave Lenny a warm smile. "Thank you for that." Remembering Barbara's comment, she said, "It's nice to know chivalry isn't dead."

Lenny puffed out his scrawny chest. "Not as long as Lenny Fink's around."

"I hope Evelyn was appreciative."

Lenny grunted. "She wasn't as gracious as you."

Later that day when Barbara jogged past the clubhouse, Olivia called her over. As they sat down at a patio table, the activities director surveyed the area to make sure they wouldn't be heard. "You know how you were asking if anything else out of the ordinary happened at bingo the other night?"

Barbara nodded.

"I found out one of the bingo players lost her credit card, and since then, someone's racked up thousands of dollars in charges on it."

"Did this player say she lost her card when she was at bingo?"

"She couldn't remember. Shirley was one of the women at the table who'd had too much to drink that night," Olivia said. "The same one who nearly fell when she got up to go buy another bingo card." She pinned her eyes on Barbara. "The one Lenny Fink prevented from falling. After Lenny helped settle Shirley back in her chair, I noticed he went and bought her bingo card for her, paying with a credit card."

Barbara lifted an eyebrow. "Is that right? I wonder if Lenny used Shirley's card and then conveniently forgot to give it back to her."

"I've been wondering the same thing," Olivia said.

At home, Barbara freshened her makeup, adding another layer of mascara and giving herself a lush red lip. Smiling, she smacked her lips in the mirror. "Hello, gorgeous," she said, mimicking Barbra winning the Oscar for *Funny Girl*. Pulling on a V-necked red tank top and her Georgia O'Keefe yoga leggings with the red and purple flowers, she headed out to seek her quarry.

Fluffing her hair and adjusting her ear buds, Barbara did a slow jog around the perimeter of Cedar Glen. If she timed it right, she would run into Vince on the way to his weekly poker game. She smiled and waved at a few of the seniors out on their daily walks. Most of the men at Cedar Glen were sweet old guys, pleasant and polite. Unlike Vince and Lenny, the resident flirts. Lenny had a reputation for going after anyone in a skirt, while Vince appeared content to reserve his flirting for Barbara.

Which is why she planned to take advantage of Vince's crush on her. Spying him locking his front door, Barbara hit her Golden Oldies playlist. "Oh, Pretty Woman" filled her ears. Turning up the volume, she jogged in Vince's direction, humming along to the '60s classic.

Overhearing the song, Vince stopped her on the sidewalk. He mimicked Roy Orbison's signature growl. "Hello there, pretty woman. Lookin' gorgeous as ever."

Barbara jogged in place, smiling as she removed her ear buds. "You always say the sweetest things, Vince."

"I only speak the truth." His eyes skimmed her perfect physique, lingering on her boob job before coming to rest on Barbara's taut, wrinkle-free face. "You are hands down the most beautiful woman around here. Hell, you're the most beautiful woman in Santa Bonita."

"Why, thank you." Continuing to jog in place, Barbara resurrected her Texas drawl. "My mama always said, 'It hurts to be beautiful.'"

"Does your mother still live in Tyler?"

Barbara shot Vince a surprised look. "How did you know I'm from Tyler?"

"I heard you mention it once."

"I was born and raised in Tyler, Texas, but I left the Lone Star State as soon as I could. I still have kin there, but Mama and Daddy passed on a few years ago."

"My folks have been gone a while, too. Guess it's all part of the aging process, huh?"

Barbara grimaced.

"Not that we're old," Vince hastened to add. "Especially not you. Why, you don't look a day over fifty. Make that forty."

Barbara preened. "I like to keep in shape and stay active. Luckily, our wonderful weather helps—it's not humid here like Texas. I'm glad I made the move to the Golden State—I'm a California girl through and through."

Grinning, Vince sang a snatch of the Beach Boys' "California Girls."

Time to find out his connection to Dmitri Glazatovsky. "Are you a California boy, Vince?"

"I'm a California transplant. I was born in the Windy City but didn't like those Chicago winters, so moved here in the sixties. Best move I ever made."

"What kind of work did you do?"

His eyes took on a shifty look. "A little of this, a little of that. Some construction, some maintenance, a little transport. I was a long-haul trucker for a while."

"Did you like that?" Barbara pretended to be interested as they walked toward the clubhouse.

"At first. There's nothing like being on the open road. It got old after a while, though."

"I can imagine. I love traveling, but I'm not a big fan of being stuck in a vehicle for ten or twelve hours at a time."

"Me neither. That's why I got out of trucking."

"And then what did you do?"

"Worked for an import-export firm for a while."

And what exactly did you import and export, I wonder?

But she didn't want to press Vince too much and make him suspicious. "Here in Santa Bonita?" Barbara asked innocently.

"Nah, Sacramento. I retired more than a decade ago, though. That's when I moved here."

"So you're not working at all anymore?"

"I'll do the occasional odd job here and there for my old boss, but I'm happy living the life of leisure now."

"Me too," Barbara said as they reached the clubhouse. She was dying to ask Vince if his old boss was Dmitri Glazatovsky, but knew that would tip her hand. At least she could tell Cagney what she'd learned.

Vince touched her arm. "How would you like to enjoy a little leisure with me now? I'm supposed to play poker with the boys, but I'd much rather spend time with you. Maybe take you out to dinner. How does that sound?"

"I'd love to, but I have plans with the girls. Can I take a rain check?"

Barbara grimaced as she jogged away. Wrinkly Vince gave her the creeps. She needed to cleanse herself. She texted her personal trainer.

BARBARA: Hey Ryan, you up for a little afternoon delight?

NINETEEN

The Alphabet Sleuths reconvened at Barbara's that night to compare notes over wine and a vegetarian charcuterie board their health-conscious hostess had prepared.

Daphne brought a bag of Doritos and Velveeta nacho sauce along with a Sprite. "Hope you don't mind, B. I knew I'd need something to stick to my ribs. I brought dessert too." She held up a box of Twinkies with a flourish.

"You shouldn't have, Cagney."

"I try to do my part." Daphne winked as she lowered herself onto the Pottery Barn sofa.

"If it's all right, I'll start with what my investigation uncovered," Barbara said. "First, shortly before you all arrived, I arranged to accidentally run into Vince. I learned he used to work for an import-export business in Sacramento more than a decade ago."

Daphne snorted. "Import-export, huh? That's usually a cover for drug smuggling."

Atsuko looked thoughtful. "That's also the same time that Dmitri Glazatovsky was in Sacramento when he was suspected of real-estate fraud."

"Exactly," Barbara said.

"We already know Glazatovsky's into drug trafficking." Daphne crunched on a Dorito. "Rick and I busted him for it a few years ago, but he managed to weasel out of it."

"Did you ask Vince if he worked for Glazatovsky?" Claire asked Barbara.

"I couldn't without it looking suspicious. But Vince did say he occasionally does the odd job for his old boss."

"Which could explain his conversation with Dmitri in front of the Cedars," Daphne said. "Leave it to me. I'm on it."

Barbara then recounted the Mabel Brown cheating incident. "And that's not all; Olivia said a group of women were pretty tipsy at bingo. She thought they'd been mixing vodka with their Sprite, which would have been against the rules. Since vodka is odorless, though, she couldn't prove it. Olivia said one woman was so drunk she nearly fell, but a knight in shining armor rode to her rescue." Barbara smirked. "Any bets as to who Lancelot might have been?"

"Hmm, let me guess." Claire put a finger to the side of her nose. "Would that by chance be Lenny Fink?"

"Bingo. You win the prize."

"Is it a four-pound box of See's?"

"Nope." Barbara extended the charcuterie board to Claire. "Have some edamame." Then she told them about drunken Shirley nearly falling and how she suspected Lenny had used Shirley's credit card on her behalf. Later, that credit card went missing, with huge charges on it. "Granted, we don't know if Lenny used Shirley's credit card for the bingo-card purchase and then pocketed the card," Barbara said, "but it seems a little suspicious."

"We'll have to do some more digging on that," Atsuko said. "Talk to Shirley and interview her to get all the details. I'm happy to do that."

Daphne raised her good hand. "Can I go next? My report builds on what B discovered." Leaning over the round coffee table, she dragged a Dorito through the nacho sauce.

Claire shoved two napkins on the edge of the acacia-wood table between Daphne and the nacho sauce and placed another napkin on her friend's lap.

Oblivious, Daphne gave her report of Mabel Brown accosting Evelyn outside bingo. "Evelyn told Mabel she'd cheated and called her a . . ." Daphne frowned, trying to remember what George had said. Her forehead cleared. "A pathetic creature. Mabel got mad and pushed the candy off Evelyn's walker, and suddenly, it was raining chocolate."

Barbara crossed her long legs. "I prefer it when it's raining men."

"George told me Mabel was all over that chocolate in a heartbeat," Daphne said. "Shoving candy into her mouth, her pockets, her purse, wherever she could."

Claire grinned. "Sounds like Lucy and Ethel on the chocolate factory assembly line."

"I love that episode," Atsuko said.

"Me, too. It's a classic. But get this, girls. There's more to the story." Daphne fastened her eyes on them. "Mabel threatened Evelyn the night before she died, told her she had better watch out, that Evelyn would get hers one of these days."

"Mabel has quite a temper," Claire said.

"That's what George said too. He also said Mabel wouldn't hurt a fly, that she's all talk. But I've heard that before," Daphne said. "When I was a cop, I saw the results of some of those people who wouldn't hurt a fly. Folks with bad tempers who get so enraged one day that they just snap and lose it. And bam, someone loses their life as a result." Her lips tightened, and she fisted her good hand, remembering.

Barbara patted Daphne's knee.

Claire handed her a Twinkie.

"And *that* is one of the many reasons I'm no longer a cop." Lifting her shoulders, Daphne bit into the Twinkie.

Claire followed suit, and Barbara crunched on a carrot.

Atsuko went next. "I didn't find out too much from Doris, although she also mentioned the fight with Mabel. Doris wondered whether the fight so upset Evelyn that she might have had a stroke or heart attack."

"Anger *can* trigger a stroke," Claire said, "although usually it's within an hour of the fight or emotional event. Angry outbursts can also increase the risk of a heart attack, but it's usually a cumulative effect over time, and happens to someone who has frequent outbursts."

"Doris said Evelyn remained calm and collected while Mabel went off on her," Atsuko said. "Said she was cool as a cucumber."

Claire sipped her wine. "In that case, it's Mabel who would be most at risk of stroke or heart attack, not Evelyn."

Barbara drained her wine glass and poured another.

"There is one other thing Doris told me," Atsuko said. "She mentioned Lenny is always slinking around at night. Last night, Doris saw him behind Evelyn's condo"—she paused for effect—"running away."

"Oh my God." Claire's eyes grew as big as her Royal Albert dessert plates. "Lenny killed Evelyn! He let it slip when we were talking he'd been inside her house and seen her bookcases. When he realized what he'd said, he broke out in a cold sweat. Proof that he's guilty."

Daphne shook her finger at Claire. "Hang on there, Miss Marple. Lenny could have been in Evelyn's house at any time and seen her bookcases. That doesn't prove a thing."

Barbara snorted. "Cagney, you clearly did *not* know Evelyn. That woman did not let *any*one in Cedar Glen across her threshold, apart from Connie and Claire here."

"That's right," Claire said. "Evelyn was a very private person. She didn't like having other people inside her house. She considered her home her sanctuary and didn't want anyone invading it. It was months before she invited me in." Claire's eyes misted. "She showed me all the art she'd collected from Europe. Evelyn adored Paris and made me promise I'd go one day." Claire regarded Daphne. "Never in a million years would Evelyn have let Lenny into her home. He *must* have killed her."

"But why?" A frown creased Atsuko's forehead. "What would his motive have been?"

Claire replayed Evelyn's message again in her head. "He must have been involved in the shady dealings Evelyn was talking about. She must have seen or heard something, and Lenny realized it and knew he had to silence her before she told anyone." Her eyes filled with tears. "If I hadn't missed Evelyn's call and then decided it was too late to go see her once I listened to her message, I might have been able to prevent him from killing her. Evelyn's dead because of me."

Atsuko hugged her. "No, she's not. You couldn't have known."

"Atsuko's right," Daphne said. "This is *not* your fault, Claire. It's the fault of whoever did this. *If*, in fact, someone did kill her, that is. We still don't know if that's the case." She pulled out her phone. "I'm going to let Rick know we have more information about Evelyn's death, and ask him to come over."

* * *

An hour later, Detectives Bartlett and Miller sat across from the Alphabet Sleuths in Barbara's condo.

"Would you like some wine?" Barbara offered.

"No thanks, ma'am," Jessica said. "Not on duty."

Ma'am? Although she'd grown up in Texas where the word was as common as cowboys, Barbara had never liked the title being applied to her. *Ma'am* was for women of a certain age. *Old* women. She narrowed her eyes at the detective busy pulling out her notepad. *You're not such hot stuff, Missy.* Barbara was gratified to spot several gray hairs on the detective's bent head.

Before the police arrived, Daphne told the girls it would be more efficient to have one person tell the detectives what they knew, rather than have several people talking at once. Since Daphne was the one with law enforcement experience, they agreed she would act as their spokeswoman.

Daphne did so now, recounting what they'd learned about Evelyn's movements leading up to her death. When she got to the part about Mabel confronting Evelyn and pushing the box of candy off her walker, Jessica interjected, "This fight was all for a box of chocolate?"

"Not just *any* chocolate, Detective," Claire said. "This was a four-pound box of See's. Do you know how much that costs? A hundred and fifty bucks. That's a lot of money. And a lot of chocolatey goodness." Licking her lips, Claire daydreamed of her favorite Bordeaux.

Daphne shot her a look and resumed her account, telling the detectives about Lenny's reputation as a ladies' man and how he'd been with a group of women who got drunk during bingo. She said they suspected he'd likely provided the forbidden alcohol to the women to advance his own agenda—perhaps palming their credit cards? Then Daphne delivered the coup de grâce. "Lenny Fink was seen running away from the back of Evelyn's condo the night she died. We also know for a fact that Lenny had been inside Evelyn's home."

Jessica frowned. "And how exactly do you know that? Did someone see him inside the deceased's residence that evening?"

"No," Claire interjected, "but when I was investigating Lenny, discreetly pumping him for information, he let it slip he'd been inside Evelyn's house and seen her bookcases." Her face flushed with triumph.

Rick sent a sideways glance to his partner before replying. "*Investigating* him? Pumping him for information? Have you ladies been playing detective?"

"We're not *playing* at anything, Detective Bartlett," Atsuko said, bridling at the amusement she heard in Rick's voice. "We conducted a discreet investigation among some Cedar Glen residents and personnel into Evelyn's movements to see what we could learn. Daphne has now distilled our findings and presented them to you, and we'd like to know what you're going to do about it."

"This is a matter for the police," Jessica said, dismissing Atsuko. "Not civilians."

"Does that mean you're not going to do anything with the information we gave you?" Barbara asked.

"Detective Bartlett and I will discuss what we've learned here tonight and then decide what further actions to take. We still don't know whether the deceased died of natural causes or not. Should we find out she didn't, we will follow up with this"—Jessica peered at her notebook—"Lenny Fink. Until then, ma'am, I suggest you leave the investigative work to the professionals."

Barbara saw red. She wasn't accustomed to being treated with such condescension. Not anymore. Those days were long behind her. The second *ma'am* didn't help. She stood, eyes blazing. "Don't you talk down to me, Missy. And don't you dare dismiss us. Every single one of the women in this room is an accomplished professional."

She jerked her head at Atsuko. "Take Atsuko. She's a retired journalism professor with a master's degree who graduated summa cum laude and has multiple teaching awards to her name." Barbara nodded to Claire and told a little white lie. "Claire is a retired paralegal from one of the top law firms in the Midwest *and* she has a medical background to boot." Finally, she zeroed in on her best pal, the one she'd christened Cagney. "Daphne, as I'm sure you know, is a retired police officer with the Santa Bonita Police Force, who has received commendations for bravery, including a police purple heart."

As Barbara singled out each woman, the Alphabet Girls went and proudly stood by her side.

The B member of the Alphabet Sleuths concluded her list. "And *I* am a member of the National Association of Realtors™ who made agent of the year seven years in a row. I am also a former actress and professional model who appeared in *Vogue* magazine." Barbara drew herself up to her full height of five foot ten. "Together, we are the Alphabet Sleuths, and if you don't follow through with the probable murderer in our midst, we will make our own citizen's arrest."

"We certainly will." Atsuko put on her professor voice. "Under California Penal Code 837, we are entitled to make a citizen's arrest when a felony has been committed and we have reasonable cause to believe the person we arrest has committed the felony."

Jessica's face flamed, and Rick puffed out his cheeks. "Now, ladies, no need to get upset," he said. "Let's everyone calm down now, shall we?" He side-eyed his partner. "I'm sure Detective Miller did not mean to question your abilities. We appreciate the information you have given us and will definitely look into it." His phone buzzed with a text. Glancing down, Rick's mouth thinned to a grim line. "Excuse us a moment." He gestured for his partner to follow him.

TWENTY

An hour later, at ten o'clock, when most of Cedar Glen's inhabitants were bedded down for the night, the Alphabet Sleuths and a handful of residents watched as the cops took Lenny Fink away in handcuffs. Lenny, missing his usual bravado and bad rug, looked old and frightened.

Eighty-two-year-old Shirley Robinson, standing beside Doris Franklin and George Hansen in curlers and a housecoat, said, "I can't believe Lenny murdered Evelyn. He's such a nice man. So charming and attentive."

Doris grunted. "Too charming if you ask me. Always sniffing around the ladies. You should thank your lucky stars that all he did was steal your credit card, Shirley. It could have been a lot worse. You could have wound up dead, like poor Evelyn."

"We don't know for sure Lenny stole my card," Shirley said.

The Alphabet Girls exchanged glances.

Doris squinted at Shirley from beneath raised eyebrows. "The police found it in his house."

"Lenny could have found it after I lost it and picked it up, planning to return it to me."

Doris groaned. "Wake up, Shirley! The man's a thief and a murderer. I heard the cops also found Evelyn's emerald ring, which her son had reported missing, *and* Tammy Sue's Rolex watch. How do you explain *that*?"

Shirley dug in her heels. "Maybe Lenny's a kleptomaniac. That doesn't mean he's a murderer."

"I saw him with my own eyes, running away from Evelyn's patio the night she was murdered," Doris said.

George interjected. "I knew a kleptomaniac once. A guy I worked with. Another stonemason. Did I ever tell you about the time—"

Behind George's back, Daphne rolled her eyes and slipped away with her fellow Alphabet Sleuths.

As they walked back to their condos, Barbara's body thrummed with excitement. "Congratulations, girls," she said, high-fiving Daphne. "We solved a murder! Can you believe it?" She began singing "We are the Champions."

Claire put her finger to her lips. "Shh. It's late. People are sleeping."

"It's only a few minutes after ten," Barbara said. "Come on, we need to celebrate. I've got a bottle of champagne in the fridge." She led the girls inside. "Cagney, since you're not driving anywhere, you can have a glass too. Right, Claire?"

Claire faced Daphne. "When was the last time you had a pain pill?"

"Six hours ago."

"Sorry. You'll need to stick to Sprite or water. Unless, of course, you want to wind up with organ damage or bleeding in your stomach and intestines."

Daphne popped open a Sprite.

Barbara poured champagne for the rest of them and raised her glass. "Here's to the Alphabet Sleuths and solving our first case."

"Here, here," Atsuko said. They clinked glasses, but Claire seemed subdued.

"Why the long face?" Barbara asked. "We got the bad guy. Served him up to the cops on a silver platter."

"I was thinking of Evelyn—how terrified she must have been in those last moments of her life when Lenny was killing her. What a terrible way to die. Evelyn should have died in her sleep, or at least with her son beside her at the end. Lenny took that away from her." Tears fell from Claire's eyes. "Sorry if I don't feel like celebrating."

"No," a chastened Barbara said, "*I'm* sorry. I was so caught up in the excitement of solving the case, I didn't think of Evelyn. Or you." Somberly, she raised her glass. "To Evelyn."

"To Evelyn," they chorused in subdued tones.

Inside her bedroom, Claire shucked off her clothes and left them on the floor. She didn't bother folding her pants and blouse and putting them away. Elinor cocked her head as Claire pulled on her robe and opened the sliding glass door to the patio.

With her dog on her heels, Claire made her way to the hot tub on leaden legs. It took all the energy she had to sit on the edge of the spa and lower herself into the water. She was tired. Bone-crushingly tired. Tonight, Claire felt every one of her sixty-nine years. Turning on the jets, she leaned her head back, resting it on the top of the spa, and closed her eyes, reliving the past two hours.

After Detective Bartlett had gotten the text from the coroner and shared it with his partner, he informed the self-proclaimed Alphabet Sleuths that Evelyn had been murdered. Rick asked the women for the contact information of the residents they had interviewed and called Connie, arranging to meet the Cedar Glen manager at her office. Connie, in turn, called her activities manager Olivia and asked her to report to her office ASAP.

Meanwhile, Jessica called for back-up, stationing herself near Lenny's condo until the officers arrived. Once officers had been posted to the rear and the front of Lenny's home, cutting off his line of escape, Detective Miller rejoined her partner in Connie's office.

The two detectives questioned the nervous young activities director first. Olivia, who still lived at home, had brought her parents along for support. Olivia repeated to Rick and Jessica the information she had given Barbara, and, belatedly, her boss, about Lenny's actions on the night of bingo. The detectives then moved on to George and Doris's homes to question them.

Afterwards, they rang Lenny's doorbell.

Lenny had been in bed reading a Clive Cussler novel. Seeing the cops through the peephole, he grabbed his keys and tried to flee out the back patio, but the officer posted there stopped him. While Rick and Jessica questioned the pajama-clad Lenny, the officers, using the emergency search warrant the detectives had procured, searched his home. They found three credit cards belonging to other Cedar Glen residents and a sock full of women's jewelry in his underwear drawer next to a bottle of Viagra.

When Rick and Jess saw Evelyn's credit card and the missing

emerald ring matching the description Chuck Blair had given police, they bagged the evidence and arrested Lenny on suspicion of theft and murder.

Tears leaked down Claire's face now as she thought of her dead friend. She and Evelyn hadn't been close, but she'd admired the ninety-four-year-old and enjoyed talking to her about books and listening to her stories about her frequent trips to Paris over the years. Knowing how much Claire loved gardens, Evelyn recounted her first magical trip to Giverny and insisted Claire visit Monet's garden one day.

Claire resolved the next time she returned to her beloved Britain, she would add in a few extra days and go to Paris in Evelyn's honor. When her head hit the pillow that night, she exhaled a sigh of exhaustion as Elinor snuggled in bed beside her, relieved that the drama of the past couple of weeks was now behind them.

Atsuko meditated before she went to bed, clearing her mind of all the negative energy the recent deaths had engendered. She'd done a follow-up interview with Shirley as she'd promised the girls she would, but Shirley refused to even entertain the idea that Lenny—who she was obviously sweet on—had stolen her credit card. *I need an escape*, she thought. She decided to join the bus trip to Lake Tahoe tomorrow with the other residents who enjoyed gambling. Atsuko hadn't played the slots in a while, and her fingers were itching to return to those South Shore casinos.

She missed the original slot machines. She had always found it so satisfying to pull down the lever and hear the ding-ding-ding when she got three cherries. Now the levers were gone and everything was touch-screen, but the machines still ding-ding-dinged and paid out, so Atsuko wasn't going to complain.

Yawning, Daphne glugged another Sprite as Barbara finished off the bottle of champagne. Barbara couldn't sit still. She moved around her home with a frenetic energy, fluffing pillows, sweeping the floor, and putting away the remains of the charcuterie board.

"Is it always such a rush when you solve a case and arrest a criminal?" she asked Daphne, with flushed cheeks and sparkling eyes. "No wonder you became a cop. I think I was in the wrong profession."

Daphne bit into a Twinkie. "It wasn't always a rush, but it was definitely satisfying to get a perp off the street and put them behind bars."

"I wonder if Lenny will get the death penalty," Barbara mused as she picked up her Barbie.

"Whoa, slow down there, Sparky," Daphne said. "This is only the beginning. There's a lot more involved before it gets to that point. *If* it gets to that point."

"Who'd have ever thought sleazy Lenny would turn out to be a murderer?" Barbara played with her vintage doll's ponytail. "I wouldn't have thought he had it in him."

"You'd be surprised what people are capable of." Memories of Rick's betrayal resurfaced. Daphne pushed them down. "I don't think Lenny intended to kill Evelyn. My guess is he was in the midst of robbing her, she woke up and caught him, and he panicked. If that's the case, he'd likely be charged with second-degree murder. That can carry a sentence of fifteen years to life in prison, but not the death penalty."

"At his age, that means Lenny would probably die in prison."

"Yep."

"Guess old Lenny-boy should have thought of that before he decided to embark on a life of crime. Isn't that right?" Barbara said to the figure in her hand.

"What's the deal with you and that doll, anyway?" Daphne asked. "For someone who's a feminist, I can't believe you have a Barbie."

"Cagney, do you know what Barbie's slogan is?"

"She has a *slogan*?"

Barbara bobbed her head. "'You Can be Anything.' Barbie has always been ahead of her time. She started out as a fashion designer, but since then she's held a variety of jobs, including doctor, pilot, astronaut, judge, and police officer, to name only a few. Barbie even ran for President in the nineties." The retired model's eyes kindled with girlish memories. "Growing up in

Texas, I fell in love with Barbie when she made her debut. I begged my mom for a Barbie doll for my tenth birthday, but she refused, calling her cheap and vulgar, even though all my friends had one. At fifteen, I got a job at Woolworth's and used my first paycheck to finally buy my own doll. I wanted to be like Barbie, sexy and glamorous, and not a housewife like my mother. I wanted a profession. A career."

Barbara's gaze returned to Daphne. "If you think about it, Barbie is a feminist icon. You really need to watch the *Barbie* movie."

"Well, I guess that's me schooled," Daphne said. "I didn't know all that."

"Did you know Barbie never married Ken?"

Daphne's eyebrows shot up. "Really?"

"Uh-huh. That's the one area I didn't follow in her footsteps, to my everlasting regret. Although"—the corners of Barbara's mouth turned up—"if I had, I'd never have gotten the great community property settlement I did from my last husband."

Before she went to bed that night, Daphne got a text from Rick.

RICK: Hey, Daph, still no sign of Benny? The prison doc said he developed diabetes in the joint and a-fib too. We're thinking he may have croaked somewhere. Odd no one's found his body, though.

TWENTY-ONE

Friday afternoon, Daphne grunted as she did her PT exercises. She'd started physical therapy yesterday morning and was determined to get her shoulder back in fighting shape again. The doctor said she could remove her arm from the sling several times a day to bend and straighten her elbow and do range-of-motion exercises. Afterwards, though, she had to put the sling back on and continue to wear it at all times, including to bed at night.

Daphne was counting the days until she could sleep unencumbered. Meanwhile, she had decided to cut back on all the junk food and try to eat more healthily. She didn't own a scale, refusing to be a slave to one like Barbara, but she'd been taken aback when they'd weighed her at the doctor's office to learn she'd put on thirty pounds in retirement. No way would she tell the girls, especially not Barbara. She crunched on a carrot as she checked her phone. She was still waiting to hear back from her sources on Vince's connection to Glazatovsky. So far, nothing had turned up. Daphne had a sneaking suspicion, though, that Vince might be part of Dmitri's drug-running operation.

Reading Rosamunde Pilcher's *Coming Home* for the third time, Claire felt the familiar prickling sensation behind her eyes that presaged a headache brought on by tiredness. Time for a power nap. Claire loved her power naps. Twenty to thirty minutes of sleep recharged her and got her through the rest of the day, renewed and refreshed. When she didn't heed her body's sleep signal, she felt exhausted and out of sorts, snapping at the slightest thing.

Closing the curtains and slipping the Paddington Bear "Do Not Disturb" sign over the outside doorknob, Claire padded down the hall to her bedroom, Elinor in her arms.

* * *

Barbara flicked through the hangers in her closet, rejecting one outfit after another. Too summery. Too plaid. Too long. Too short. Too loose. Too purple. She wanted the right outfit for her date tonight. Pulling out one of her little black dresses, she examined it. In her opinion, a woman could never have too many LBDs. Holding the sleeveless dress up against her, she looked into the mirror. Very Audrey Hepburn. Or Tippi Hedren in *Marnie*. In her twenties, when she used to wear her hair in a French twist for an evening out, people always commented how Barbara resembled the blonde actress Hitchcock made famous in *The Birds*.

Two days ago, Barbara had signed up for a high-end online dating site for professional people over fifty. Although she enjoyed the occasional afternoon delight of gymnastics with her personal trainer, Ryan wasn't someone she'd want to date. The steep membership fee of the online dating site had given her a moment's pause, but she decided she'd be happy to pay extra to weed out the con men and other undesirables. Tonight's date was a retired plastic surgeon. His photo showed a silver-haired fox with Paul Newman eyes in an Armani suit. His wife of more than forty years had died a year ago, and Lincoln James was lonely and looking for companionship. In his profile, Lincoln said he loved the ocean, traveling, skiing, yoga, hiking, and good wine.

On paper, he ticked all the right boxes.

Barbara hoped he would do the same in person. She wanted something new and exciting. The girls shooting down her great idea had bummed her out. She had tried talking her pals into making the Alphabet Sleuths an ad-hoc detective agency. She remembered the conversation as if it had only just happened:

"We should hang out a shingle," she'd suggested to the girls after Lenny's arrest. "After all, by pooling our combined skills and talents, we caught a thief and a killer. Why not continue? Going forward, though, we charge for our services and make some money in the process." Her blue eyes gleamed. "Three people have already approached me since Lenny's arrest, saying they'd like our help." She ticked them off on her fingers. "One wants us to find a long-lost relative; another, an old boyfriend;

and the other one wants us to find a missing lucky charm she thinks a friend may have stolen."

"You can't decide to be a private investigator out of the blue, with no experience," Atsuko pointed out. "I'm sure there's training involved, and who knows what else. I don't know about the rest of you, but personally, I'm done with school."

"And I hate guns," Claire piped up. "You can't be a private eye without a gun. Remember *Magnum, P.I.*? I'm never going to carry a firearm."

Daphne added her two cents. "You also can't be a PI without certification and a state license."

"Well, how long does that take to get?" Barbara asked.

Daphne shrugged. "I don't know. I'd have to look it up."

"I'm going to Google it right now." Moments later, Barbara read aloud: "In the state of California, the requirements to be a private investigator are a total of six thousand hours of paid, investigative work over three years, *or* a total of five thousand hours of paid, investigative work over a two-and-a-half-year period with an associate degree in criminal justice, law, or police science; *or* a total of four thousand hours of paid investigative work over two years with a bachelor's degree in law or police science."

Barbara fastened her eyes on Daphne as she read the next part, "Acceptable investigative work includes sworn law enforcement officer." Extending her arms in front of her, she made a fist, pulled her arms into her torso, and executed a victory dance. "Cagney, you already meet the requirements!"

"I'm pretty sure there's more involved than just having been a cop," Daphne said.

Barbara skimmed through the rest of the entry. "It says you have to submit an application packet with an ID, a certificate to support your experience, two passport-type photos, firearms qualification, and a check or money order for fifty bucks." Her eyes sparkled. "Piece of cake. Once your application's approved, you schedule a private investigator exam—a two-hour multiple-choice test. After you pass the test, all you have to do is pay a hundred and seventy-five bucks to get your PI license. You got this, Cagney! You can be the official PI and we'll be your support staff. Your back-up." Barbara eyeballed Atsuko and Claire. "Right, girls?"

Claire shook her head. "I don't think so."

"I'm seventy-five years old," Atsuko said. "I'm not going to start a new career at this age. I'm content with my life as it is."

"Also, B, that assumes I'd even *want* to be a PI," Daphne said. "And the answer to that would be a big N-O. Sorry."

Barbara pleaded and cajoled, but Daphne remained steadfast in her refusal.

So, instead, Barbara had sought new avenues of excitement, signing up with the discreet online dating agency for "mature" adults. Now, sitting in front of her dressing table, she carefully applied her makeup, starting with foundation and blush, and adding false eyelashes, mascara, and eyeliner. She ended with a red lip, swiping on Bobbi Brown's Parisian Red. Smacking her lips at the image in the mirror, she screwed in the diamond earrings she'd bought with her last divorce settlement.

Lincoln James was not who he'd pretended to be.

Barbara had arranged to meet her date at the Gourmet Dragon, the upscale Asian fusion restaurant downtown. When she walked in, dressed to the nines in her LBD and black strappy sandals, her heart sank when a short, wrinkled guy in his mid-eighties wearing a cheap knock-off of an Armani suit and a bad rug approached her in the restaurant lobby.

Shades of Lenny Fink, she thought.

"Barbara." The wrinkled old geezer extended his hand. "You're even more beautiful than your photo. Has anyone told you that you look like Tippi Hedren?"

Ready to make her patented get-out-of-bad-date excuse of suffering from a debilitating migraine by wincing and putting her hand to her head, Barbara stopped short. Across the restaurant, she spotted the gorgeous Rick Bartlett at a table, deep in conversation with a man she recognized as Dmitri Glazatovsky. A bottle-blonde in heavy makeup, a push-up bra, and a cheap red dress with a plunging neckline completed the trio. As Barbara watched, the blonde giggled and rubbed Rick's arm while the heavyset Russian gangster beamed.

I thought you had better taste than that, Rick. What are you playing at?

Barbara decided the B member of the Alphabet Sleuths needed to do a little undercover work. Smiling, she shook her date's hand. "Well, aren't you the sweetest thing, Lincoln." As the maître D' approached, she adopted a wan smile. "Would it be possible to seat us over there where the light's not so bright?" Barbara pointed to an empty table behind Rick in a dark corner where the detective wouldn't see her, but she could watch him, unobserved. "I'm afraid I feel the beginnings of a migraine coming on, and the light hurts my eyes."

"Of course, madam. I understand. I too suffer from the occasional migraine."

"Thank you so much," Barbara murmured to the attractive maître D' with gray-flecked hair. Her eyes flicked to his left hand. No wedding ring. *Why couldn't you have been my date tonight instead of Mickey Rooney here?* She followed the tall sixty-something man in the fitted black suit as he led them to the secluded table.

"Isn't this nice and cozy?" Lincoln James said once the good-looking maître D' left. He put his hand on Barbara's thigh. "Great minds think alike. Now, why don't we get acquainted, pretty lady?"

Barbara removed his hand. "Slow down, Speed Racer. Tell me about yourself. Where are you from, and what made you decide to become a plastic surgeon?" She made her eyes wide. "Is it true you have to go to medical school for years before you can become a doctor? I can't even imagine. Tell me all about it." Barbara fluttered her false eyelashes.

As her date puffed out his chest and launched into his autobiography, she feigned an absorbed interest, all the while scoping out Rick Bartlett and his tablemates. From this vantage point, Barbara could see the woman in red had on a silky, too-tight dress that strained against her mid-section. She appeared to be in her early fifties. Her voice was loud and animated as she gestured with her hands. Barbara noticed the glossy red manicure and glittering diamond on the blonde's left hand—emerald-cut with a band of small diamonds surrounding it.

That's got to be at least three carats, she thought. While Lincoln droned on about how he'd been top in his class at medical school, Barbara made the appropriate sounds of admiration, straining to hear the conversation of the trio in front of her.

The blonde stretched out her left hand, admiring the massive rock on her finger.

Glazatovsky gave her a proud smile and took the blonde's hand in his. "It will be a beautiful wedding."

"The likes of which this town has never seen," Rick added.

"Nothing but the best for my Irina," Glazatovsky said.

Dmitri Glazatovsky's getting married? But why is Rick involved?

At that point, the waiter appeared to take their order, and Barbara couldn't hear any more.

"Shall we start with oysters?" Lincoln smirked. "I've always found them to be quite the aphrodisiac."

TWENTY-TWO

That afternoon while Barbara was trying to decide what to wear for her date, Claire shelved the boxes of books Chuck Blair had given her from his mother's condo. On their morning walk that day—after Atsuko's trip to Tahoe had been cancelled—she and Atsuko had seen Chuck go into Evelyn's home and stopped by to pay their respects. Inside, they'd found the salt-and-pepper-haired man in his sixties standing in the living room, staring at the floor-to-ceiling bookcases, a lost expression on his face.

"I have no idea what to do with all these books," Chuck said. "There must be thousands here." He grimaced. "I've never been a reader like Mom, to her everlasting disappointment. If you ladies would like any books, please feel free to take as many as you want."

"I'd love to." Claire pulled out a tissue. "That was one of the things your mom and I had in common—our love of books. We agreed one can never have too many books."

"Unless you die and make no arrangements for their dispersal, and your heir is now stuck with them."

Claire heard the bitterness in Chuck's voice, but Atsuko saw the grief in his eyes.

"I'm tempted to throw them all in the dumpster." Chuck pulled a book off the shelf. "Who even reads Plato anymore?" He held up another book. "Or Socrates? No one I know." He began yanking books off the shelves and throwing them on the couch.

Atsuko laid a gentle hand on his arm. "Why don't you let Claire and me sort through this for you? There are plenty of places we could donate these books, starting with the Cedars, our nursing home and assisted-living facility. Their library is always short on books, and so is our clubhouse." She patted his arm. "You're upset. Why don't you take a break and let us handle this? We'd be happy to, wouldn't we, Claire?"

"Absolutely. It would be a treat to go through all these books. And many nursing homes and senior centers would welcome a donation. So would the library. There's lots of little Free Libraries around town as well."

"You wouldn't mind?" Chuck asked.

"Not at all."

"Thanks." Evelyn's son puffed out a sigh. "I'll gather my mother's papers and some personal things I'd like to keep, but beyond that, I'll let an estate agent handle the rest."

"Sounds like a good plan," Atsuko said.

"Feel free to take whatever you want." Chuck disappeared into his mother's bedroom and began making phone calls.

And so Claire and Atsuko began going through Evelyn's prodigious library, choosing the books they wanted and boxing the rest. After three hours of Chuck's antsy-ness and continual glancing at the clock, though, Claire decided the best thing would be to move all the books to her house, where she could sort through them at her leisure.

"I know you're in a hurry, Chuck, and these books are in your way. Would you mind if I took them over to my house so I could take my time going through them?"

"That seems like a lot of work. Wouldn't it be easier to just toss them all?"

Claire tried not to wince in front of the non-reader. "Actually, the handyman here is a friend of mine. I'm sure Mark wouldn't mind wheeling the books over to my house. It's not far."

Chuck inclined his head. "Mark, huh? Nice guy. I met him the morning"—he paused—"the morning you found Mom. That'd be great if you don't think he'd mind. If he's got a second dolly, I can wheel a load or two over as well." His eyes went to the grandfather clock. "I don't have much time, though. I have some appointments and a business dinner in San Francisco tonight."

"I'm sure Mark would be grateful for any help you can provide," Claire said. "I'll text him."

Ten minutes later, the handyman appeared with two dollies. The men loaded up the books and wheeled the first set of boxes over to Claire's. Then they did it again. When they returned after delivering the second load, Chuck looked askance at the boxes still remaining. "I'm afraid I can't help with the rest. I have to leave; I've got an appointment with Mom's lawyer."

"No problem," Mark said. "I got it."

Atsuko, who had finished packing up the last box of books, piped up. "Claire and I will help, Mark. Between the three of us, we'll manage. Right, Claire?"

"Right." Claire added one of the expressions she'd picked up in England. "We'll have this done and dusted in no time."

Chuck looked from Atsuko to Claire, uncertain. "Well, if you're sure." He gave Claire a key. "Would you mind locking up when you're finished? I still have the spare key Mom gave me for emergencies."

Claire patted his arm. "Don't worry about a thing. Now go, before you're late."

Chuck nodded at them. "This has been a tremendous help. A huge weight off my shoulders. I'll take you all out to a thank-you dinner once everything settles down."

After he left, Mark loaded both dollies. His eyes scanned the remaining boxes. "One more trip and we're done," he said.

"Great." Claire moved to the second dolly and gripped the handles.

"Oh no, you don't," Atsuko said. "Not with your sciatica. I've got this."

Claire cast a dubious look at her petite friend. "Atsuko, those boxes are way too heavy for you."

"Which is why we're using dollies." Atsuko angled the red metal hand truck back. "It's all a matter of balance—right, Mark?"

"You've obviously done this before."

"This isn't my first rodeo."

Claire stuck out her bottom lip. "I feel bad leaving here empty-handed while you two do all the work."

"You can carry those prints Chuck said I could have and the frame with the quote you wanted," Atsuko said.

Mark angled his head at Claire. "What's the quote?"

"'The person, be it gentleman or lady, who has not pleasure

in a good novel, must be intolerably stupid.' From *Northanger Abbey*."

"Jane Austen knew what she was on about," Mark said. "She's one of my favorite authors."

"Mine, too. Which of her novels do you like best?" Claire asked the retired teacher.

"It's a toss-up between *Pride and Prejudice* and *Sense and Sensibility*. How about you?"

"I love both of those, but I have to say *Persuasion* is my favorite. I'm partial to Anne Elliot."

"And the dashing Captain Wentworth," Atsuko teased. "Claire and I swooned over Ciaran Hinds in the movie version."

"So did my wife," Mark said. "She told me, 'Ciaran Hinds can put his shoes under my bed any day.'" He smiled, remembering. "I told her that was fine by me as long as she didn't mind Helen Mirren putting her shoes under my side of the bed." He winked at Claire.

Claire flushed, pushing down the image of Mark and bed, and locked the door behind them after Atsuko and Mark wheeled the dollies out.

On their way to Claire's, the trio passed Vince coming out of his house in one of his ubiquitous '60s bowling shirts, carrying a six-pack of Miller High Life. Vince waved and headed to his vintage T-bird.

Mark shook his head as Vince peeled rubber leaving the parking lot, blasting the Beach Boys. "That guy's an interesting character. I was in his place last week fixing a broken toilet. Have either of you been inside?"

"No," Atsuko said, "but he keeps inviting Barbara. He's got the hots for her."

"His entire condo is an homage to the sixties. Surfboards on the wall, posters of sixties groups, including a huge one of the Beach Boys, and a soda fountain booth in the dining room. It felt like being inside Mel's Diner. The guy's got a huge record collection too." Mark paused. "*And* a mysterious locked room."

Claire arched her eyebrows. "A locked room?"

Mark gave a rueful nod. "I asked him if that's where he kept all the bodies, but Vince didn't think that was funny. Some people have no sense of humor."

"Maybe that's where he hides his crazy wife, like Rochester in *Jane Eyre*," Claire said.

Mark grinned. "Or perhaps it's his laboratory, where he conducts secret experiments."

"You're both wrong," Atsuko said. "I think he's hiding his collection of porn." Then she remembered. They'd never found out what Vince's connection to Dmitri Glazatovsky was. Evelyn's death had knocked it clear out of their minds. *Could Vince be on Glazatovsky's payroll, doing something criminal for him in his locked room?*

Later, Claire took a power nap. Rested and renewed, she squeezed through the stack of boxes in the den she'd turned into a library. As she set the framed *Northanger Abbey* quote that had lived atop Evelyn's bookcase in front of her Jane Austen collection, her phone pinged with a text.

MARK: Brontë would like to invite Elinor on a play date. She graduated with honors from obedience training and promises she'll be on her best behavior. We'll be at the dog park if you'd like to join us.

She texted back.

CLAIRE: Elinor gratefully accepts Brontë's kind invitation.

Then Claire donned a pretty floral blouse over her capris and added a touch of lipstick. She pulled out the puppy chew toy she'd bought for the occasion—a plush giraffe with thick, braided cotton rope legs so the dogs could play a game of tug-of-war.

Sprawled in her recliner, Daphne reconsidered Barbara's suggestion that the Alphabet Sleuths form a PI agency—the suggestion she'd so quickly shot down. *Maybe it's not such a bad idea after all.* Truth is, she could use the cash. Plus, she realized she'd let herself go after retiring early from the police force and feeling depressed and bored. *I'm only sixty-two*, Daphne reminded herself. *Once I finish PT and get back in shape, I can easily envision myself working another decade or more.*

Would the other girls want to, though? Daphne knew Barbara would, but what about Claire and Atsuko? They seemed content in retirement. As a former legal secretary, Claire would be the perfect office manager. She was good on the phone and at dealing with people, and she had the etiquette thing down pat.

Claire hates computers, remember? And she's technologically impaired.

Daphne deflated until she realized: Atsuko can take care of the computer end of things. She's great with research and ferreting out information. On the drive home from the cabin, Barbara had told Daphne how Atsuko had done the research and got the skinny on Dmitri Glazatovsky and shared it with them. The retired professor's journalism skills would come in handy during investigations.

And what would Barbara do? Daphne asked herself.

The answer came to her in an instant. Undercover work! B would be great at interviewing men—most of them were putty in her hands. She can also go out on stakeouts with me. Although, knowing B, she'd want to wear a trench coat like Columbo and oversized sunglasses as a disguise.

Daphne started thinking about logistics. They would need an office space, and that cost money. Maybe the Alphabet Sleuths could work out of her spare bedroom to start, until they could afford an office. *Conducting a business in a private residence, Sherlock? A retirement community? There may be zoning laws against that.* While Daphne scrutinized zoning codes through the city planning office online, the doorbell rang. Peeking through the keyhole, she saw Barbara looking as though she'd stepped out of an Audrey Hepburn movie.

Daphne opened the door wide. "Wow, B, you look great. Did you have a hot date? What was his name?"

Barbara grimaced. "I had a date that was anything but hot. And his name was Lincoln James—supposedly." She kicked off her strappy sandals and rubbed her foot. "I think I'm going to give up online dating. Even the upscale sites don't vet their clients well enough. The men still lie through their teeth and pretend to be something they're not."

"Guys usually do." Rick's handsome face filled Daphne's head.

Barbara went to the fridge and pulled out a bottle of Stella Artois.

"Go ahead. Help yourself, B. Mi casa es su casa."

Opening the beer, Barbara took a long swig. "I needed that. But enough about my lousy date, I have something to tell you." Her eyes sparkled with the juicy morsel she was about to impart. "Guess who I saw at the Gourmet Dragon?"

Knowing her friend's penchant for celebrities, Daphne's forehead creased. "Daniel Dae Kim? I know he lives in the Bay Area. One of my old coworkers thought she saw him at the Dragon once. Rumor is he has family in Santa Bonita." She scrunched up her face. "An aunt or cousin maybe?"

Barbara shook her head. "It wasn't Daniel Dae Kim, although that would have been cool. I loved him in *Lost*. He's a hottie." Her eyes gleamed. "It was *another* hottie I saw tonight. Someone local." She paused to stretch out her big reveal. "Your old partner, Rick. And guess who he was with?"

Daphne went still.

Smoothing down her little black dress, Barbara inclined her head, eager to show off her investigative chops to Cagney. "*Dmitri Glazatovsky*, the Russian mobster," she announced with élan. "Not sure why Rick was there, but he seemed pretty friendly with Glazatovsky and his girlfriend."

"Girlfriend?"

Barbara wrinkled her nose. "A cheap-looking blonde in a push-up bra named Irina. Although"—she sent Daphne a smirk—"this Irina is more than Glazatovsky's girlfriend. She's his *fiancée*. She was waving this huge rock around, and I heard Dmitri say it would be a beautiful wedding."

Daphne's heart clenched. "Did Rick have anything to say?"

"As a matter of fact, he did." Barbara pulled a face, trying to remember. "Something about it being a wedding the likes of which Santa Bonita has never seen." She tilted her head. "I still can't figure out Detective Gorgeous's connection to a Russian mobster and his fiancée, though."

"Irina is not Dmitri Glazatovsky's fiancée," Daphne said in a quiet voice as she fought down the urge to hurl. "She's his daughter."

TWENTY-THREE

Barbara stared. "The chick with the push-up boobs is Glazatovsky's *daughter*?"

Daphne nodded.

"But that means . . ." Barbara's mouth dropped open. "She's engaged to *Rick*. Your former partner? The gorgeous detective?" She gaped at her pal. "Is the man blind, crazy, or what?"

"Or what." Daphne sank into her recliner, feeling sick. *I never thought it would get this far.*

"What is one of Santa Bonita's finest doing marrying a mobster's daughter?" Barbara's eyes widened. She sat down on the couch. "Rick's a crooked cop?"

Daphne's throat went dry. "Yes."

"How long have you known?" Barbara narrowed her eyes. "Is that why you retired early?"

"That and other reasons."

"Did you confront Rick?"

Daphne nodded, feeling miserable all over again about what happened. "He said I was imagining things—that I'd misunderstood."

"What exactly did you supposedly misunderstand? C'mon, Cagney, out with it. Tell me the whole story."

"I don't want to talk about it."

"Too bad. It's high time you did." Barbara crossed her legs. "Now spill."

"OK, but if I do, I'll need a drink."

Barbara gave her a look.

"Don't worry; I'm done with the pain pills. Last night I took the final one."

Barbara pulled out two beers from the fridge. Handing one to Daphne, she opened a second Stella and returned to her seat.

Daphne took a long drink and sighed. She closed her eyes,

remembering. "It was soon after I returned to work after being shot—"

"Wait, *what*? You were shot? How come you never told me this before?"

"No big deal. Ancient history."

"How did you get shot?"

Daphne blew out another sigh. "We responded to a robbery at the Santa Bonita Bank. When we got there, the robbers were having a shoot-out with our guys. We exited the car, guns drawn, keeping down." She released a rueful grin. "Only I didn't crouch down far enough and took a bullet in the chest."

Barbara's hand flew to her throat. "Oh my God."

"It's OK. It didn't do much damage—missed my vital organs, and the doc got it out without a problem."

"I thought cops were issued bullet-proof vests."

"They were. Are." Daphne didn't meet Barbara's eyes. "Those vests are super uncomfortable, though, and you sweat like a pig all day long wearing one, so I only wore the vest cover."

"Well, that was pretty effing stupid, Cagney."

"Agreed."

Barbara's eyes narrowed. "And where was your partner when you got shot?"

"Like me, Rick was moving forward, gun drawn. When I got hit, he was by my side in an instant, shielding me with his body." Daphne got a lump in her throat, remembering how Rick had cradled her in his arms. "He came to the hospital every day."

She left out the part about her partner and his wife being separated, and how she and Rick had started to regard one another with new eyes. "Rick brought me flowers, candy . . ." Daphne's eyes flicked to the Tommy Lasorda bobblehead doll on the shelf. "And that."

Barbara's brows drew together. "A Wolverine bobblehead?"

"No, the one next to Wolverine—Tommy Lasorda. Rick knew what a huge Dodgers fan I was. Am." Daphne shook her head to clear it of the bittersweet memory. "Anyway, it was shortly after I'd returned to work. We'd stopped at a dry cleaners owned by some members of the Glazatovsky family. We'd been keeping an eye on the shop for a while. Irina Glazatovsky had an office in the back. Word on the street was she cooked the books for her old man, and the dry cleaners was a front for one of Dmitri's operations—money laundering, we suspected."

Daphne took another pull from her beer. "That day, we'd gotten a call about a robbery at the shop and went to investigate. I was interviewing the guy who worked the counter, and Rick was interviewing Irina in the back." Her stomach filled with bile. "That's when I saw them together."

"What do you mean *together*?" Barbara raised a perfectly arched eyebrow. "Do you mean in the biblical sense?"

"No. You know—that dance a man and woman do when they're attracted to each other. Irina was pressing up against Rick in her low-cut top and tight jeans, all over him like a cheap suit. When Rick saw me, he got all red and embarrassed. Afterwards, in the car, he told me Irina was coming on to him."

"What?" Barbara affected Streisand's Yiddish accent from *Funny Girl*. "He couldn't push her away?"

"That's what I said. A few days later, we returned to the shop with more questions, and I saw Irina give Rick some money." Daphne took a deep breath, surprised at how much her partner's betrayal still hurt after all this time. *You think you know someone . . .*

"Money?" Barbara's eyes widened.

"Yep. A wad of bills. I confronted Rick when we got back in the car, but he said I was seeing things. Gave me some lame excuse, saying what I saw was Irina giving him flyers for her cousin's dance studio for his daughter and her friends. I knew Sami had been wanting to take modern dance classes." Daphne scrutinized Barbara. "I also know the difference between flyers and cold hard cash." She bit her lip. "I thought Rick and I were friends." *Starting to become more than friends.* But she didn't say that part aloud. "I was an idiot."

"Why didn't you turn him in? I know he was your partner and all, and you probably felt a sense of loyalty to him, but if he was on the take, I'm surprised you didn't report him."

"I did report him." Daphne gave a short laugh. "I told my boss. *Our* boss, Captain Dunlap, my superior officer. Someone I thought was a straight shooter—one of the good guys. He thanked me and said he'd look into it. The captain told me to keep it on the down-low, though, because accusing another officer of being corrupt was a serious charge and could destroy his career. I knew that, which is why it was so hard for me to report Rick in the first place, but I kept quiet as the captain asked." Daphne's lips tightened as she remembered. "The next day, I saw Dunlap talking to Rick in his office. Later, when we went out on patrol, I tried to pretend that nothing had changed between us, even though we both knew it had. I kept waiting to see what Dunlap was going to do, but nothing happened. A few nights later, when I was off duty, I followed Glazatovsky to this seedy bar on the other side of town where I knew he liked to go."

Daphne's stomach clenched, reliving the scene. "Inside, I found Rick and the captain with Dmitri. I watched as the three of them drank and laughed together like best pals. Then I slipped out the back." She shook her head at the memory. "One of them must have seen me, though, because the next day the captain pulled me off patrol and put me on desk duty. He said he thought I'd returned to work too soon after my injury and didn't want me to overtax myself. Said I needed to take it easy." She snorted. "He suggested I take some time off—stress leave—reassuring me the leave would be covered by my insurance and wouldn't impact my pay."

Barbara made a sound of disgust in the back of her throat. "Are you frickin' kidding me? Did he think you were stupid or what?"

"Something like that."

"So what happened?"

Daphne rubbed her forehead, feeling the beginnings of a headache coming on. "I went to my partner, my friend, and told him what I'd seen, what I suspected, and how the captain suggested I take stress leave." She sent Barbara a humorless glance. "And do you know what Rick said?"

Barbara shook her head, transfixed by the sordid tale unfolding in front of her.

Daphne swigged down the rest of her Stella. "He looked me straight in the eye and said that was probably a good idea. I told Rick exactly where he could put that good idea, and he said I didn't understand—it wasn't what I thought. I needed to trust him." A small belch escaped from her mouth. "Ha. Trust *him*?" Daphne slammed her empty bottle down on the coffee table.

"That's when I realized Rick and the captain were both bent, and it was their word against mine. Who would believe me? It's not like I had pictures or a recording or anything." Her eyes flashed. "I wasn't going to go out on any damned stress leave, and I sure as hell wasn't going to spend the rest of my career chained to a desk. That's not why I became a cop." Daphne picked at the label on her beer bottle. "Instead, I took early retirement. The last time I saw Rick was at my retirement party nearly two years ago."

"Until he showed up here, warning you about Benny," Barbara said. "The Benny we'd dumped in the quarry the night before."

"Yep. When I saw Rick that day, I asked him how his wife was. He said they'd gotten divorced, but he never said a word about getting engaged to Irina." Daphne splayed her feet out on the coffee table. "Don't you think that would have been the perfect time to mention it?" *How could she have been so stupid? To think for even a moment that Rick had romantic feelings for her, when all the while he'd had his eye on the bottle-blonde with the push-up boobs.*

"They deserve each other," Daphne said. "Rick will be set for life now, married to Glazatovsky's only daughter and heir, and turning a blind eye to his father-in-law's dirty dealings." She angled her head to the side, considering. "I wonder if that was his plan all along."

"Do you think Rick's partner, Jessica, knows what's going on?"

"No idea."

"Someone should clue her in."

"Well, it's not going to be me. I've learned my lesson."

Barbara nudged Daphne's foot. "Don't worry, Cagney. I've got this."

TWENTY-FOUR

Claire met Atsuko at the clubhouse for Saturday morning croissants and coffee. She nuked her Yorkshire Gold and stuck an almond croissant on her plate, then made her way over to their table, passing by the group of regulars clustered around the flat screen, laughing at the antics of *The Golden Girls*.

Claire sometimes thought their Alphabet Girls were Cedar Glen's own Golden Girls. Barbara was obviously maneater Blanche, and Atsuko, the wise and pragmatic Dorothy, albeit nowhere near as sarcastic. Claire knew the girls would label her naïve Rose, which left Daphne, the youngest, as Sophia, the oldest, most opinionated Golden Girl and Dorothy's mother. Sophia always had the best insults. *Maybe it's time for me to take a page from Sophia's book and come up with some snarky one-liners myself*, she thought.

Atsuko rolled her neck to get a crick out of it. "Are you as sore as I am after packing up Evelyn's books yesterday?" she asked as she sat down.

"A little, but the hot tub helped."

"Did you get all your new books shelved?"

"No, I still have several more boxes to unpack. I got side-tracked taking Elinor on a play date with Brontë."

"A date, huh? Was that only between Elinor and Brontë?" Atsuko teased.

Unfortunately. Claire shoved the thought down. "Don't go playing matchmaker," she said. "Mark is a friend, but that's all. He's a lovely man, but I have no interest in getting involved with anyone again," she lied to herself as she sipped her tea. "Besides, he's still grieving his wife. I'm enjoying Mark's friendship. He's a nice guy." She looked at Atsuko. "I just realized . . . I've never had a male friend before."

"Men can be wonderful friends. Kenichi and I were friends

before we got romantically involved. Friendship is a great foundation for marriage."

"Atsuko . . ." Claire warned.

"I'm not talking about you and Mark. I'm telling you about my experience with my husband. Kenichi was my best friend," Atsuko said simply. "I miss him every day."

"I'm sorry."

"It's OK. I'm grateful for all the years we had together. We were blessed with fifty years of marriage, and fifty-four years of friendship. I consider myself lucky."

"Not many women can say that. Look at our Alphabet Girls. I was married nearly as long as you, but it wasn't a happy marriage." Claire snorted. "And Stan was definitely *not* my best friend. His best friend was golf." She went on. "Barbara's had three husbands, and none of them are still in her life, which says a lot. Then there's Daphne, who's never been married—"

"*So?*" Daphne came up behind them. She slammed her plate on the table and glared at Claire. "What does that matter? Marriage is not the be-all and end-all of everything, you know. Some people actually *like* being single."

"I know. I didn't mean—"

"And *you* of all people should talk, Claire." Daphne scowled. "You had a lousy marriage. I'd rather be single any day of the week than be stuck in a bad marriage."

"So would I." Claire lifted her shoulders. "I wasn't touting the joys of marriage, Daphne. You're right; I have no idea what a good marriage is like. That's what I was saying to Atsuko before you arrived. We were talking about how lucky she was to have been married to her best friend for fifty years. I said not many women could say that, including me."

"Claire was only using the Alphabet Girls to illustrate her point," Atsuko said.

Daphne stabbed a piece of cantaloupe. "Well, I don't like being used to illustrate a point. It's not like I haven't had offers, you know." She glared at them. "I'm not some lonely loser on a shelf. I prefer my independence and not being tied down."

"I understand," Claire said. "I feel the same way. It just

took me a lot longer to get there. Please accept my apology, Daphne. What I was actually saying—badly, apparently—was that you, Barbara, and I are all in the same boat compared to Atsuko."

"I don't compare myself to *any*one," Daphne said. "I'm my own person. What you see is what you get. Take me as I am, or not at all. I don't give a flying fudge." Only, like Ralphie in *A Christmas Story*, she didn't say fudge.

Atsuko winced at the f-bomb. "Looks like someone got up on the wrong side of the bed today." Her eyes slid to the hard-boiled egg and fruit on Daphne's plate.

"Don't you start, Atsuko."

"Did something happen, Daphne?" Claire asked, shooting her friend a look of concern. "Is there anything you want to talk about? Anything we can do to help?"

"Not really." She salted her hard-boiled egg. "I'm not in the mood to talk."

"We can leave you alone if you prefer," Atsuko said. "Right, Claire?"

"Of course. If you need your space, Daphne, please say so. We can finish our breakfast at my house."

"Nah, you don't have to leave. Sorry. I'm in a crappy mood." Daphne's phone pinged. Picking it up, she read Rick's text.

RICK: Lenny Fink didn't kill Evelyn Blair. We're bringing him back to Cedar Glen now.

Daphne cursed and texted back.

DAPHNE: WTF?!

Typing bubbles appeared. She waited for Rick's answer.

RICK: I'll explain when I get there.

Daphne turned her phone face down. *So much for setting up the Alphabet Sleuths Agency.* Could the last twenty-four hours *get* any worse?

"What is it?" Claire asked.

Daphne shoved her breakfast aside. "Evidently, Lenny didn't kill Evelyn. Detectives Bartlett and Miller are on their way back here with Lenny now as we speak."

"*What?*" Atsuko said.

"How can that *be*?" Claire asked. "He was caught

red-handed with Evelyn's things and seen running away from her place the night she died."

"I know. Apparently, though, he's not guilty, or the cops wouldn't be releasing him." *Or else he has a really good lawyer*, Daphne thought.

Barbara approached, green smoothie in hand.

Vince jumped up from a nearby table. "Hey there, Barbara, lookin' good." He slid his hand over his combover, his diamond pinky ring glittering against his Grecian Formula Black. "How'd you like to go to Sacramento and have dinner at Cracker Barrel tonight? They do a great country-fried steak. Maybe catch a movie after?"

"Sorry, Vince, I already have plans," Barbara said. She gave him a sweet smile. "Maybe another time."

"I'll hold you to that, doll." Lacing his hands together, Vince thrust his forefingers toward her in a playful motion while making a clicking sound at the back of his throat.

Sipping her smoothie, Barbara took the seat next to Atsuko. "What's going on, girls?"

"Tell her," Claire said to Daphne.

"Tell me what?"

"Lenny Fink is being released."

Barbara stared at them. "But he killed Evelyn."

"Evidently not," Daphne said. "The cops are bringing him back now."

Barbara's eyes narrowed. "*Who's* bringing him back?"

"Detectives Miller and Bartlett," Atsuko said.

"Is that right? Well, I have something to say to Detective Bartlett. A few things, in fact."

"B, you're not going to say anything to Rick," Daphne warned.

Atsuko's head swiveled from Daphne to Barbara. "What did we miss?"

"What's going on?" Claire asked.

"Not here," Daphne said. "I'll tell you later." All at once, a hot flash hit. It felt as though someone had lit a fire beneath her. Daphne grabbed Claire's half-full glass of ice water and poured it down her back, extinguishing the flames.

"Ah, the joys of menopause," Claire said. "I remember it well." She poured the youngest Alphabet Sleuth a glass of water from the pitcher and handed it to her.

Daphne chugged it down.

"I had to give away all my turtlenecks during my hot flash years," Barbara said. "Luckily, those days are long behind me."

"How long?" Atsuko asked innocently, winking at Claire.

"Never you mind."

"I was still teaching when I went through menopause," Atsuko said. "Those were the days when we still used overhead projectors. One time, a hot flash hit out of the blue, and the palms of my hands were sweating so much the pen I used to write on the slide smeared and ran."

"I remember feeling like Gypsy Rose Lee the way I had to strip when a hot flash hit," Claire recounted. "Sometimes I'd barely make it through the door before I whipped my bra off. If I had something in my hands, like a bag of groceries, I'd drop my bra on the nearest surface and forget about it. Once, I was putting away groceries in the kitchen when my son walked in with one of his high school friends. They'd come in for a snack and saw my bra on the table. Douglas was mortified, but his buddy assumed I'd been engaging in some afternoon delight and branded me a 'cool mom,'" Claire said, using air quotes.

"Go, Claire," Atsuko said.

Barbara sang a snatch of "Afternoon Delight." Which reminded her—she wanted to schedule another session with Ryan this week.

Daphne tilted her head, a puzzled look on her face. "Who's Gypsy Rose Lee?"

Before Claire could tell her about the famous stripper immortalized by Natalie Wood in the *Gypsy* movie, and countless others on Broadway, the clubhouse erupted in angry chatter.

The girls turned as one to the entrance to observe the two detectives walk in with Lenny Fink and Connie. No longer wearing his hairpiece and clad in one of his polyester leisure suits, Lenny's arm linked with Shirley Robinson's. The eighty-year-old was holding on to Shirley for dear life.

"What's that killer doing here?" Doris shouted. Several others echoed her question.

"My Lenny didn't kill anyone," Shirley said. "He's innocent." She sent a side-eye to Rick Bartlett. "Isn't that right, Detective?"

Rick stepped forward. "Hello, everyone. In light of new evidence, it is clear Mr. Fink did not kill Evelyn Blair, which is why we have released him. Our investigation into Ms. Blair's murder is still ongoing. Please contact me or Detective Miller if you have any information that might prove helpful. Thank you."

Shirley shot a triumphant look at Doris and pushed a cowed Lenny forward. "Go ahead, sweetie."

Connie gave the resident flirt an encouraging nod.

Pressing a shaking hand to his forehead, Lenny said in a quavering voice, "I'm sorry for all the hurt and pain I've caused. I admit to being a thief and a conman, but I'm not a murderer. I could never kill anyone." His faded blue eyes sought those of the plump, white-haired woman next to Doris. "Tammy Sue, I apologize for stealing your watch. Stealing has been a compulsion of mine for years, and I never knew why. Recently, thanks to Shirley, I've learned that kleptomania is a mental health condition where a person feels an urge to steal things. I am now seeking treatment for this condition. To anyone else I've done wrong, please accept my humble apologies."

Shirley beamed. "And not only that," she said. "I'm tickled pink to announce that Lenny and I are getting married."

There were gasps all around.

Barbara side-eyed Daphne. "There must be something in the water."

Atsuko and Claire exchanged glances.

As a group surrounded the happy couple, Detective Bartlett walked over to the Alphabet Girls. "Hello, ladies," he said. "Daph, could I talk to you in private, please?"

Why? So you can tell me about your engagement?

Barbara looked at Rick as if he were bubblegum stuck to the bottom of her shoe. "Want me to go with you, Cagney?"

"That's OK, B. I'm good." Daphne led Rick to a corner table away from everyone. "You've got something to say?" Her manner was cold. Abrupt.

Rick scrutinized his former partner. "Daph, I told you I'd explain about Lenny Fink. Yes, he went into Evelyn Blair's house to steal from her, but he's no killer. Lenny's a con man and a two-bit thief," Rick said. "He told us he'd been watching Evelyn's house and knew she left her patio door cracked open when she went to bed. On the night in question, Lenny waited until eleven thirty when he knew Evelyn would be asleep—along with all the other residents. That's when he slipped inside her bedroom through the patio, to steal whatever he could."

Unwrapping a stick of gum, Rick stuck it in his mouth. "Once Lenny got inside, though, he saw Evelyn wasn't in bed. Hearing the shower running, he looked around for her purse, finding it in the living room. Lenny said he began rifling through the purse, but then he heard the shower stop and knew he had to get out of there fast. He grabbed Evelyn's credit card and the ring on her nightstand, and ran out the back. That's when Doris Franklin saw him running away."

"And you believe this cock-and-bull story?"

"Yes, because according to the pathologist, Evelyn was killed between the hours of one thirty and three thirty a.m., during which time Lenny Fink was in Shirley Robinson's bed. And they weren't sleeping." Rick rolled his eyes. "I now know more about the miraculous powers of Viagra than I ever wanted to know." He waited for one of Daphne's snarky comebacks, but none was forthcoming.

"Thanks for telling me. Is there anything else?"

"As a matter of fact, there is."

Here it comes. Daphne's hands clenched into fists, her nails digging into her palms.

"I also have some information on Benny Popov that I thought you'd like to know."

Daphne paled. Her stomach roiled. *Oh my God, they found Benny's body wrapped in my Dodgers blanket. Rick recognized the blanket and is going to arrest me.* Her nails dug crescents into her palms. "Oh yeah," she said, with a casual air. "What's that? Did he finally turn up like the proverbial bad penny?"

"No, but it turns out Benny had a cache of child porn hidden in the attic of his former house." Rick's jaw worked.

"Pretty nasty stuff. We also learned he had been abusing young girls."

Daphne recoiled. "How come we didn't know this back in the day?"

"Because he kept it well hidden. His ex-wife found out, and that's the real reason she left him. When Sheila learned Benny was about to be released from prison, she contacted Dmitri Glazatovsky and gave him the information. Said she wanted Dmitri to know the kind of sicko he'd had working for him. Thought he might want to think twice before giving Benny a job again."

Rick pinned his eyes on his former partner. "Glazatovsky may be a criminal, Daph, but he can't abide someone abusing children. Says those who do that kind of thing are animals—animals that deserve to be put down. And as a father, I happen to agree." His mouth thinned to a grim line. "Dmitri would never employ a known child abuser. In fact, I wouldn't be surprised if the ten grand he offered for information was his way of flushing Benny out so he could get rid of him." He delivered a measured gaze to Daphne. "I think we've seen the end of Benny Popov, Daph. I don't think you need to worry about him coming after you anymore."

If she hadn't been sitting down, Daphne would have crumbled to the floor. *Wait until I tell the girls*, she thought, knowing that Claire, in particular, would be relieved. "I appreciate your telling me." She longed for a Coke to wet her dry mouth. Daphne cleared her throat. "While we're talking, I hear congratulations are in order."

Rick gave her a blank look.

"Your engagement." Daphne could hardly get the words out. "I wouldn't have thought Irina was your type, but then what do I know?" She shrugged. "I've been wrong before. Turns out I'm not a very good judge of character." She eyed her former partner. The man she thought she knew. She hadn't known him at all. "You've got the brass ring now, haven't you, Rick?"

"Daph, I—"

Barbara rode to the rescue. "Congratulations on your engagement, Detective. That's quite a rock your fiancée has.

A bit flashy for my taste, but I guess it takes all kinds." She linked her arm with Daphne's. "Come on, Cagney." She wrinkled her nose. "It smells funny in here—like fish that's gone bad."

TWENTY-FIVE

The girls reconvened at Claire's, where she brewed a large pot of tea and set out some English shortbread. They had lots to talk about.

"What did Detective Bartlett have to say?" Atsuko asked Daphne.

Claire dunked a shortbread finger in her tea. "We've been dying to know."

Daphne recounted her conversation with Rick.

There were gasps, scattered "Oh my Gods," and stunned silence.

"He really thinks Dmitri Glazatovsky did away with Benny?" Claire said.

"Uh-huh."

"So we're in the clear?" Atsuko asked.

"Yep."

Claire burst into tears, and Atsuko hugged her. Blowing her nose, Claire wiped her face with a napkin. "Ever since that night, what we did—what *I* did—has been weighing on my conscience."

"Not mine." Barbara shrugged. She smirked. "But then I've never had much of a conscience."

"Love your honesty, B." Daphne decided one piece of shortbread couldn't hurt.

Nodding at the others, Claire said, "With this new information about the not-so-dearly-departed, I have to say I'm not sorry I killed the guy." Then she called Benny a name the girls had never heard pass her prim lips before.

Atsuko applauded. "I feel the same. And now, may I suggest we lay that subject to rest and move on?" She turned to Daphne. "Are you going to tell us why you've been in such a foul mood all morning and what it has to do with Detective Bartlett?"

Daphne rubbed her hand across her face and sighed. "I don't want to have to explain the whole thing again."

"I'll give them the *Reader's Digest* version." Barbara faced Claire and Atsuko. "The long and the short of it is that Rick Bartlett, Cagney's former partner in the Santa Bonita Police Department, is in bed with local mobster Dmitri Glazatovsky."

Atsuko's eyes widened.

Claire stole a glance at Daphne whose head was bent over her plate as she made mincemeat of her shortbread.

Barbara filled in the details her friend had given her last night. When she finished, Atsuko's eyes flashed. "I'm so sorry, Daphne. What a betrayal."

"I'm sorry too," Claire said, having difficulty taking it all in. "Detective Bartlett seems like such a nice man. I thought he was one of the good guys." She shook her head. "I guess he was another sheep in wolf's clothing."

The girls exploded in laughter. "You mean wolf in sheep's clothing," Atsuko said.

Claire furrowed her forehead. "Isn't that what I said?"

"I almost forgot," Barbara said. "At the time Cagney discovered the rot in her department, she had only recently returned to work after being shot on the job—and that's how they rewarded her. Nice, huh?"

Claire and Atsuko's eyes swiveled to Daphne. "WTF!" Atsuko said, refusing to say the actual f-word.

Daphne flapped her hand. "Ancient history."

"The more recent history, however, is that Detective Bartlett is now engaged to Dmitri Glazatovsky's daughter," Barbara said.

Claire's eyes widened. "The local crime lord's daughter?"

"You have *got* to be kidding me." Atsuko side-eyed Daphne.

Daphne wanted to hurl. "Let's focus on something else." She recounted how the police had come to believe Lenny Fink was innocent of Evelyn's murder.

Barbara shuddered at the thought of wrinkled Lenny and Shirley in bed together. "Thanks for putting that picture in my head, Cagney. Now I can't unsee it."

"Close your eyes and think of George Clooney instead."

Atsuko's face wore a contemplative expression. "If Detective

Bartlett is crooked, how can we trust him to do a proper investigation into Evelyn's death?"

"We can't," Daphne said, her voice flat.

Barbara jumped up from her chair. "You know what this means, don't you?" She pumped her fist. "The Alphabet Sleuths are back in business."

Daphne's mood lifted, and the girls discussed what they needed to do next.

"The first thing is to start from the beginning," Atsuko said. "In journalism, when a reporter writes a story, in the first paragraph—or lead as we call it—they must include the five Ws and an H." She ticked them off on her fingers. "Who, what, where, when, why, and how."

Daphne gave an approving nod. "Cops use those same questions in a police investigation to gather the basic information when interviewing witnesses and interrogating suspects. Once all those questions are answered, we've got the whole story."

Barbara smoothed down her yoga pants. "We need to get cracking if we want to solve Evelyn's murder."

"So . . . we're not going to let the detectives know we're back on the case?" Claire asked.

"No way," Atsuko said. "Detective Bartlett is untrustworthy. As for his partner—"

"Jessica Miller thinks we're a bunch of little old ladies." Barbara made a face. "She doesn't take us seriously."

"I guess we'll have to prove her wrong, then, won't we?" Claire said.

"Works for me," Daphne said. "This time around, though, we need to be more methodical."

Atsuko bobbed her head. "Agreed. We jumped to conclusions with Lenny before we had all the facts. We won't do that again."

"The first thing we need to do is make a list of suspects and write down what we already know." Daphne pulled a pen from her pocket and turned her napkin over.

"Like they do on *Vera*," Claire said. "They put the murder victim's picture on a white board along with photos of the possible suspects. Then they add notes beneath the pictures."

Barbara pouted. "But we don't have pictures of Evelyn, or anyone else for that matter."

"We write their names instead. Hang on." Claire darted from the room and returned moments later with an easel and whiteboard. "We used to use this for Pictionary." Pulling the curtains shut, she set the easel in a corner of the kitchen, then removed a dry-erase marker from her junk drawer. "Right then, let's start with Evelyn." She wrote Evelyn's name at the top of the board and drew spokes out from her name. "Who did Evelyn interact with?"

"Not very many people that I can think of," Daphne said, "besides her son and you."

Claire wrote down Chuck Blair's name and her own. "OK, who else?"

"The chocolate-grubbing Mabel Brown." Barbara wrinkled her nose. "And Lenny and Vince. Remember, Mark said he saw them helping Evelyn on her way to bingo?"

"That's right," Atsuko said. "Evelyn also had to have interactions with Olivia, the activities director, and, of course, Connie." She cocked her head at Claire. "Did Evelyn have any other family members?"

"Not that I know of. Her husband died years ago, and they only had the one child."

"What about Evelyn's son as a suspect?" Barbara asked. "If he's her only child, her estate would go to him, right? He could be in line for a hefty life insurance policy or inheritance."

Claire bit her lip. "I don't think Evelyn had much money."

"We don't know that for sure though, do we?" Atsuko said. "The first thing we need to do is get to know more about Evelyn. Who was she? Where did she go? What did she do? Did she have any enemies?" She patted her lip with her forefinger. "Claire, remember when we were boxing up Evelyn's books and Chuck Blair said he had an appointment with his mother's lawyer? The lawyer will know about Evelyn's estate and the contents of her will. That's who we need to talk to."

Daphne snorted. "Good luck with that. There's this little thing called attorney–client privilege. Lawyers don't give up information easily. Besides, we don't know who's Evelyn's lawyer."

"I'm sure Detective Miller does," Atsuko said. "I can talk to her and try to find out what she knows. Not only the name of the lawyer, but also what's going on with their investigation and any new leads they might have."

"How exactly are you going to do that?" Claire asked.

Atsuko gave a serene smile. "I have my ways."

Claire wrote Jessica Miller's name on the board and put Atsuko's name beside it. "OK, Atsuko will talk to Detective Miller, and I'll talk to Evelyn's son. Who wants to take on Vince and Lenny?" She grimaced. "The only good thing to come out of all of this is Lenny's engagement to Shirley. Now he'll finally leave me alone."

"Quite the change in old Lenny-boy," Daphne said.

"I think he was scared straight," Atsuko mused. "Although a leopard doesn't change its spots overnight. It's good he's getting therapy, but Lenny's been a player his whole life. Shirley's going to have to keep a tight rein on her fiancé."

"I wish Vince had a fiancée," Barbara grumbled. "Then he'd stop hitting on me."

"Why don't you go out with the poor guy, B?" Daphne said. "Put him out of his misery."

"Then I'd never get rid of him."

"*Get rid of him*," Claire murmured. She regarded the girls. "Mark told Atsuko and me that Vince has a mysterious locked room in his house. Mark said he teased him when he was doing repairs in Vince's bathroom and asked him if that's where he kept all the bodies. Vince didn't find that funny."

"That's right," Atsuko said. "I'd forgotten about that. We were joking around about what he could be hiding, and Claire said perhaps Vince has a secret laboratory. I said it's probably where he keeps his porn stash. Then I remembered that Claire had seen Vince with Dmitri Glazatovsky. Daphne, you were going to check with your sources to see if you could find out their connection. Did you ever do that?"

"I did, but they haven't gotten back to me yet. Evelyn's murder knocked it clear out of my head, but I'll follow up on that right away." Daphne got a thoughtful look on her face. "I wonder if the something shady Evelyn was referring to in her message to Claire has something to do with Vince. We need to find out what's behind that locked door in his house."

The three Alphabet Sleuths turned as one to Barbara.

TWENTY-SIX

Later that morning, Atsuko settled in with her laptop and green tea. They needed to learn all they could about Evelyn. Since most of the Cedar Glen residents hadn't known the nonagenarian well, Atsuko decided to look online to see what she could discover. Typing in Evelyn's name, she did a quick search.

Instantly, the dead woman's name, age, and address popped up. Evelyn had lived at her current address for the past twenty years. Under relatives, Chuck Blair's name was listed along with Evelyn's husband, Chuck Sr., who had died the year before she moved to Cedar Glen.

Doing a deeper dive, Atsuko discovered that prior to living in Santa Bonita, Evelyn had resided in San Francisco for more than forty years. She also found out Evelyn had worked at an art gallery in the City by the Bay for several years. Writing down the name of the gallery, Atsuko wondered if they were still in business. A quick Google search showed they were. She punched in the phone number.

"The Devereaux Gallery," a cultured, female voice answered.

"Hello, my name is Atsuko Kimura. I'm trying to find out information about a woman who worked at your gallery. Evelyn Blair?"

"I'm sorry, there's no Evelyn working here."

"My apologies, I didn't make myself clear. Evelyn worked there more than twenty years ago; apparently for some time."

"I wouldn't know. I've only been here a few years. If you'd like to give me your name and number, though, I'll have Miss DuBois call you back. She's been here for ages."

After providing her details to the woman, Atsuko resumed her online search for further information on Evelyn Blair.

* * *

Elinor regarded Claire from the armrest of the Scotch plaid loveseat as she finished going through another box of Evelyn's books in the den she'd made into a library. When Claire moved into her condo after selling the beige behemoth, the first thing she did was unpack her myriad boxes of books. She had taken her time placing the volumes on the bookcases—her favorite thing to do. Some people arranged their books in alphabetical order by author, some by color, others by size, but Claire's system was more eclectic. She arranged her books loosely by subject matter, genre, and similar authors, ensuring they weren't all matchy-matchy, color-wise.

Claire hated matchy-matchy. She liked to mix things up.

Once, she'd been watching a popular HGTV show where a famed designer was decorating the living room of an old Victorian. Claire watched in ever-increasing dismay as the designer filled a bookshelf with books, turning the colorful spines displaying the titles and author names to face the wall. The interior decorator left the books' front edges with their matching cream-colored pages face out, to complement her neutral design aesthetic. Claire yelled at the TV. "You're no reader!" When she saw the same sacrilege happen again on another home makeover show, she stopped watching HGTV in protest.

Opening another box of Evelyn's books, Claire pulled out the top one, a cream-colored, leather-bound hardcover with the title *Kahlil Gibran Diary for 1977*. The subtitle indicated there was a selection for each week from *The Prophet*. Claire remembered reading *The Prophet* in high school and being captivated by the words of the Lebanese American poet and philosopher. Idly, she flipped through the pages. A blue-inked entry caught her eye.

April 12, 1977

Chuck grows ever more tiresome. He knew when he married me I was a free spirit and would not be caged, yet he continually tries to clip my wings. He got angry because after Sebastian's show we went to the Tadich Grill for a late supper. Chuck was afraid some of his business colleagues might see me out with my lover . . .

Claire let out a puff of surprise. Flipping to the front of the book she read the first entry.

January 1, 1977

Happy New Year! A new year always holds such promise. I wonder what adventures await this forty-seven-year-old in 1977. Could it be that I will finally divorce Chuck? I agreed to stay in the marriage until Chuck Jr. graduates high school, but I'm not sure I'll be able to stick to my agreement. Three more years seems an eternity . . .

Claire rocked back on her heels. *Oh my God. This is Evelyn's diary from nearly fifty years ago.* She wondered if there were any more. Digging into the box, she pulled out seven leather-bound journals from the 1970s, noticing the color of the leather changed from cream to blue in 1980. She opened the blue diary to a random page.

May 13, 1980

Chuck Jr. is becoming his father—boring, conventional, and obsessed with money. How could I have given birth to a child who not only doesn't read but has no interest in the arts? He'll be attending college at Case Western, majoring in something called computer engineering. I was dreading taking him to Cleveland; the city is the butt of so many jokes. When we arrived, though, I was pleased to discover Cleveland actually has a vibrant arts scene, including the Cleveland Museum of Art, the Cleveland Orchestra, and the Great Lakes Shakespeare Festival. Who knew? Naturally, my Philistine son will not avail himself of any of these cultural activities. He did, however, tell me he's excited to see the local football team play.

Just shoot me now.

Claire tapped her fingers on the leather-bound journal, considering. Chuck must not have known his mother kept diaries, or he'd never have allowed her and Atsuko to remove such personal items from her home. She pulled out her phone to call him and tell him what she'd found. Then she stopped herself. *What if Evelyn continued writing in a diary up to the present?* she wondered. *She might have written something about the shady dealings she mentioned, which may provide a clue to the identity of her killer.* Putting down the phone, Claire began searching for more diaries. She was halfway through a second box of books when Elinor began to bark, running to the front door.

The doorbell rang. Picking up her dog and shushing her, Claire looked through the peephole and got a shock. She opened the door slowly to Shirley Robinson and Lenny Fink.

"Hi, Claire," Shirley said. "Lenny has something to tell you."

Elinor growled at the man in the polyester suit.

Lenny took a step back.

"Elinor, stop that," Claire said.

The spaniel-mix released a final bark before settling into her human's arms, keeping a wary eye on the visitors.

Shirley pushed her fiancé forward. "Go on now."

Lenny extended *The Greatest Showman* CD to Claire. "I'm sorry for vandalizing your house and stealing this." A trickle of sweat appeared on his brow. "There's no excuse for my behavior, Claire. I was angry and lashed out." He couldn't look her in the eyes. Lenny pulled out his wallet. "I'd also like to pay you for the cookies I took. They were delicious."

Daphne rapped on Connie's open office door and poked her head in. "Got a few minutes?"

"If it's about the broken coffeepot in the clubhouse, three other residents have already informed me, and a new coffeepot is on its way as we speak."

"It's not about a broken coffeepot." Daphne pulled out the chair in front of Connie's desk. "May I?"

"Be my guest." Connie's eyes flicked to her Apple Watch. "I have an appointment with the police in fifteen minutes, though, so I can't talk long. Not that I have anything new to tell them." She expelled a sigh. "I know the detectives are only doing their job, but I have a job to do too, and with all that's been going on around here lately, the work is really piling up."

Daphne gave her head a shake. "I don't know how you deal with the constant complaints and demands of all these old geezers." She sent Connie a sly grin. "Naturally, I don't count myself in that group since I haven't even hit the age of Medicare yet."

"Thank God for that." Connie swigged her Diet Coke. "We've reached our limit of crotchety curmudgeons."

"Any of those curmudgeons have problems with Evelyn?" Daphne asked with an innocent air.

"Besides Mabel Brown and George Hansen, you mean?"

Daphne's ears pricked up. "George? What was his beef with Evelyn?"

"She was always complaining about his music." Connie pursed her lips. "I make sure the hours of quiet are strictly enforced at Cedar Glen. No noise before eight a.m. and after nine at night. George said Evelyn griped when he played his music at three in the afternoon. She told him it sounded like caterwauling and that if he got a new hearing aid, maybe he wouldn't have to turn his music up so loud and force everyone else to have to listen to what she called 'that country crap.'"

"I'll bet that didn't go over well with George."

"Not at all. Especially when Evelyn started playing *her* music in retaliation. George said he saw her put a CD player in the window and turn it towards his house and blast him with opera." Connie took a deep breath and released it. "The two of them went at it like cats and dogs. It became quite a game of musical one-upmanship. I had to tell both of them to keep the noise down. I said if they wanted to listen to loud music, to put on headphones."

"Sounds reasonable."

"That was only the beginning of the George and Evelyn war." Connie's mouth twisted. "Evelyn then complained that George always put his trash can on her property. She said she told him time and time again to respect her boundaries and keep his trash in front of his home." Connie sighed. "George countered that it was a public street and she didn't own it—he would put his trash wherever he wanted. The next day, Evelyn shoved George's full trash can in front of his house, tipping it over so there was garbage all over his petunias." She made a face. "There was no love lost between those two."

"Well, isn't that interesting—George never mentioned a word of this when I talked to him." Daphne leaned forward with a conspiratorial air. "Connie, do you think maybe Evelyn pushed George too far? And one day, he decided he'd had enough and was going to end the war of the neighbors permanently?"

Connie got up to shut her office door. "Are you asking if I think George might have killed Evelyn?" she whispered.

"I guess I am."

"The thought crossed my mind." Connie put her finger to her lips. "Don't say anything, though." She tugged at the sleeves of her russet blazer. "It's not my place to gossip about residents."

"I'll be silent as the grave." Daphne flinched, realizing what she'd said. She reached into the bowl of candy Connie kept on her desk and pulled out a Hershey's miniature. Unwrapping the milk chocolate, she popped it into her mouth.

I thought you were trying to lose weight.

Ignoring her inner weight watcher, Daphne asked, "Is there anyone else you can think of who might have wanted to kill Evelyn?"

"Well, now that you ask . . . actually, I'm not convinced Lenny is as innocent as they say. I've been wondering if Shirley might be lying to give her boyfriend an alibi."

"Is that right?" Daphne unwrapped a second Hershey's.

Connie nodded. "I wouldn't be at all surprised if Shirley's forcing Lenny to marry her as a way to ensure her silence."

"That's an interesting suggestion. You should pass your suspicions on to the police."

There was a rap at the door. "Ms. Adams," Rick's voice called out.

"Speak of the devil."

Claire pushed her favorite feel-good musical into the DVD player. Whenever she was out of sorts or needed to escape from everything, *Mamma Mia* never failed to deliver. The knowledge that Lenny had been the one to break into her house and vandalize it had given her pause. *It was simply a prank*, Claire told herself, recalling Daphne saying the vandalism was likely caused by teens. *Lenny may be eighty, but he has the impulse control of a teenager.*

Still, the idea of him having been in her home creeped her out. *What if he rifled through my underwear drawer or something?* Claire shuddered and hit play on the DVD remote. Rocking out to "Dancing Queen" along with Meryl and her older gal pals, Claire heard a knock. Opening the door, she found the Alphabet Girls on her doorstep.

"We have some news," Daphne said.

"Ooh, I love this song!" Barbara exclaimed. She began to dance to the ABBA classic, and Atsuko and Claire followed suit.

Daphne busted a move, and Barbara burst out laughing.

"What?" Daphne said with an injured air.

"You know I love you, Cagney," Barbara swiped at her eyes, "but you have absolutely no rhythm."

"Not all of us were glued to *American Bandstand* growing up, B." Daphne gave her older pal an innocent look. "In fact, I'm not sure that show was still on TV when *I* was a teen."

"It most definitely was. *Bandstand* ran until the late eighties." Barbara gave Daphne a sweet smile. "I will acknowledge, however, that you've got one dance move down pat."

"What's that?"

"The white man's overbite." Grinning, Barbara imitated Billy Crystal in *When Harry Met Sally.*

Daphne stuck out her tongue.

"Moving on." Claire stopped the DVD. "You said you had some news, Daphne?"

"Yeah. My source finally came through. He said Vince did work for Dmitri Glazatovsky back in the day when they were both in Sacramento. Rumor is he was part of Glazatovsky's drug-trafficking operation."

Atsuko slammed her hand on the coffee table. "I *knew* it! Did your source say whether or not Vince still works for our local crime lord?"

"He doesn't think so. He said Vince retired a while ago after that big real-estate fraud went down and Dmitri was caught in the crosshairs. As far as he can tell, he's kept his nose clean ever since." Daphne gave the girls a look. "That doesn't mean our boy Vince's nose hasn't started to itch recently. Don't forget, he told B he does the odd job occasionally for his old boss."

"I wonder what kind of odd job that might be," Atsuko mused.

"Which is why we need to find out what's in Vince's secret room."

"No worries," Barbara said. "I've got it covered."

TWENTY-SEVEN

Peering in the mirror, Barbara sighed. Was that another gray hair sprouting among the blonde? Leaning to the light, her hand reached up and plucked out the hair, her mother's voice echoing in her head: *Remember, it hurts to be beautiful.*

Preparing to ambush Vince, Barbara knew she needed to look her best. She also knew she would have to call upon all of her Method acting training to make this work. She got into character as she applied her makeup. Knowing Vince was a fanatic for all things '60s, Barbara teased her hair and applied false eyelashes. With black eyeliner, she drew on cat eyes, creating a winged effect in the corners.

Next, she pulled on vintage orange-and-white polka-dotted bell-bottoms and a snug white cardigan with little flowers at the top, unbuttoning the top three buttons of the classic sweater to show a hint of cleavage. Barbara liked to maintain a fashion record of the times and kept pieces of clothing from each decade in the back corner of her closet, beginning with her teen years in the 1960s. The second '60s outfit she pulled out, she reserved for the actual date with Vince.

Date with Vince. The foreign phrase echoed in her mind.

Barbara wrinkled her nose. *How has it come to this?* "A girl's gotta do what a girl's gotta do, right?" she said to her pink bell-bottomed Barbie. "Or, in this case, an Alphabet Sleuth." Channeling her inner Charlie's Angel, Barbara asked herself, *What would Farrah do?* For a final touch, she sprayed on Chantilly, overnighted from Amazon. She had been amazed to discover the '60s perfume mainstay was still being produced.

She headed out to seek her prey.

* * *

Atsuko spotted Rick's partner going door to door. She hurried over to the forty-something woman. "Detective Miller, could I talk to you when you have a moment?"

Jessica cocked her head to one side. "You sure you want to do that? The last interaction we had, your friend Barbara copped quite an attitude and told me off. Said I was dismissing the four of you." *And made my partner read me the riot act afterwards.* She still smarted from Rick's criticism of how she'd handled the old ladies.

"Barbara gets a little defensive," Atsuko said. "She's fighting a losing battle against time and can be sensitive about her age and her abilities. She's determined to prove numbers don't mean a thing and that she's as active and together as she was in her forties." Atsuko grinned. "Whereas I have fully accepted old-ladyhood." She pointed to her face. "I've earned every one of these wrinkles."

"Good for you. I actually think women who allow themselves to age naturally grow more lovely with time," the detective said. "My wife is a decade older than me, and I love her crow's feet and every one of her wrinkles. Maggie's beautiful—inside and out."

"Do you have a picture of her?"

Pulling out her phone, Jessica extended it to Atsuko with a proud smile. "That's us on our wedding day. We got married at Bodega Bay."

Atsuko looked at the photo of two women in long white dresses standing on the beach. "What a pair of beautiful brides. Maggie's gorgeous—I'd kill to have hair like hers."

"I know, right? For years she straightened it, until finally one day she said, 'Why the hell am I doing that?' and embraced her natural fro."

"She looks a little like Angela Bassett."

Jessica's lips curved upward. "I'm always telling her that." She fastened her eyes on Atsuko. "How about you? Are you married?"

"I was, for fifty years. My husband passed away a decade ago."

"I'm sorry." The detective placed her phone back in her pocket.

"I'm grateful for the time we had," Atsuko said, "although I had hoped Kenichi and I would grow old together." She fluttered her hand to her face and went into full-on old-lady mode. "Aging on your own has its downsides. One of the things that can happen with age is fear." She fastened anxious brown eyes on the detective. "Now that we know Lenny didn't kill poor Evelyn, some of us—the other ladies, I mean—are worried the killer could strike again, and one of us might be next."

"I don't think you need to worry about that." Jessica patted her hand. "I think this was an isolated incident."

"So you don't think there's a modern-day Boston Strangler targeting old ladies at Cedar Glen?" Atsuko laid the anxiety on thick.

"Not at all. I think we're going to find the killer is someone who knew Evelyn and had some type of grudge against her." Jessica's lips tightened. "Murder is often personal."

"Well, that's a relief. Thank you for easing my mind, Detective. I feel so much better."

"No problem."

"Sorry to have taken up so much of your time. I'll let you get back to work now," Atsuko said. "Oh, and please pass on my congratulations to Detective Bartlett."

"Congratulations?"

"On his recent engagement." Atsuko frowned. "Now, what was his fiancée's name again? Something exotic." Her face cleared. "Oh, now I remember. Irina Glazatovsky."

"*What?*"

Atsuko clapped her hand over her mouth. "Oops. I didn't realize it was a secret."

Claire opened another box of books in search of more diaries. She and Atsuko had packed in such a hurry under Chuck's impatient gaze that she had no idea which box might hold more of Evelyn's journals. Or even how far back the journals went and whether Evelyn had continued keeping a diary in the present day.

A worn, green leather-bound book without a title caught her eye. Holding her breath, Claire opened it.

April 17, 1947

I can't believe I'm finally in Paris! I've longed to visit since reading the opening lines of Madeline *when I was ten about the old house where twelve little girls lived. Sadly, Paris after the war is not the glamorous city of the '20s and '30s that I dreamed of—the Paris of the intellectuals, writers, and artists like Hemingway, Fitzgerald, Cole Porter, and Josephine Baker.*

France is still suffering from wartime shortages. Electricity is rationed, and I read there is little coal. Many of the buildings are in a state of disrepair, with peeling paintwork and smoke-blackened stone facades. Here and there, though, I can still catch glimpses of the beauty and grandeur of the City of Light.

Mother and I will be here for six glorious weeks to take in the sights and attend the fashion shows to choose my wardrobe for my coming out in five months. (Personally, I think "coming out to society" and the debutantes' ball tradition is archaic and should be shelved. As the only daughter of Charles and Henrietta Blackwell of the Denver Blackwells, though, and since I'm not of age, I am forced to go through the motions of "proper" society.) I voiced my objections, but my opinion doesn't matter.

My parents control my life—Mother, in particular.

When I realized indulging Mother in this silly ritual meant I would be in Paris for six weeks, though, I decided to put up with the absurdities to spend time in this magical city. The contrast between the haves and the have-nots here has been illuminating and disturbing.

Two months ago, an unknown couturier named Christian Dior debuted designs that sparked a return to femininity and fantasy. His clothes have nipped-in waists and full, billowing skirts in stark contrast to the utilitarian, masculine styles of the war. The salons are crowded with wealthy French women and the upper echelons of society (including rich American tourists like Mother and myself) who are willing to pay a fortune for Parisian designs.

Meanwhile, rationing is still in place and the working class is starving . . .

Claire flipped a few pages.

April 20, 1947

Today, I had my picture painted by a street artist in Montmartre. Mother wanted to visit Sacré Coeur, but to get to the church we had to pass through the artists' square at Place du Tertre. It used to be the central square of the village of Montmartre and is centuries old. Imagine: Picasso used to live and work nearby! Seeing the artists sketching tourists, I begged Mother to let me have my picture done as a souvenir from our time here. She agreed, albeit reluctantly.

That's when I met the most beautiful man I've ever seen.

His name is François—he's the street artist I chose. He has curly black hair and eyes the color of the ocean. I could get lost in those eyes. When he finished his sketch and handed me my picture, his hand brushed against mine. It felt as if an electric current ran through me. François felt it too; I could tell from the way he looked at me.

Mother hustled me away quickly, though, before I could even say thank you.

April 22, 1947

I sneaked out of the hotel while Mother was sleeping. She has one of her migraines, so she'll be out for hours. I had to return to Montmartre and see François again—to see if what I'd felt when his hand touched mine was real or a momentary aberration. The crowds were so thick it took me a while to find him.

When I finally located François, he had finished sketching an American tourist with three chins and fingers thick as sausages. I saw the size of the woman's fingers because she was waving her hands in the air—hands covered in diamond rings so tight the flesh bulged out. She was obviously wealthy, yet she was yelling at François, refusing to pay the price he quoted and calling it "highway robbery." It made me ashamed to be an American.

Then François looked up and saw me. His whole face lit up.

He handed the rude woman her sketch and waved her away, hurrying over to me. François took my hands in his and said, "Ma belle." The same electric current I'd felt yesterday coursed through my body again . . .

Claire knew she should open more boxes and continue searching for more recent journals, but she was transfixed by the teenaged Evelyn's diary entries—so different from the reclusive woman she had known. *Besides*, she thought, *maybe there would be a clue from Evelyn's early life that could be helpful in solving her murder.* She turned the page, eager to read more about the young Evelyn.

April 25, 1947

I am in love! Sublimely, supremely, head over heels in love. I've never felt this way before. Every night I slip out of our hotel after Mother's sleeping pills have taken effect to meet François. He waits for me in the small park across the street and we steal away to his friend Alain's apartment in the fifth arrondissement where we make love for hours.

Since Alain works the night shift, we have the place all to ourselves. Mother would be appalled by the condition of the run-down studio with its cracked linoleum and peeling wallpaper—not to mention the shared toilet down the hall—but to me it is heaven on earth. In that shabby little room, François and I can be alone together . . . We can't keep our hands off each other. The human body is truly a thing of beauty. According to the church and society, what we're doing is wrong and immoral, but for the first time in my life, everything makes sense.

Chin in hand, Claire sighed, captivated by the tale of the young lovers.

May 29, 1947

François and I are making plans to elope. I am going to have a baby! We are over the moon and excited to begin our new lives together as husband and wife. I know Mother will never let me marry François—she's determined I marry "a good boy from the right family" back in Denver and already has her eye on a few candidates. François's parents have picked out a girl for him as well—the daughter of friends he has known all his life. Her family has a good pedigree and more money than his own, he told me.

François and I are determined not to let our families keep us apart. We are soulmates. We belong together—

The doorbell rang. Cursing the interruption, Claire set down the journal, marking her place. "What is it?" she snarled, flinging open the door.

Atsuko took a step back. "Whoa. Did I interrupt your power nap? There's no Paddington Bear on the doorknob."

"Sorry. I was in the middle of reading something fascinating." Claire pulled her friend inside. "You won't believe what I've found." She stared into Atsuko's eyes. "Evelyn's diaries. She was pregnant when she was seventeen years old in 1947."

Atsuko's eyes widened. "I was born in 1949. That means Evelyn has a child my age."

TWENTY-EIGHT

Barbara entered the clubhouse. Hearing the music, she made her way over to the baby grand, knowing she'd find Vince holding court. Every Saturday morning, an hour before the lunch crowd arrived, a cluster of Cedar Glen residents gathered around the piano for a singalong, accompanied by piano player Vince.

Barbara spied her quarry tickling the ivories as George, Doris, Lenny, and Shirley sang along to "Fly Me to the Moon," led by the poor man's Sinatra.

Spotting her in her orange bell-bottoms and cardigan, Vince's face lit up. He started singing the Beach Boys' "Barbara Ann." The others tried to follow Vince's musical about-face, but Shirley and Doris had a hard time keeping up.

Flashing back to her youth dancing along to Dick Clark's *American Bandstand* in front of the TV, Barbara's feet moved of their own volition. She flung out her arms and began doing the Mashed Potato. As Vince sang one Beach Boys hit after another, she segued into the Pony and the Swim and ended with the Locomotion. Belying her age, Barbara danced her heart out.

Vince stood, applauding madly when she finished. George and Lenny followed suit, but Doris and Shirley's applause was more muted, with Shirley looking as if she'd sucked a lemon.

Barbara flapped her hand in front of her face to cool off. "That was so much fun. I haven't danced like that in years."

"You can't tell," George said. "You're quite the dancer, Barbara."

"You certainly are." Lenny's eyes fixed on her cleavage.

Shirley captured Lenny's arm, snuggling up against her fiancé and looking Barbara up and down. "Are you going to a costume party?"

"I was in a sixties mood."

Vince beamed. "I'm always in a sixties mood. Best decade ever."

Lenny started to say something, but Shirley cut him off. "Come on, honey, we have to get going. We've got that appointment for you to get fitted for your tux." She delivered a fake smile to Barbara and Doris. "I'd forgotten how much there is to do to prepare for a wedding."

"When's the date again?" Doris asked.

"November eleventh—Veteran's Day. My sweetie's a Navy vet, so we thought that would be appropriate." Shirley giggled, gazing up at her fiancé. "Also, since men are notoriously bad at remembering anniversaries, this way he won't forget. Right, honey?"

Lenny tugged at his collar. "Right."

Shirley waved to the group as they departed. "You'll be receiving your invitations soon. Just wait until you see them. They're stunning. Isn't that right, sweetheart?" she cooed to Lenny.

"Yes, dear."

Vince watched the couple as they exited through the main doors. "Shirley's got Lenny completely whipped."

"Whipped?" Doris asked.

"Guy talk." Winking, George gave Vince a thumbs-up. "I don't know about the rest of you, but I'm off for my daily nap." He shuffled off, holding onto his walker.

Doris followed him. "It's about time for my siesta too."

"Guess it's just you and me, babe." Vince sidled up to Barbara.

Barbara called upon all her Method acting training. Adopting her breathy Marilyn voice, she said, "I never realized you were so musical, Vince. You're quite the piano player. Such a good singer too. I had no idea." She made her blue eyes wide. "Thank you for that trip down memory lane, The Beach Boys always take me back to my days in SoCal."

"That's when you were in *How to Stuff a Wild Bikini*. You looked great in that movie," Vince said.

Barbara stared at him. "You must be the only person on the planet who saw me in that."

Vince ducked his head. "I doubt it. Your dancing was amazing. You really stood out from all the other girls."

"That's sweet of you to say."

"Do you mind if I ask you something?"

"Fire away."

"Was Annette Funicello as nice as she seemed in the movies?"

"Annette was an absolute sweetheart." Barbara smiled, remembering. "Kind to everyone, even a nobody like me."

"You could never be a nobody. Those Hollywood directors were idiots for not putting you in more movies," Vince said. "You could have been a big star. With your looks and talent, you could have gone straight to the top."

"You should have been my agent," Barbara teased.

"I shoulda."

She gave a little laugh. "Oh, well. Spilled milk." She pouted, sticking out her bottom lip. "You haven't said anything about my outfit."

Vince's eyes started at the bottom of Barbara's bell-bottoms and traveled upward, coming to rest on her cardigan-clad chest. "Groovy, baby."

"I found it in the back of my closet and thought it would be fun to mix it up a bit." Fully getting into character now, Barbara released a girlish giggle. "You won't believe what else I found—this super-cute minidress and my old go-go boots. Isn't that a scream?"

"I've always had a thing for women in boots."

Barbara sang a snatch of "These Boots Are Made For Walkin'."

"Whaddya say you put on that miniskirt and those boots tonight and walk all over me on the dance floor?" Vince's eyes gleamed. "There's a club in Sacramento that does retro dance night."

Barbara thought fast. *How will that allow me to learn what's in his locked room?* She wasn't comfortable getting into a car alone with Vince and leaving town. *What if he is Evelyn's murderer? Who knows where he might take me, what he might do?* No, she needed to stay on-site where the Alphabet Girls could provide back-up support. She also needed more time to prepare.

"I have a better idea." Barbara looked up at Vince through her lowered false eyelashes. "How about if I make you a fabulous dinner at your place tomorrow night, and after dinner we dance. That way, we can choose the music we like. Plus"—she walked her fingers up his arm—"it's cozier that way."

Barbara thought the Sinatra wannabe might need a bib to catch his drool.

"Perfect," Vince said. "I'll provide the wine and the music. We'll make it a night to remember."

"I'm looking forward to it. See you tomorrow at seven." Barbara gave a little wave and left, feeling his eyes on her as she departed the clubhouse. *I should get an Oscar for that performance.*

While Barbara acted out her scene with Vince, Atsuko and Claire dove into Evelyn's diary, eager to find out what happened to her, François, and their baby.

June 1, 1947

We have been betrayed! François's friend Alain, who let us use his apartment, sold us out to his parents for a few francs. He told them my name and the name of the hotel where we've been staying. François's parents contacted Mother and told her of our plan to elope. Then the three of them, along with François's older brother, Michel, and Mother's high-society friend, Mrs. Quinn, ambushed us at Alain's apartment as we tried to leave.

They informed us there would be no marriage, saying they refused to allow it since we were underage. Mother said she wouldn't let me throw my life away on a penniless artist. François's family took umbrage at that, but Mother ignored them and said if we persisted in this insanity, she would bring charges of rape against François. Rape! Can you believe it?

I looked her right in the eye and told her if she dared do such a thing, I would tell the gendarmes she was lying. I said I would tell them François and I were in love, and I had given myself to him willingly.

Mother cringed at that, but without batting an eye, she said she'd tell the police I was barely seventeen, prone to hysterics, and that this Frenchman had taken advantage of me. "Who do you think they'll believe?" she asked me. "A respected woman of means or a hysterical child?" She stared at me with that icy look she gets and said, "Do you want to ruin your lover's life and livelihood with a charge of rape? A charge that will hang over his head the rest of his days. Who will buy his paintings when it gets out that he raped one of his subjects?"

I knew then Mother had won. She always does. In that instant, I hated her more than I've hated anyone in my life. François and I sobbed as they pulled us apart and Mother led me away. I promised my love I would be back with our child the minute I turned eighteen and we would start our lives together. This is only temporary, I reassured him.

François fought against his brother and father, but they held him tight. He called out, "Je t'aime, ma petite choux. Je t'aime!"

"Je t'aime, mon amour," I screamed. "I'll be back soon with our baby."

How little I knew . . .

Tears slid down the faces of the two grandmothers. Atsuko cursed and called Evelyn's mother a name Claire had never heard pass her friend's G-rated lips.

Claire flipped through the pages of the diary. "The rest of the year is blank."

"Where's the diary for the following year?"

Claire had already begun digging through the open box of books. "Hopefully, in here." She handed Atsuko stacks of books as she searched. At last, at the bottom of the box she pulled out another worn green journal with a triumphant flourish.

Opening the 1948 diary, they were met with more blank pages. Until the end of February.

* * *

February 27, 1948

My baby is gone and so is François.

The ink was blurred.

After we left Alain's apartment, Mother hustled me into a waiting car Mrs. Quinn had hired. They took me to a small convent outside the city where they stashed me away with a discreet group of nuns for my entire pregnancy. One of the nuns was a midwife and delivered my baby when the time came—a beautiful little girl I named Lisette . . .

"Lisette," Atsuko breathed. "That was the name Evelyn gave one of her good-luck bingo trolls." She brushed away a tear.

Lisette looks like her father. The same gorgeous dark hair, the same beautiful eyes as the ocean. She has my nose, though—a Roman nose, my father always told me, a Blackwell characteristic. She also has a birthmark on the back of her neck, a small strawberry spot that looks like a kidney bean.

The midwife, a nice nun named Sister Marguerite, wrapped Lisette in a blanket and brought her to me. The moment I held my daughter in my arms and looked into her eyes, I fell in love. A love like I've never known. I only got to hold her a few minutes, though. Sister André came into the room and scolded Sister Marguerite, saying, "What are you doing? You know better than to let her hold the child." She snatched my baby from my arms and said, "This child's family is waiting downstairs for her."

"I'm her family," I said. "Lisette is my daughter." Sister André ignored me and headed to the doorway with my child. I screamed, "Don't take my baby! You can't take my baby!" I tried to get out of bed, but I was too weak. "Lisette, Lisette," I screamed and then fainted.

When I came to, my baby was gone.

Claire let out a cry, her hand flying to her mouth.

"Oh my God," Atsuko said. "I've read about this kind of

thing. It happened to unmarried girls in Ireland who got pregnant. Good Catholic girls—including some who'd been raped at twelve or thirteen. Rapes that resulted in pregnancy." Her eyes blazed. "Their families were ashamed of their daughters, considering it a sin for them to be unwed mothers. They turned the girls over to the nuns during their pregnancy, and once the girls gave birth, the nuns gave the newborns away to "proper" homes. Those poor girls never saw their babies again. That was Ireland, though, where the Catholic Church had a stronghold. I never dreamed such a thing could happen in Paris."

Claire's fingers gripped the diary. "Evidently, Henrietta Blackwell decided to take a page from Ireland's book."

"What a horrible mother. But what happens next? What about François?"

Daphne returned to the bench outside George Hansen's condo. Time she had another talk with garrulous George. Glimpsing him leaving on his daily walk, she affected an absorbed interest in her phone. Moments later, she heard the squeak of the walker as the retired stonemason approached.

"Hello, Daphne," George said. "Enjoying this nice cool day?"

"Sure am. I'll take fall anytime over the dog days of summer."

"Me too. Did I tell you years ago I lived in Phoenix? Talk about hot. That desert is a real scorcher. I remember once—"

Daphne cut him off, having no patience for one of his long-winded stories. She looked him in the eye. "George, you weren't honest with me the last time we talked."

"What do you mean?"

"You neglected to tell me about your ongoing feud with Evelyn Blair."

Beneath his white hair, George's ears turned red. "That's because it wasn't relevant."

"Really? I understand there was no love lost between you two."

"Evelyn was always complaining about my music." George's hands tightened on his walker. "I'm entitled to listen to whatever music I want. Last time I checked, America's still a free country. Although who knows for how much longer," he muttered.

"It is, but there's also showing consideration for your neighbors."

"The same consideration Evelyn showed me when she'd blast that opera crap full volume?"

"It wasn't only that, though, was it?" Daphne asked. "I hear you made a habit of sticking your garbage cans in front of Evelyn's condo, rather than your own. Why was that?"

George huffed. "The streets belong to the county, not the residents. I pay my taxes. I have a right to use public property."

"True. But would it have killed you to move your trash cans eight feet so they were in front of your house, rather than Evelyn's?"

George flushed. "It's hard managing those heavy trash cans at my age. It takes all my energy to roll them down to the street. I'm not going to move them an extra eight feet to please my crotchety old neighbor."

"Well, you don't have to worry about that anymore, do you?" Daphne tilted her head. "With the cops releasing Lenny, it will be interesting to see who they arrest next for Evelyn's murder."

"It sure as hell won't be me. I never touched that old biddy."

Daphne decided to take a long walk before paying a visit to Shirley and Lenny. She needed the exercise. Meandering through Cedar Glen's walkways, she admired the last roses of the season, wondering how long it would be before the leaves started to turn. As she approached the front parking lot, she noticed Rick and Jessica engaged in a heated conversation in Rick's car. Ducking down and using the other cars for cover, Daphne sidled closer. A car away from the two detectives, she sneaked a peek. Jessica's face was contorted in anger, and she gestured wildly with her hands. Although the car windows were cranked up most of the way, Daphne heard the female detective say, "Glazatovsky."

Then, clear as a bell, she heard Rick say, "Jess, it's not what you think."

TWENTY-NINE

Atsuko's phone rang as she and Claire were about to read the next entry in Evelyn's diary, eager to find out what happened to François.

"Is this Atsuko Kimura?" a woman with a lilting French accent asked when she answered the phone.

"Speaking."

"This is Remy DuBois, Director of the Devereaux Gallery in San Francisco. I understand you were asking about Evelyn. Is she a friend of yours?"

Atsuko put the gallery director on speaker so Claire could hear. "An acquaintance."

"How is Evelyn? I haven't talked to her in a few days. We try and chat every week." She chuckled. "As you probably know, she doesn't text or email. Things have been crazy here of late with a new collection, though. I'm hoping to call her tomorrow and catch up."

Claire and Atsuko exchanged looks.

"I hate to have to tell you this," Atsuko said, "but Evelyn passed away."

"*No!*" They heard the woman suck in her breath. "When?" she asked in a quavering voice—a voice full of tears.

"Last Thursday."

"How?" Remy DuBois sniffled. "Did she die in her sleep?"

"I'm afraid Evelyn was killed," Atsuko said.

"Killed? In an accident?"

Claire gave Atsuko an encouraging nod.

"I'm so sorry, but Evelyn was murdered. The police are investigating her death."

"*Murdered?*" The gallery director gasped. "But why? Evelyn was ninety-four years old. What possible reason could anyone have for killing her? It makes no sense."

"That's what we're trying to find out," Atsuko said.

"We? Are you with the police?"

Claire spoke up. "Hello, Ms. DuBois, my name is Claire Reynolds. Evelyn was a friend of mine." She cleared her throat. "I'm the one who found her. As you can imagine, it was a terrible shock. I want to find out who is responsible for her death."

The sound of crying came over the speaker. "I can't believe this. It's so horrible. Evelyn was my friend, my mentor." The weeping increased. "My daughter's godmother."

"I'm so sorry for your loss, Ms. DuBois."

"Please, call me Remy."

Ever the journalist, Atsuko said, "Remy, we're trying to build a picture of who Evelyn was, so we can try to figure out who may have wanted to kill her. Evelyn was very private, so we didn't know much about her."

Claire piped up. "Apart from the fact that she was a widow, mother to Chuck, and loved books, bingo, music, and art. Oh, and Paris. Can you tell us more about Evelyn? Anything that might give us a more complete picture of who she was?"

"Oui. Whatever I can do to help. Evelyn was a dear friend. I've known her for years—since I first started working here, actually."

"When was that?" Atsuko asked.

"The summer of 1976—America's bicentennial and the year I got married." Remy released a throaty chuckle through her tears. "It was a time of great celebration, both for the U.S. and for me as a bride embarking on a new career as an art gallery attendant. Evelyn was the curator of the Devereaux Gallery then, and she took me under her wing."

"Evelyn was the curator of an *art gallery*?" Claire asked, surprise evident in her voice.

"Not just *any* gallery," Remy said. "One of the finest boutique galleries in San Francisco." She tinkled out a laugh. "Of course, I'm biased since it is my family's gallery."

Atsuko wrinkled her forehead. "I thought your last name was DuBois?"

"Devereaux is my husband's name. I kept my maiden name because I am a DuBois, my parents' only child. I did not want our name to die out with them."

"Good for you," Claire said.

"How long was Evelyn the curator at your family's gallery?" Atsuko asked.

"About twenty years, give or take. I don't recall the exact number, but if it's important, I can find out."

"I don't think that will be necessary," Claire said. "Do you know how Evelyn became a curator?"

"Now, that I *do* know. She'd started out as a painter—"

"*Evelyn?*" Claire said. "I didn't know that. She never said."

"That's because she didn't paint for very long." Remy chuckled. "Evelyn once told me she soon realized she wasn't a good painter. In fact, she said she was rather terrible, so she gave it up. But she loved art, particularly French art, and she had a good eye. Evelyn said if she couldn't paint, she wanted to at least be surrounded by beautiful works of art. She began her career here as a gallery attendant, as I did, and worked her way up to curator."

"What does a gallery attendant do?" Atsuko asked.

"Open and close the gallery, promote exhibits, monitor the artwork and keep it safe, plan gallery events, ensure the gallery is always clean and tidy, and do all the necessary clerical and admin tasks."

"That's quite a job," Claire said.

"Not everyone is cut out for it. You must have a great love of art and artists to be good at it."

Claire felt a prickle of excitement. Evelyn did have a great love for one French artist in particular. Perhaps Remy knew about François. Her brows drew together. *What was François's last name?* That's when she realized Evelyn had never mentioned François's last name in her diary, at least not as far as she had read.

"Did Evelyn's husband and son spend much time at the gallery?" Atsuko asked.

Remy snorted. "Non. Neither of them ever set foot in the gallery. Evelyn told me they were Philistines with zero interest in the arts or any kind of culture. She said her husband's driving interest was money and moving in the right circles, and that her son followed in his father's footsteps."

Claire recalled Chuck's complete disinterest in his mother's library. "Why in the world did Evelyn ever marry that man?"

"That's another story for another day," Remy said dryly. "I do know she and her husband had an open marriage. Evelyn was a free spirit. She had a succession of lovers when she worked here—mostly artists."

Claire spit out the water she was drinking.

"Might any of those lovers have had a reason to kill her?" Atsuko asked.

"No. Those relationships were fleeting. They only lasted a matter of weeks. Besides, this would have been over thirty years ago now."

Claire and Atsuko heard a murmur in the background.

"Forgive me," Remy apologized. "I must go. There's something requiring my urgent attention. May we talk again later? Please let me know when Evelyn's funeral will be. I assume her son is handling the arrangements?"

"I believe so," Claire said, "although the medical examiner hasn't released her body yet. We'll keep you posted."

When Atsuko ended the call, the two Alphabet Sleuths stared at one another.

"Who'd have guessed quiet Evelyn led such a colorful, exciting life?" Claire said.

Atsuko lifted an eyebrow. "Goes to show that little old ladies are more than their bingo cards—Evelyn's journals are proof of that. Speaking of her journals, I know we're both dying to find out what happens with François and their baby, but if we have any hope of cracking this case and finding Evelyn's killer, I think we need to set aside her early years for now and try to find her most recent diaries. They might provide clues to who killed her."

Claire sighed. "You're right. That's what I started to do when I first found her diaries, but I got sidetracked by Evelyn's Paris romance. Also, I didn't have a chance to tell you, but in those diaries from the seventies, Evelyn mentioned a lover named Sebastian, who was clearly an artist." She gave Atsuko a wry look. "Evelyn mentioned how tiresome her husband Chuck was, and wrote she was considering divorcing him after Chuck Jr. graduated high school."

"No love lost there."

"From the sound of it, Evelyn's marriage reminds me a lot of my marriage to Stan."

Atsuko stuck her hands on her hips. "Claire Reynolds, are you going to tell me you had a string of lovers too?"

"No, but now I wish I had."

Claire settled her helmet on her head, making sure it was snug. Then she donned her knee pads and elbow pads before lacing up her skates. Putting on her wrist guards, she set off.

Elinor gave her a mournful look and retreated to her doggie bed.

When she'd first learned to rollerblade a few years ago, Claire thought it would be fun to take her dog along as she skated down Cedar Glen's pathways. She envisioned Elinor trotting happily by her side as they zipped along the sidewalk, the wind in her hair and Elinor's fur as she and her canine daughter got their exercise together.

But Elinor wasn't having it.

Her rescue dog hated the rollerblades and barked and whimpered the whole time. So Claire skated solo. She'd loved skating ever since she was a kid. Growing up in the Midwest, she'd fallen in love with ice skating and skated every chance she got. Crowded around the Zenith console TV along with her family, she had watched, enraptured, as Peggy Fleming glided elegantly over the ice in her chartreuse skating costume to win the gold medal at the 1968 Winter Olympics.

The only gold the Americans won.

Six months later, Claire's dad got a job out west and moved his family to a place that never snowed—central California. That was the end of ice skating and the beginning of Claire's roller-skating addiction. An addiction she gave up when she married Stan.

After her husband died, Claire decided to learn how to rollerblade and fell in love.

Whooshing along Cedar Glen's pathways on rollerblades took Claire back to her skating youth—the only time she felt free as she escaped the confines of her restrictive upbringing.

When she skated as a child, she imagined herself to be Peggy Fleming traveling around the world to exotic places, doing something she loved.

Claire had a vivid imagination. Listening to Peter, Paul, and Mary on her transistor radio as a pre-teen, she daydreamed of being Mary Travers singing around the country with the folk trio at music festivals. When Claire wasn't imagining herself as the singing Mary or skating Peggy, she envisioned herself as the strong, smart Emma Peel in *The Avengers*, a master of martial arts doing feats of derring-do on par with any man.

Now, as a senior in a retirement community fast approaching seventy and rollerblading, Claire didn't feel one bit of her advancing years.

Skating kept her young. Fit. And free.

As she skated Cedar Glen's curving pathways, Claire hummed "Defying Gravity" from *Wicked*, determined nobody would bring her down.

Turning the corner, she smacked into Mark and Brontë and went down.

"Claire, are you OK?" Mark bent down to help her up, struggling to untangle her from barking Brontë's leash.

"I'm fine." She brushed off the seat of her leggings and stood up, grateful she'd been wearing her protective gear. "It's my fault. I was daydreaming and not watching where I was going. Sorry if I scared you, Brontë."

The dog licked her hand, and Claire winced.

"Let me take a look at that." Mark took her hand in his and examined Claire's palm. "You scraped this pretty well. Looks like you've got some road rash. Come with me."

Claire tingled at Mark's touch. A tingling she resisted. "It's OK. I'll go home and put antiseptic on it."

"My place is closer." He nodded at the red door in front of them. "Besides, I think Brontë could do with a little reassurance in the form of a treat."

"Well, when you put it that way . . ."

Mark knelt, undoing Claire's rollerblades, and she stepped out of them, feeling awkward. She wasn't used to a man being solicitous.

Leaving the skates at the front door, Mark led her inside. "Have a seat; I'll be right with you." He unclipped Brontë's leash and headed to the kitchen, the terrier scampering after him.

Claire followed and sat at the counter, taking in her surroundings as Mark gave Brontë her treat. Everywhere she looked, there were books.

On the table. Counter. The floor beside the couch. And myriad bookcases ringing the great room.

"Read much?" she asked.

Mark pulled out hydrogen peroxide from beneath the sink. "Only in my spare time." He grinned. "I'm a retired English teacher—what did you expect?"

"No wonder you didn't want any of Evelyn's books."

"No place to put them. I had to make a rule: for every book that comes in, another book must go out."

"I've thought of doing the same thing, but it's so hard deciding which book to let go."

Humming "Let it Go," the teacher-turned-handyman sat beside Claire and opened the bottle of peroxide.

And he likes Idina Menzel too? Who knew?

Stan hated musicals and refused to watch them, except for *White Christmas*. Now, in Mark's kitchen, Claire had to restrain herself from flinging her flat-chested body at this dream man.

Mark gently took her hand. "This is going to sting a bit," he said, looking into her eyes.

"I'm a big girl, I can take it." *I can take anything you want to give me.*

Claire immediately chastised herself. *Stop it, you silly old woman. You're as bad as Barbara. It's obvious this man is still in love with his wife.*

THIRTY

The Alphabet Girls reconvened at Claire's for a late lunch to share their findings. Claire set out shrimp-salad stuffed avocadoes, pub cheese and crackers, carrot sticks, and homemade chocolate-chip cookies. Then she pulled out the whiteboard.

Daphne tucked into her stuffed avocado. "Thanks to Connie, I learned George Hansen and Evelyn had a long-running feud." She recapped the music wars and trash-can debacle between the two neighbors.

Barbara munched on a carrot stick. "Interesting that Georgie-Porgie never mentioned this when you talked to him right after Evelyn's death."

"I thought so too, which is why I paid him another visit." Daphne dragged a carrot stick through the pub cheese. "George is not our man, though. Whoever entered Evelyn's house through the sliding glass door would have had to jump the fence to get onto her patio. No way George can do that; he's too dependent on his walker." She finished her carrot stick and grabbed another. "Lenny, on the other hand, is still pretty spry."

"But he's in the clear." Atsuko reached for a cookie. "Lenny was with Shirley during the time Evelyn was killed."

Daphne cast a look of longing at Claire's homemade cookies. "According to Shirley, yes, but Connie wonders if she might be lying to cover for Lenny. She thinks Shirley may be giving Lenny an alibi to force him to marry her."

"I can't believe anyone would want to marry Lenny," Claire said.

"It takes all kinds." Barbara turned to Daphne. "Did you put the screws to Shirley and Lenny to get them to 'fess up, Cagney?"

"I'd intended to, but then I saw something that knocked that clean out of my head." Daphne recounted how she'd seen the two detectives arguing in their car and heard Jessica say the name Glazatovsky. Her mouth twisted in a bleak approximation of a smile. "Rick fed Jessica the same tired line he gave me when I confronted him, saying, 'It's not what you think.'"

Barbara snorted. "Detective Miller's a smart cookie. She's not going to buy that. I wouldn't be surprised if she goes straight to the top and informs the powers-that-be of Ricky-boy's corruption *and* her boss's."

Daphne grimaced. "Unlike me, who turned tail and ran."

"That's not what I meant, Cagney."

"I know, but face it, B. If I hadn't caved when I discovered Rick and the captain were in bed with Dmitri and reported it, we wouldn't have crooked cops still running the Santa Bonita Police." She took a drink of her lemonade, then raised her glass. "More power to Jessica if she can bring them down."

"I wonder how she found out about Rick Bartlett's connection with the Glazatovsky family," Claire mused.

Atsuko held up her hand. "I planted that seed. I told Jessica to pass on my congratulations to Detective Bartlett on his engagement."

Barbara smirked. "Way to go, Atsuko. I wouldn't be surprised if the dominoes start to fall soon."

Daphne clicked her glass against Barbara's. "Here's hoping."

"Back to Evelyn," Atsuko said. "I found out she worked in a San Francisco art gallery for years. Claire and I spoke to the director of the gallery, who was a close friend of Evelyn's. They were so close, in fact, that she made Evelyn her daughter's godmother." She stole a glance at Claire. "But that's only the tip of the iceberg. We also discovered Evelyn and her husband had an open marriage. Back in the day, she had several lovers—mostly artists."

Barbara lifted a plucked eyebrow. "Who'd have thought our resident curmudgeon would turn out to be such a wild woman?"

"There was much more to Evelyn than met the eye," Claire said. She proceeded to tell the girls about her diaries and what she and Atsuko had uncovered so far.

"Wait." Daphne held up her hand. "So you don't know what happened to Evelyn's daughter, who was basically snatched from her mother's arms, or this François, who sounds like he was the love of her life?"

"Not yet," Claire said, "and it's killing me. Since we're trying to track down Evelyn's killer, we thought we should set the old diaries aside for now and go through the newer ones. If we're lucky, there may be information in her last diary that will point us to her killer."

"So where is this final diary?" Daphne asked.

Claire cut her eyes to the stack of boxes in the den. "In one of those boxes, we hope."

Barbara jumped up. "Well, what are we waiting for? Let's get cracking. Didn't your mother ever tell you, 'Many hands make light work'?"

As the girls sat on the floor hunting through the boxes for Evelyn's latest diary, Barbara relayed her earlier Oscar-caliber performance with Vince.

Daphne shook her head. "Only you, B, would have vintage sixties clothes at your disposal."

"Not just the sixties. I also have a peasant blouse, tube top, and maxi dress from the seventies," Barbara said. "And for the eighties, I kept my favorite legwarmers and leotard along with my Madonna bustier top and fishnet gloves."

Atsuko looked at Claire over the top of an open box. "Have *you* ever worn a bustier?"

"Not yet. Maybe I should, though, and show off my tatts." Claire blushed, wondering what Mark might think of that.

Barbara gave her a thumbs-up. "Go, Claire."

"I found it!" Daphne held up a moleskin journal covered in Van Gogh's irises. "This is dated this year."

"Let's take it to the dining-room table where we can read it together," Claire suggested.

The Alphabet Girls sat at the table and Daphne handed the journal to Claire. "You do the honors. You were Evelyn's friend, and you're the one who found the diaries in the first place."

Opening the diary from the back, Claire flipped through the empty pages until she found the final entry. She read aloud.

September 17

Taco Tuesday and bingo night.

I talked to Chuck briefly yesterday. He's not happy with me. But then again, when has he ever been? My son is a carbon copy of his father. The only thing Chuck and I share is DNA. We're from completely different planets. I remember that book Men are from Mars, Women are from Venus, *but in our case I think it's more like I'm from Mercury and Chuck is from that new dwarf planet I read about a few years ago—the one that's even more distant than Pluto.*

C'est la vie. I made my peace with our relationship, or, rather, lack of a relationship, long ago, and I know Chuck's done the same.

I'm so glad Remy and I have stayed in contact. I love chatting with her every week. I'm going to ask her to come for a visit this weekend and bring Fleur. It's been ages since I've seen my goddaughter, and I have a surprise for the two of them. I hope they like it.

"Fleur." Daphne interrupted, looking at the girls. "That's what Evelyn called one of her good-luck trolls."

Claire nodded. "She named the other one after her daughter, Lisette. Both French girls she loved." She blinked back a tear.

"What else does Evelyn say?" Barbara asked.

Claire resumed reading.

Bingo was exciting on several levels tonight. Lenny Fink was in his usual sleazy form. He was panting after Claire for a while, but now it seems he's latched onto Shirley Robinson. Not surprising, since Shirley's loaded. I can't understand what she sees in him, but lonely women make stupid choices. I'm living proof. I still can't believe I ever married Chuck. I noticed Lenny palm Shirley's credit card when she was falling down drunk. I wonder if I should say something. Shirley may not appreciate my telling her the man she's crazy about is a two-bit thief and God only knows what else.

Atsuko mused. "I wonder if Lenny's thievery is the shady goings-on Evelyn talked about in her voicemail?"

"Maybe," Daphne said. "Or maybe there's more. Keep reading."

The biggest surprise of the night was I won the grand prize at bingo—a four-pound box of See's Candy! I love See's. So does Remy. I was planning to share my box of candy with her and Fleur this weekend, but that crazy Mabel Brown spoiled everything. She accosted me outside bingo, claiming we'd tied for the win and I should split the candy with her. I told her I would do no such thing and called her a liar and a cheat.

Mabel went mad. She pushed the box of See's off my walker, and chocolate went flying everywhere. Then she scrabbled on the ground like a rabid dog, grabbing and gobbling as many chocolates as she could. I've never seen such a thing. It was quite disturbing. Mabel swore at me and called me names, even threatened me. I'm not worried, though. She's all bark and no bite.

The person I find most disturbing is Vince Merlucci. That man has a twisted side. I was quite unsettled by what I glimpsed in his spare room when I walked past his condo after bingo. Usually, he keeps the drapes drawn, but I guess he'd forgotten to close them that night. I need to tell someone what I saw. Not Chuck; he'll say I'm crazy and dismiss me out of hand as he always does. I considered telling Connie, but she has a lot on her plate and something like this might tip her over the edge. (Or, like Chuck, she'll think I've got dementia and shouldn't be living alone anymore. Chuck's been trying to push me into the Cedars for years now.) I think I'll tell Claire what I saw. She has a good head on her shoulders; she'll know what to do. I'm going to call her right now.

Claire looked up at her friends through blurred eyes. "If only I had listened to Evelyn's voicemail that night."

"Don't go down that road," Atsuko said. "We've already talked about this. You are not to blame."

"That's right," Daphne said. "The good news is, now we have a good idea of who the killer is."

"Yeah," Barbara said in a bleak voice. "Vince. The guy Evelyn said has a twisted side. The same guy I have a date with tomorrow night." Her throat went dry. "The guy I'm going to be alone with, trying to find out what's hidden in that secret room."

"You won't be alone, B," Daphne said.

"Planning to make this a double-date, Cagney?" Barbara gave a short laugh. "Somehow, I don't think Vince will go for that. Besides, I only have one pair of go-go boots."

"You won't be alone because the Alphabet Sleuths will be close by, ready to ride to the rescue. Right, girls?"

"Right," they chorused.

Daphne leaned forward. "Let's put our heads together and figure out how we're going to do this."

An hour later, they had a plan.

Daphne's phone buzzed with a text. She read the message and released a strangled cry.

"What is it, Cagney?" Barbara asked.

Wordlessly, Daphne passed her the phone.

RICK: We found Benny.

Barbara paled beneath her makeup.

"What?" Claire and Atsuko said in unison.

Claire snatched the phone from Barbara. Reading the text, she crumpled to the floor.

THIRTY-ONE

Claire came to on the couch, the girls clustered around her. "What happened?" she asked.

"You fainted." Atsuko handed her a glass of water. "Take a drink."

Claire did. Then she remembered. She gazed at Daphne, horror-struck. "They found the body?"

Daphne nodded, her mouth a grim line.

"H–how?" Claire asked, wondering how long it would be before the cops showed up to arrest her.

"According to news reports, late last night a guy walking his dog saw a car go over the edge of the quarry," Atsuko said. "He called 911 and they sent a dive team, hoping for survivors."

Claire's heart clenched.

"While the divers were searching for the car, they found Benny," Barbara said.

Stomach roiling, Claire asked, "Did the news identify him?"

"Not yet," Daphne said. "They're calling it an unidentified body, but Rick knows it's Benny. He's on his way over to talk to me."

Claire sat up, pushing down her fears. "I'm coming, too. I'm going to confess."

Barbara stood tall. "We all will."

Daphne's nostrils flared. "You'll do no such thing!" She puffed out a breath. "Girls, I need you to hold on for now. Let me hear what Rick has to say. Remember, he hinted at the prospect of Glazatovsky getting rid of Benny. Maybe that's what he's coming to tell me."

Claire wavered. "I still think I should make a clean breast of it—tell the detective what really happened and that I was only trying to stop Benny from killing you."

"And that it was self-defense," Atsuko said.

"It's a little late for that at this point," Barbara said. "I'm with Cagney. Let her talk to Rick and get the scoop before we rush into anything that could come back and bite us all."

Daphne shot her a grateful look. "Thanks, B."

"What do you think, Atsuko?" Claire asked, turning to her friend.

Atsuko considered. "I think we should let Daphne talk to Detective Bartlett and see what he has to say. Then we can make a more informed decision."

Claire puffed out a sigh. "OK," she said reluctantly.

Daphne's phone buzzed. Glancing at it, she said, "That's Rick. I need to go. Just chill out, guys, act natural. It's all going to be fine."

It will *be fine*, Daphne told herself as she headed home. *I'll make sure of that. I won't let Claire or the others take the fall for what is all my fault. I'm the one who got them into this, I'm the one who will get them out of it. Whatever it takes.*

To distract herself from worrying about the detective's conversation with Daphne, Claire decided to continue reading through Evelyn's diaries. Picking up the ones they'd found so far, she set them on the dining-room table and arranged them in chronological order by decade. That's when she discovered gaps. Either Evelyn hadn't kept a diary for every year, or Claire hadn't found all of them. She quickly went through the two remaining boxes of books. No diaries, but some beautiful coffee-table art books she intended to keep for herself.

Elinor whined and scratched at the front door.

"I'm sorry, sweetheart. Mommy forgot to take you on your walk today, didn't she? We'll go right now." Clipping on Elinor's leash, Claire headed outside. As she approached Evelyn's condo, she noticed the front door standing open and heard a crash and a curse.

Elinor released a loud bark.

Claire called out. "Everything OK in there?" as Elinor continued barking.

Chuck Blair appeared in the doorway, unshaven and with bloodshot eyes. "Sorry for the noise. It's all such a mess."

Claire's heart went out to her friend's grieving son. "I thought you were going to have estate agents handle everything."

"I am, but I realized there were a few things I'd forgotten to get."

Claire felt a twinge of guilt thinking about the stack of his mother's diaries on her dining-room table. *Should she say something?*

If you do, you'll never find out what happened to François or Evelyn's daughter, she told herself. Claire warred with her conscience. *These are his mother's diaries. They belong to Chuck now. You need to give them to him.*

I will. Not yet, though. Once I find out what happened to the love of Evelyn's life and her daughter, Lisette, I'll return the diaries to Chuck.

"Claire?" Chuck gave her an odd look.

"Sorry. I was wool-gathering."

Elinor growled.

"Stop that, Elinor," Claire scolded. She gave Chuck a rueful look. "I think someone's telling me she needs to go to the dog park. I'd better go."

Daphne took a deep breath and answered Rick's knock. "Come in. You want a beer? Soda?"

"Nothing for me, thanks, but you go ahead." Rick followed her into the kitchen.

Daphne opened a Stella and took a long drink. "So, Benny finally turned up, huh?"

Rick gave her a speculative look. "Yep. Like the bad penny he was."

"The news said a car went into the quarry—was Benny in the car?"

"Nope. The car had been used in a liquor store robbery earlier, then ditched by the robbers. Some of Glazatovsky's guys, we think. We're still sorting through the evidence." Rick sat on the couch, regarding his former partner perched on the edge of the recliner.

Daphne took another swig of Stella, her heart beating wildly.

"We think Benny might have been stuffed in the trunk, and the impact of the crash threw his body out."

"Seems plausible."

"Benny-boy was neatly wrapped up in a blanket and some carpet and placed inside a couple of trash bags, which seems appropriate," Rick added dryly. He stretched his arm out along the back of the couch atop Daphne's new Dodgers blanket. "We think whoever whacked Benny was a Dodgers fan, since that's the blanket he was wrapped in."

Outwardly, Daphne maintained her cool, although it felt as if her heart was going to explode from her chest.

Rick pinned his eyes on her. "Somehow, though, the sports blanket went missing from the evidence room. Magically disappeared into thin air." He flicked his fingers. "Poof."

"Is that right?"

"Yep. I can't figure out how that happened. The guys are getting sloppy, I guess. What I do know, though, is Glazatovsky has season tickets to the Dodgers." He gazed at Daphne. "He's almost as big a fan as you." Rick cleared his throat and stood. "You don't need to worry about Benny anymore, Daph. The guy got what was coming to him."

Home from walking Elinor, and with still no word from Daphne, Claire grabbed a handful of diaries, including the one from 1948 she and Atsuko had been reading together earlier. She set the small stack next to her wingback and resumed reading.

March 1, 1948

It is after midnight and I am still weak, but I have escaped from the convent. The nuns told me Mother would be returning today to take me home, so I had to leave before she arrives. I am returning to Paris and François. I will tell him about his daughter, and together we will find our baby girl. I fainted after Sister André took Lisette from me, and I tried to go after them. When I came to, Sister Marguerite, the midwife who had been so kind, was gone, and Sister

André was standing over my bed. She told me to stop being a silly girl, that my baby had been given to a good family, a married couple who had been unable to have children of their own. Sister André said I needed to forget about what had happened and be grateful my parents were still allowing me back into their home after the way I had shamed them.

I nodded and pretended to listen, all the while planning my escape.

Late that night, when the nuns were asleep, I slipped out the kitchen door and caught a ride into Paris with a farmer taking his vegetables to market. Once I got to the city, I went straight to Alain's apartment. Someone else was living there, though. The concierge told me Alain had moved out months ago. (Probably to a much better apartment with the money he'd gotten for betraying us.)

I was feeling weak and feverish, but knew I had to find François. I went to Montmartre to look for him. I asked the other artists if they knew where he might be, but they all shrugged and said, "Désolé." Finally, one of the older men told me he'd heard François had moved to the country with his family. He didn't know where, though.

When I heard that, I collapsed. How will I ever find my love?

I wound up in the hospital, drifting in and out of consciousness. That's where Mother found me. I had not escaped after all . . .

Tears pricked Claire's eyes. The following pages were blank until April.

April 3, 1948

I have not had the energy to write. It took me weeks to recover. Mother brought me back to Denver where I hoped there might be a letter from François waiting for me. I had given him my address and knew he would write or figure out a way to come and get me, and we would return to Paris. I can't wait to tell him he has a daughter—our beautiful Lisette. Together, we shall find her.

May 7, 1948

Still no word from my love . . . Where is François? Why doesn't he write? Father tries to comfort me, but Mother will not allow his name to even be mentioned. She hopes to wipe him out as if he never existed. But François does exist and so does my baby. Somewhere . . .

June 13, 1948

Weeks have passed and still no word. No letter. No phone call. Nothing. Was it all a dream?

September 1, 1948

It has been six months without a word from François. I have given up hope. Apparently, he did not love me as much as I loved him. Either that or his family somehow prevented him from communicating with me. Whatever the reason, my love is gone and so is my child.

My mother has destroyed my life. I have nothing left. Today, I packed a bag and left, telling her I never want to see her again. This time, since I'm of age, she couldn't stop me.

The tears leaked down Claire's face. She could feel the desolation in Evelyn's words. She wept for the young lovers and their lost daughter. There were no diaries again for five years. Not until 1953. Claire picked up the diary from that year, but the first few months were blank. Then she found a sentence that made her heart leap.

April 15, 1953

François and I have been reunited!

Claire gasped, skimming the entry. Evelyn wrote she had finally saved up enough money to return to France and resume the search for her daughter. In Paris, she had seen a painting of Montmartre with the artist's signature, François Dumont, in a small art gallery. Evelyn was examining the painting when a man's voice behind her asked if she liked it.

The man was François.

I couldn't believe it, Evelyn wrote. *I thought I'd gotten over my first love, the man who'd abandoned me. The man who never came for me. But the moment I looked into his eyes again, I knew I'd been lying to myself. François asked me why I never answered his letters. As we talked, I realized that once again Mother had kept us apart. François told me he had sent letter after letter to our Denver address. For six months, he said. Letters I never received.*

I told François he had a daughter, Lisette. A daughter with his blue eyes and black hair. Then I told him our daughter had been snatched from my arms and taken away. We wept together. François promised me, his petit choux, that we would find our child, as we'd found one another.

"Nothing will ever separate us again," he vowed.

Then my lover told me that after waiting more than a year to hear from me, he had at last given up, thinking I had rejected him and that he would never see me again. Surrendering to family pressure, he married the girl his parents had chosen for him all those years ago, his childhood friend, Colette. Then, in a halting voice, François revealed to me—the love of his life, the woman he thought he'd lost forever—that he had a two-year-old son named Jacques.

Oh, Evelyn. Claire's heart ached. She glanced at the mantel clock, knowing she had to meet Atsuko to rehearse her part in tomorrow night's scheme. She realized she'd have to save the rest of the diary for later. Before she left, though, she had to at least find out if Evelyn stayed with François.

Pulling the last diary from the stack—1960—Claire did a quick skim, relieved to discover the couple had lived together in Paris since they'd been reunited. They couldn't marry because Catholic Colette wouldn't give her husband a divorce, but Evelyn wrote that she didn't care. She and François didn't need to be bound by convention; they were together now and refused to let anything separate them ever again. The couple continued to search for Lisette, but still hadn't found their daughter.

Claire read the final entry.

November 12, 1960

My love is gone. François was killed in a car accident.

The writing blurred, the page splotched with tears.

Claire wept.

There were no more diaries until 1976. But Claire didn't have time right now to read anymore. Hurrying over to Atsuko's, she filled her in.

Atsuko's eyes filled when Claire told her about François. She sniffled. "I'm so happy they found one another again."

"Me too. Although it breaks my heart they only had seven years together."

"Better seven years than none. Those two were meant to be together. François was the love of Evelyn's life. Her soulmate. Not everyone is fortunate enough to experience that."

Claire side-eyed her friend. "And they didn't need a piece of paper to legitimize their love either."

"Point taken." Atsuko held up her hands in surrender. "Sorry for banging the marriage drum so loudly."

Both their phones pinged at the same time with a text.

DAPHNE: **Never fear; all's well that ends well. Elvis has left the building.**

Claire looked at Atsuko. "Does that mean what I think it means?"

Atsuko nodded. "We're in the clear."

Claire burst into tears.

Daphne gave them a *Reader's Digest* version of her conversation with Rick, omitting the bit about the Dodgers blanket. "Rest easy, girls, Benny Popov is out of our lives forever. Rick and the captain think he was stashed in the trunk of a stolen car used in a liquor store robbery last night—a robbery committed by some of Glazatovsky's goons, who then ditched the car in the quarry. There's no need to worry about Benny anymore—we got away with it."

"That calls for champagne," Barbara said.

Later, Daphne paid Claire a private visit. "There's no need to tell the others this, but I wanted you to know"—she pinned her eyes on her friend—"Rick vanished the Dodgers blanket Benny was wrapped in. I think he recognized it as mine and made the evidence disappear, figuring I offed Benny."

Claire gasped. "But you didn't. *I* did."

"You know that, and I know that, but Rick doesn't, so let's let sleeping dogs lie. No need to muddy the issue at this point."

Claire gave Daphne a speculative gaze. "He must care for you an awful lot to have done such a thing for you."

"You'd think so, huh?" Daphne's lip curled. "But if Rick cares for me so damn much, why the hell is he marrying Irina Glazatovsky?"

Late that night in her hot tub, Claire stood, letting the breeze caress her naked body. Sitting down on the flat ledge, she swung her feet over the side and reached for her robe—a luxurious white terry-cloth bathrobe like the ones the ritzy hotel spas provide. Pulling on the thick robe, she glanced down at her floral tattoo, recalling when she'd got it.

Claire had found out about Stan's latest infidelity, begun after she had come home from the hospital after her double mastectomy. Her husband refused to look at his wife's flat chest and sought comfort elsewhere. Something he had done throughout their marriage.

The first time Stan cheated on Claire, she had been heartbroken. She thought it was her fault. She hadn't been pretty enough or sexy enough to keep her husband from straying. Claire tried to become sexier for Stan, and it worked. For a while.

Until it didn't.

After years of Stan's cheating, she finally realized she wasn't the problem; he was. That's when Claire moved into the spare bedroom and the couple became roommates, staying married for the kids. After the children moved out, she remained in the marriage, afraid she couldn't make it on her own. She started taking steps to independence, though. Like getting her chest tattoo—

Elinor raced onto the patio from the bedroom where she'd been sleeping, barking up a storm and scratching at the fence. Glimpsing an eye between the wooden slats, Claire yelled, "Hey!" as she belted her robe. The eye disappeared, and she heard the sound of running feet as Elinor continued to bark.

From the patio next door, Atsuko yelled, "Claire, are you all right?"

"There's a peeping Tom out here." Stepping onto the metal patio chair, Claire peered over the top of the fence. In the moonlight, she caught the gleam of a shiny head before it disappeared around a corner.

Daphne's patio light went on. She peered up at her robe-clad neighbor, visible over the fence. "Claire? What's going on?"

"There was a bloody peeping Tom staring at me, but he's not going to get away with it. Come on, girl, let's get him!" Stepping down from the chair, Claire grabbed her phone and turned on the flashlight. Then, unlocking the gate, she let Elinor loose and ran after her.

"Hang on," Daphne yelled. "He could be dangerous."

But Claire was a woman possessed. Barefoot, she ran after her barking dog, the moonlight spotlighting her white robe.

Daphne, who'd been asleep in her t-shirt and flannel sleep pants, cursed and grabbed her glasses and her SIG. Opening her patio gate, she raced after Claire and Elinor, followed closely by Atsuko in a nightgown and red kimono robe.

Atsuko dialed 911 as lights began turning on all over Cedar Glen.

Elinor's barking grew more frenzied as she drew near Shirley Robinson's condo. Alerting at the door, she scratched at it and howled. Catching up to her dog, an out-of-breath Claire pounded on the front door. "Lenny Fink, show yourself! I know it was you."

Elinor continued to bark, and Claire continued to pound. When at last the door opened a crack, Claire reached down and scooped up her dog.

Shirley poked her bedhead out, clutching at her robe. "Claire, what on earth? It's the middle of the night."

"Lenny," Claire yelled into the condo, "you can't hide behind

Shirley this time. Now get out here and face the music, you filthy pig."

Daphne and Atsuko arrived with Daphne holding her gun.

Shirley paled. "What's he done now?"

"Your fiancé is a peeping Tom," Claire said. "He was staring through the fence at me when I got out of my hot tub."

Atsuko noticed movement at the back of Shirley's patio. "He's trying to make a run for it!" She shone her flashlight that direction.

"Don't even try it, Lenny," Daphne yelled, "unless you'd like to take a bullet to the gut."

"Don't shoot, don't shoot," the peeping Tom cried.

"Raise your hands where I can see them and walk this way," Daphne ordered. "Slowly."

Sirens blared as a sniveling Lenny made his way over to the former cop with the blue gun trained on him. "I'm sorry, I'm sorry," he blubbed, snot-nosed, a wisp of white hair blowing in the breeze.

"You *are* sorry," Shirley said. "A sorry excuse for a man, you pervert." Running to her fiancé in her quilted robe and curlers, she cold-cocked him.

The police appeared, and Daphne filled them in. After getting statements from a sobbing Shirley and Claire, who said, "I'm pressing charges," they arrested Lenny and took him away.

And Barbara slept through it all.

THIRTY-TWO

Cedar Glen was buzzing the next day.

Passing by Doris Franklin and George Hansen after grabbing a low-fat yogurt from the clubhouse, Daphne overheard their conversation.

"I told Shirley that Lenny was bad news, but she wouldn't listen," Doris said to George, her eyes sliding to Shirley's condo, where the curtains were closed.

"Poor Shirley." George clucked his tongue. "Lenny really fooled her. Fooled all of us. He reminds me of a guy I used to work with when I was a stonemason. Did I ever tell you about the time . . ." His voice trailed off as he and Doris made their way to the clubhouse, where everyone was gossiping and holding forth on the subject of Lenny Fink.

Everyone except Shirley and the Alphabet Girls, that is.

Shirley had not left her condo all day, refusing to come to the door for anyone. Mabel Brown set an eight-ounce box of See's truffles on her welcome mat, and Atsuko texted Shirley that she'd left a container of mochi outside her door. She warned Shirley not to leave the mochi out too long as it needed to be refrigerated.

Ten minutes later, when she passed by Shirley's condo, Atsuko saw an age-spotted hand slide out the front door and grab the mochi and chocolate.

Claire slipped away, needing to run an important errand. She pulled into the back of the abandoned strip mall on the outskirts of town, where the man she was meeting had instructed her to go. Two minutes later, a dark, nondescript car pulled up alongside her. The driver gestured for her to get in.

Claire took a deep breath and slid into the passenger seat. "Hello, Detective Bartlett."

"What's this all about?" Rick asked.

Claire proceeded to tell him what happened to Benny Popov, beginning with that fateful night when she saw the ex-con strangling Daphne and charged at him with a shovel, and ending with the Alphabet Girls dumping him in the quarry. "I didn't want you to think Daphne killed him," Claire said. "It was me, trying to save her life—I never meant to kill him."

Rick drummed his hands on the steering wheel. "Is that all?"

Claire nodded.

"Do you feel better now that it's off your chest?"

Claire exhaled. "Much. Ever since that horrible night, my conscience has been bothering me about what I'd done—I'm usually quite the rule follower, you see."

"Thank you for telling me." Rick gazed at her. "Now, leave well enough alone. This conversation never happened. Got it?"

Claire nodded and returned to her car.

"I can't believe I slept through all the excitement last night," Barbara said as the Alphabet Sleuths gathered in her kitchen to go over final plans for Operation Vince. "When I've got my earplugs in and my eye mask on, I'm dead to the world." Her eyes darted to Claire. "You sure you'll be up for this tonight? We can always reschedule."

"We're not rescheduling," Claire said. "I owe it to Evelyn. Her killer is still out there, and I have a sneaking suspicion it's Vince. I want us to get this guy and put him away."

"You did a good job getting Lenny last night," Atsuko said. "I don't think I've ever seen you run that fast, Claire."

"I don't know that I ever have, except for once when Grace was little and started to run to the street. That was pure fear, though," Claire said. "Last night, I was so ticked off, I wasn't going to let that creep get away with it."

"Did you know it was Lenny from the get-go?" Daphne asked.

"I suspected it might be. He's always been such a lech. And as Atsuko said, a leopard doesn't change its spots."

"What will happen to him, Cagney?" Barbara asked. "Will they throw his ass in jail?"

"Lenny did what is called peeking while loitering. It also comes under the heading of an invasion of privacy," Daphne explained. "That's a misdemeanor and punishable by up to six months in county jail."

"I hope the judge throws the book at him," Claire said.

Daphne regarded her. "Even if he doesn't, I don't think you'll have to worry about the perv showing his sleazy face around here again."

Claire raised her glass. "I'll drink to that."

Atsuko clinked her glass against Claire's.

Barbara's phone pinged. Glancing down, she pulled a face. "That's Vince." She read the text aloud.

VINCE: Hope we're still on for tonight, babe. Don't lump me with Lenny. Peeping is not my style.

Sighing, she texted back a reply.

BARBARA: I never thought it was. I'm looking forward to this evening, Vince. See you at seven.

"Time for your self-defense refresher, B," Daphne said. "Not that you'll need it, but just in case. Remember: focus on the vulnerable areas—eyes, nose, throat, and groin. You're going to want to use a heel-palm strike." She demonstrated. "Flex your wrist and either aim for his nose, jabbing upward from the nostrils, or underneath his chin, jabbing upward at the throat. Make sure you pull your arm back quickly once you do, though, because that will help thrust his head up and back.

"If he grabs you and is in too close range so you can't get enough momentum to throw a punch or kick, use your elbows," Daphne continued. "Bend your arm at the elbow, shift your weight forward, and ram your elbow into his neck, chin, or temple. This will make him loosen his grip and let you run." She eyeballed Barbara. "And if all else fails, jab your fingers into his eyes."

Two hours later, the B member of the Alphabet Girls began getting ready for her date, pulling out her pink minidress, white go-go boots, and windowpane stockings. *You can do this.* Barbara reminded herself that Daphne and Atsuko would be right next door in the empty condo, keeping watch, and Daphne would have her gun. Claire would be close by at the dog park with Elinor. *And you'll have your phone on the whole time, so the girls can hear what's going on. Plus you've got that can of Mace in your purse. You're good.*

Barbara ran through Daphne's self-defense demonstration in her mind as she finished applying her makeup. Sticking the food and wine in the insulated bag, she zipped it closed. At the last minute, she grabbed her Barbie and dropped the doll in her pink purse alongside the Mace. Taking a deep breath, she texted the girls.

BARBARA: On my way.

Then she headed to Vince's.

Earlier that day, Daphne had talked Connie into giving her the key to the empty condo next door to Vince's. "I need to use it for a stakeout," she told the manager.

"Shouldn't the police do that?"

"I'm working with the police," Daphne lied. "Undercover. They asked for my help."

"OK, but please don't make a mess. I'm showing the condo to a prospective buyer first thing in the morning."

Daphne hadn't told a complete lie. She'd texted Rick, wanting to give him a heads-up.

DAPHNE: Got a minute? Something to tell you.

He replied immediately.

RICK: Sorry, D. Something big going down.

Daphne scoped out the empty condo to get the lay of the land. Happy to see the curtains in Vince's condo closed, she inserted the key in the lock of the vacant property and went inside. Canvassing the empty rooms staged with minimal furnishings, Daphne realized it was one of the larger condos: three bedrooms and two baths.

She stepped out on the kitchen patio, noting the locked gate. Then she headed to the patio off the master bedroom, crossing her fingers. As she'd hoped, the patio did not have a lock on the gate. Some owners didn't bother with locks on the bedroom patio, wanting quick and easy access to the nearby swimming pool and not wanting to have to bother with keys. Daphne tested the gate to see if it squeaked. When it did, she left it partway open so she and Atsuko could slip through it tonight if they needed to without making a sound.

"Hell-o? Anyone here?" Doris's voice sounded from inside the condo. "Show yourself, or I'll call the police. We don't hold with burglars and peeping Toms around here."

Daphne hurried into the living room where Doris's fingers were poised over her phone. "It's only me."

"What are you doing skulking around in here?"

"I'm not skulking." Daphne held up the key. "I have some friends who are looking for a condo with three bedrooms," she lied, "and Connie said I could check it out and let my friends know if I think they'd like it." Ushering Doris to the door, she locked up behind them.

"Well?"

"Well what?"

"Do you think your friends will like it?" Doris asked.

"What's not to like? Actually"—Daphne lowered her voice—"if *I* could afford it, I'd sell my place and move in here. It's got so much space. Great view of the swimming pool too."

"I've never been a swimmer. I don't like chlorine."

Daphne led Doris away, feigning an interest in her mindless chatter.

Atsuko placed the fragrant sandalwood on the coffee table next to the small ceramic container, admiring her latest ikebana arrangement of bamboo grass and chrysanthemum as she did so. Returning to the kitchen, she put on the kettle.

She did a few stretches to limber up. Then she made herself a cup of green tea. Carrying the tea to the living room, Atsuko lit the incense, closed her eyes, and began to meditate.

While she waited for the evening's activities to get underway, Claire pulled out Evelyn's next diary and began flipping through it. The first entry came in June.

* * *

June 20, 1976

I can't believe it! After all these years, I've found my daughter at last! The first time I met our new gallery attendant, newly married to the Devereaux's son René, I felt a shock of recognition. That cloud of curly black hair and eyes the color of the ocean. I told myself there are plenty of blue-eyed, black-haired French girls. But then this lovely young woman, this new bride recently immigrated from France, turned her head, and I glimpsed it; the small, bean-shaped strawberry birthmark.

And I knew it was my Lisette. Even though she had a different name.

Remy DuBois's words echoed in Claire's head. She recalled the director of the Devereaux Gallery saying she'd come to America in the summer of 1976. Snatches of their conversation came back to her. "America's bicentennial and the year I got married," Remy had said of when she'd arrived in the U.S. "A time of celebration for your country and for me as a new bride, embarking on a new career as an art gallery attendant . . ."

Gallery attendant. *Oh my God*, Claire thought. *Remy is Lisette, Evelyn's lost daughter!* The realization sent her reeling. *And Remy doesn't know. Why didn't Evelyn tell her?*

Her phone alarm chimed. *I can't think about that now, though; I have to get into position for Operation Vince.* Clipping on Elinor's leash, Claire hurried outside.

Barbara cooked steaks in a cast-iron skillet while Beach Boys music played in the background.

Vince, clad in '60s chinos and a brightly striped shirt, sat at his retro kitchen table, gazing at the woman of his dreams over a glass of wine. "Do you know how long I've dreamed of this moment?" he said. "I can't believe you're here at last." His eyes took in Barbara's go-go boots and minidress. "You haven't aged a bit. Still as gorgeous as the first time I saw you."

"Well, aren't you the sweetest thing?" Barbara laid the Southern accent on thick. Her eyes slid to the locked door next to the living room. *Is that where he keeps the drugs for Dmitri?*

Should I hint I'd like to get high after dinner, or would that tip him off I'm on to him?

"When are you going to show me what's in your secret room, Vince?" she drawled. "I'm dying of curiosity."

"I'm saving that for dessert." He winked. "I think you're really going to like it."

"As long as it doesn't have too many calories," Barbara teased. "I have to keep my girlish figure, you know."

Vince poured another glass of wine. "Your girlish figure is perfect. Don't you worry; I promise you won't gain an ounce from the dessert I've got waiting."

Listening next door, Atsuko looked at Daphne and shuddered. "That guy is so creepy. Are you sure Barbara's safe alone there with him?"

"Absolutely." Daphne checked her phone. "In another minute, Claire will be stopping by with the excuse we cooked up. That will let lover-boy Vince know B's friends are aware of her whereabouts, which will make him think twice about trying anything." She patted her SIG. "Also, I've got this bad boy close at hand. If anything starts to go down, we'll be there in a flash, and I'll get the drop on Vinnie boy."

Claire hurried to the dog park with Elinor. She'd texted Mark earlier and set up a play date with Brontë. Daphne had made her promise not to let Mark know what was going on.

"The fewer people who know about this, the better," she said. "We've got this covered, Claire. The Alphabet Sleuths are on the job."

Brontë wagged her tail when she saw Elinor, scampering over and giving an excited yip.

Mark's mouth curved as he watched the two dogs frolic. "I'm glad they're friends now. Brontë was so excited to come play with her pal."

"Elinor, too," Claire said, distracted.

"Are you all right, Claire?"

"Sorry, I've got a lot on my mind." She was waiting for her phone to buzz to give her the signal to head to Vince's. Glancing at the two pups playing together, she smiled. “They’re having a blast, aren’t they? I’m so glad Brontë’s gotten over her fear of other dogs.”

“I wouldn’t go quite that far. She still freaks out when she sees a big dog. Little steps, though. Right?” Mark smiled.

“Uh-huh.”

Mark cleared his throat. “Claire, I was wondering if you’d like to take the dogs for a long walk together—along the river perhaps. We could have a picnic and make a day of it. What do you think?”

What do I think? I don’t know what I think. Are you asking me out?

Flustered, Claire reached in her pocket to check her phone for the time.

Only her phone wasn’t there. She gasped.

“What is it?” Mark asked. “You OK?”

“I left my phone at home. I need to get it. I’m, uh, expecting an important call. Would you mind watching Elinor for me? I’ll be back in a few minutes.” She sped away.

Mark stared after her. He gave a rueful look to the two dogs. “What do you think, guys? Was that a no?”

THIRTY-THREE

Barbara peeked at Vince's vintage Kit-Cat clock on the kitchen wall. *Where the hell is Claire? She should have been here by now.*

Vince's eyes narrowed. "Got somewhere to be?"

"No, I was simply admiring your clock—I used to have one like it back in the day. It's so cute." Barbara made her eyes big as she looked around the great room. "You've got so many cool vintage items. I especially love the surfboard. Takes me back to my beach days."

Vince puffed out his chest. "Thanks, babe. It's been a while since I've surfed, but those sure were the good old days, weren't they?"

"The best." Barbara thought back to those days when she'd lived on the beach in a bikini. Her fingers involuntarily crept to the invisible stomach pooch. *Bikinis don't work with Spanx, though.* She released a sigh of regret.

Daphne echoed Barbara's thought. "Where the hell is Claire?"

"I'll text her," Atsuko said.

ATSUKO: Claire, where are you?

Opening her blue door, Claire hurried inside. Then she stopped, realizing. *Did I forget to lock the door again?*

"Hello, Claire." Chuck Blair stood up from the wingback in front of the fireplace.

The wingback that had concealed him from sight.

Chuck held one of his mother's diaries in his hand while his other hand clutched a bottle of vodka.

Claire let out a cry, her hand flying to her chest. "Chuck, you gave me a fright. What are you doing here?"

Evelyn's son cocked his head at her. He closed the distance between them. "You really should lock your door, Claire," he said. "Anyone could get inside. Lots of unsavory people out there."

Claire's mouth went dry as she saw the diary in Chuck's hand—the last diary she had been reading. The one where she realized Remy DuBois was Evelyn's daughter.

Chuck's bloodshot eyes glittered. "I see you've found out about my bastard sister."

Claire's heart scudded. She took a step back, feeling with her hands for the doorknob behind her, wishing her guard dog was with her. Elinor would have made mincemeat of Evelyn's son. Or at least, raised the roof in her attempts to do so.

"That's not very friendly, Claire," Chuck said. "Don't leave so soon. You just got here. I want to have a little chat with you. After all, I gave you my mother's entire library. The least you could do is give me a few minutes of your time."

Atsuko looked at Daphne. "Claire's still not answering. Something's wrong. You hold down the fort. I'll be right back." She ran out the door.

Vince stood, offering his hand to Barbara. "That was a delicious meal. I didn't know you could cook too. Aren't I the lucky guy?"

"I'm glad you liked it."

"And now, it's time for dessert." Leering, the aging surfer took Barbara's hand to lead her to the locked room.

"Wait a sec. Let me get my purse." *Claire, where are you?*

"You don't need your purse."

Yes, I do. It's got my Mace and my phone. The girls won't be able to hear what's going on. Barbara reached for her pink handbag.

Vince's eyes narrowed. "I said you don't need it."

Giggling, Barbara plucked out her doll. "I only wanted to get my Barbie. See, she's wearing a pink minidress like mine. You're not the only one who likes vintage. I've had this Barbie since high school." Smiling, she waved the doll back and forth. "Isn't she the cutest thing?"

"She looks like you," Vince said. "Same great body and

hair." He licked his lips. "OK, girls, let's go have dessert and a little entertainment. Trust me, you're going to love this."

Atsuko raced to the dog park where she found Mark watching Elinor and Brontë as they played. "Where's Claire?" she asked.

"She forgot her phone and went home to get it." Mark frowned. "She should have been back by now, though."

Atsuko's Spidey-sense started tingling. She grabbed Mark's hand. "Come on."

"What's going on?"

"I'm not sure," Atsuko said, "but I think Claire needs us."

Claire and Atsuko, where the hell are you? Grabbing her gun, Daphne headed to Vince's.

THIRTY-FOUR

Vince opened the locked door with a flourish. "Ta-da!"

Barbara gaped as she looked into a mirror from her past. The walls were papered from floor to ceiling with photos of her from her modeling days. She clutched her Barbie, feeling sick. Turning slowly, she squealed.

"Do you like it?" Vince's eyes shone.

Barbara found herself face to face with a life-size cardboard cutout of herself in a bikini. The pink bikini she'd worn in the dance scene from *How to Stuff a Wild Bikini*.

"I–I don't know what to say." *You sick, twisted mother—*

Vince jerked his head behind him. "Check it out." He beamed.

The entire wall was a homage to the 1965 film. Original movie posters plastered the wall, along with stills of the cast and blown-up black-and-white prints of Barbara's face.

"The first time I ever saw you was in that movie," Vince rhapsodized. "You were the most beautiful thing I'd ever seen. I watched the movie over and over again just to see you. When you moved into Cedar Glen, I recognized you immediately. I came back here and stuck my old VHS copy into the DVD/VCR player, hitting pause when I spotted you."

He goggled at Barbara. "That's her all right, I told myself: same long legs, same great figure, gorgeous face, and beautiful blonde hair."

Gripping her Barbie, Barbara put some distance between herself and her adoring fan. She examined the photos of Annette Funicello, Dwayne Hickman, and Mickey Rooney, remembering back to when she'd made the movie. Annette had been a sweetheart—pregnant during filming and having to conceal her pregnancy. Frankie had hardly been in this last installment of the popular beach movie franchise, and the aging star from the Golden Age of Hollywood was always trying to cop a feel from the girls.

"I've probably seen *How to Stuff a Wild Bikini* more than a hundred times over the years," Vince said in a dreamy voice. He sang a snatch from the Kingsmen's "Give Her Lovin'" that had played in the film. "My first VCR tape broke, so I had to get a new one a few years ago. They don't have this on DVD."

Where the hell is the cavalry? Barbara wondered. She felt queasier by the moment, but warned herself not to show Vince how much he was creeping her out. *Let him think you're flattered.* She knew Daphne and Atsuko couldn't hear anything anymore since her phone was still in her purse in the other room. *But won't the silence tell them something's wrong?* Barbara continued making her way down the wall.

Come on, Alphabet Sleuths, get over here!

She stopped in front of a life-sized black-and-white photo of herself from the film, noticing the hot-pink bikini attached with pushpins over the black-and-white swimsuit. Barbara turned to Vince, who appeared beside her, eyes wide. "Is that—"

His face flushed with pride. "The exact bathing suit you wore in the movie. I got it on eBay." Bouncing from foot to foot and drooling at the object of his obsession, Vince removed the bikini and slid his tongue over his lips. "You're going to put this on for me, beautiful Barbara. And then the party will really begin." Pinning her against the wall, he reached down to lift up her dress.

The hell you say.

"Oh no, I'm not." Realizing she was on her own, and no help was coming, Barbara kneed Vince in the groin. Then she raised her Barbie and slammed the doll into his face, going for the eyes.

Vince yelped.

Daphne erupted into the room, gun in hand. "Get away from her, you creep!"

"No worries, Cagney," Barbara said as Vince whimpered. "I got this."

"You have children, don't you, Claire?" Chuck took a gulp of vodka as he viewed the smiling family photos on the living-room wall.

Claire swallowed over the dry lump in her throat. "Yes. A son and a daughter."

"And do you love your children?"

"Very much."

"I'll bet you're a good mother, aren't you?" Evelyn's son took another swig of vodka.

"I try to be."

"And because you're a good mother, I'll bet you plan to share your estate equally with your children—isn't that right, Claire?"

She swallowed hard. "Chuck, you're upset. Why don't you let me make us a nice cup of tea, and we'll sit down and talk?"

He ignored her and took another drink. "What if one of your children—say, your son maybe"—Chuck pointed the bottle at Douglas's picture—"went through his whole life thinking he was your sole heir, entitled to inherit your entire estate." He began to pace. "And then, one day out of the blue—as you're approaching the end of your life, for instance—you inform your son he is *not* your sole heir."

Shoving his hand through his hair, Chuck glugged some more vodka, growing increasingly agitated as he continued to pace. "You tell your son he has an older sister he never knew existed. An illegitimate sister. A bastard." He stopped in front of Claire, spittle in the corners of his mouth. "One you are going to leave the bulk of your inheritance to, because your son—your *legitimate* heir—already received a large inheritance from his father."

Chuck glared at Claire through bloodshot eyes. "How do you think that would make your son feel? Don't you think it would make him angry?"

Claire nodded, trying desperately to recall Daphne's self-defense instructions.

Chuck's eyes narrowed. "Especially if you never liked your son. Never loved him the way a mother should love her child," he raged.

Feeling his spittle land on her cheek, Claire winced.

Chuck continued to rage. "If you dismissed your son and discarded him because he was like his father, your husband—a man you never loved either. Wouldn't that make your son angry?" His eyes were wild and unfocused. "So angry he snapped and killed his own mother." Chuck lunged at Claire, grabbing for her throat.

Bursting through the door, Atsuko drop-kicked Chuck with a combination Judo–Tai Chi kick.

Mark let Elinor and Brontë loose, and they swarmed the fallen man, barking and biting.

Hugging one another, the Alphabet Girls watched as the cops took Vince and Chuck away.

"Well, this was certainly a night to remember," Claire said.

Atsuko puffed out a breath. "One for the history books. That makes three bad guys in a row we've cleared out of Cedar Glen."

Barbara pumped her fist. "Alphabet Sleuths rock."

Daphne nudged her. "Sorry your Barbie got ruined, B."

"That's OK." Barbara shrugged. "After tonight, I think I'm past the age for Barbie dolls."

The girls stared at her.

"And what age would that be, exactly?" Atsuko asked innocently.

"I may be giving up Barbie, but that doesn't mean I'm giving up everything."

"Can we take this inside?" Claire asked. "I don't know about you, but I need a drink."

"A cup of tea?" Barbara said.

"Screw the tea; I want a double margarita," Claire said.

Daphne grinned. "I'm down for that."

A familiar car pulled into the parking lot. Detectives Bartlett and Miller exited, approaching the four women.

"Are you ladies OK?" Jessica asked, hurrying over to Claire and Atsuko.

"We're fine, dear," Atsuko said. "Thank you for asking."

"Where've you been, Bartlett?" Daphne asked. "You missed all the action."

"We had some action of our own keeping us busy." Rick nodded at his partner.

"Let's give Detective Bartlett and Daphne a minute," Jessica said. "Maybe we could go inside and have a nice cup of tea?"

Laughing, the three Alphabet Girls led the detective into Claire's condo.

Daphne rolled her head to get a crick out of her neck. She'd forgotten how tense things could get when you were trying to snare a perp. *Even more tense when it's your best friend in danger.* "What's up?" she asked her former partner, trying and failing not to notice how good he looked in his khakis and snug polo shirt hugging his abs.

Rick couldn't meet her eyes. He scuffed his foot on the ground. "I wanted to tell you personally, Daph, before the news broke." Finally, he looked up and said, "We busted Dmitri Glazatovsky and his crime family tonight. We've been working with the Feds for the past couple of years to bring him down."

Daphne felt as if she'd been kicked in the gut. "*What?* Why didn't you tell me?"

"I couldn't. Dunlap said we had to keep things close to the vest. I couldn't tell anyone."

"But I was your *partner*. Your friend."

"I know." Rick's jaw worked. "It killed me not to tell you, but Dmitri was suspicious in the beginning. It took us a long time to build his trust and make him think the captain and I were on the take. The Feds told us how we had to play it."

Daphne pushed down the bile she felt rising in her throat. "Did anyone else in the department know?"

He shook his head. "Only me and Dunlap."

She stared at him. "And Irina?"

Rick flushed. "Irina was our entry point. Our contact on the inside. She keeps the books and knows everything. Her father trusts her completely." His mouth twisted. "Well, *trusted* her. That will change soon when he finds out she's turning state's evidence to avoid a lengthy prison sentence. That's why Irina and I had to fake a romance, to get Dmitri to trust me."

Daphne's head spun. She couldn't take it in.

"But I gave up my career." She removed her glasses with a

shaking hand. "I thought you were bent. You and the captain both."

Rick gazed at her, eyes full of misery. "I know. Captain Dunlap's going to be calling you. He tried to keep you on the force by giving you a desk job and offering you stress leave. He didn't want to lose you, but—"

"But I stuck to my principles."

Rick closed the distance between them. "I'm so sorry, Daph." He tried to embrace her.

Daphne held up her hand and stepped away from the detective, shaking her head. "I can't do this. Not now." She dashed her hand across her eyes and put her glasses back on. "Two of my friends were traumatized tonight. One by a murderer and the other by a sicko with a twisted obsession. I need to be with them."

She walked away.

THIRTY-FIVE

"How does it feel to be seventy, Claire?" Daphne asked as music filtered into Atsuko's dining room.

"No different than sixty-nine. I'll let you know if that changes, though." Claire took a bite of her salmon. "This is delicious, Atsuko. What a fabulous birthday meal. Thank you so much."

"Seneca said, 'Let us cherish and love old age; for it is full of pleasure if one knows how to use it,'" Atsuko said serenely.

"Who the hell is Seneca?" Barbara asked.

"A Roman philosopher and contemporary of Jesus."

"Of course he is," Barbara turned to Claire. "Have you heard from Remy lately?"

"Yesterday, as a matter of fact. She called to tell me Evelyn's headstone will be finished in a couple of days. She'd like to have us all over for lunch soon and take us to the cemetery afterwards."

"Remy seems to have adjusted to the idea of Evelyn having been her mother," Atsuko said. "I remember what a shock it was to her at first."

"Well, sure," Daphne said. "You go your whole life thinking you know who your parents are, and then, in your seventies, you find out you're adopted and the woman you thought was your friend turns out to be your birth mom. That's pretty intense."

"She's been reading Evelyn's journals, and she understands why her mother never told her who she was," Claire said. "Apparently, Evelyn wrote that when she first met Remy, Remy told her how much she adored her parents, how kind and loving they were. She said they'd given her the perfect childhood—reading her bedtime stories every night, taking her on adventures, encouraging her interests, always making her feel safe and secure."

Claire gazed at her friends. "Remy told Evelyn her mother and father were never too busy to make time for her, unlike many of her classmates' parents. She also told Evelyn that when she got married, she kept her last name, because she was the last living DuBois, and when her parents died, she didn't want their name to die out with them."

Barbara took a drink of her wine. "They sound like an amazing couple."

"Which is why Evelyn chose not to tell Remy she was her daughter. Evelyn could see how much Remy adored her parents, and she didn't want to do anything to destroy that bond—to spoil her relationship with her parents. Evelyn wrote that simply being in her daughter's life, getting to know her and her granddaughter, Fleur, was enough."

"Pretty cool of Evelyn," Daphne said.

"Evelyn was a cool woman. Ahead of her time in many ways." Claire sipped her wine. "She led a fascinating life. Remy and I have been talking about that, having now read all of her journals. Fleur read them too, and loved them. She told her mom they should consider publishing some of her grandmother's journals so other young women can read them and be inspired."

"What a great idea!" Atsuko said. "Evelyn was quite the storyteller. She kept me on the edge of my seat, wondering what was going to happen with her and François."

Claire set down her wine glass. "Me too. I was so happy when I found out they were reunited and that Evelyn got to live with the love of her life at least for a few years." She thought about Mark and how he'd had forty years with his wife, the love of his life. And how, after such a terrible loss, he had opened himself up to the possibility of another relationship by asking her out. *Who knows where that might lead?*

She gave herself a little shake. "Enough about all that, though." Claire turned to Daphne, who had dropped twenty pounds and started jogging with Barbara. The D Alphabet Girl looked happier and more alive than she had in a long time. "What I want to know is how things are going with Rick."

"OK." Daphne blushed. "Captain Dunlap apologized,

explaining why he and Rick couldn't clue me in on the Feds' investigation. He said he felt terrible losing one of his best cops. He even offered me my old job back, but I told him I have other irons in the fire now."

"Would those irons by any chance be the Alphabet Sleuths?" Barbara's eyes gleamed. "You ready to become a PI, Cagney?"

"Could be. We'll see. And as for Rick, after I got past the hurt and betrayal of everything that went down, we are now resuming our friendship. We're taking it slow, though."

B snorted. "I'll say. I keep telling Cagney she needs to make it friends with benefits, but she won't listen."

"Don't go there," Daphne warned.

Barbara turned to Claire, a gleam in her eyes. "And how about you and that handsome handyman? I know you're friends, but have you taken it to the friends-with-benefits stage yet?"

"Don't go there," Claire said.

Atsuko clapped her hands. "Time for presents." Pushing herself away from the table, she returned moments later with a large box she set in front of the birthday girl. "Or, rather, I should say *present*, singular. Claire, this is from all of us."

"Thanks, girls. Before I open my gift, though, I want to say that no gift could be better than the gift of your friendship. We've been through a lot together, especially these past few weeks, and the three of you mean the world to me." Claire gave them a tremulous smile.

"Ditto," Atsuko said.

"Don't go all sappy on us now," Daphne said. "Hurry up and open your present so we can have cake."

"OK." Tearing off the wrapping paper, Claire opened the box and pulled out tissue paper. "I wonder what it could be." She pulled out more tissue paper. And more. She side-eyed the girls. "Is this a gag gift?"

"Keep going," Atsuko said. "You're almost there."

At last, Claire pulled out an envelope from the bottom of the box.

Daphne bounced on her heels. "Open it, open it,"

Claire did so, pulling out four airline tickets.

Barbara whooped. "We're going to London, baby!" she said. "With a side trip to Paris."

"Not only London," Atsuko corrected. "All over England. Wherever you want, Claire. Your favorite spots in Great Britain, for as long as you want. These are open-ended tickets. We're all retired; we can stay as long as we want. Mark said he'll watch Elinor for you."

"You know what I said about no gift being better than your friendship?" Claire said. "Scratch that." With visions of England filling her head, she mused, "Who knows? Maybe the Alphabet Sleuths will have to do a Miss Marple while we're in the UK and solve a mystery in a small English village."

"Preferably one with a hot vicar," Barbara said.

Acknowledgments

> "In the end, it's not the years in your life that count. It's the life in your years."
>
> —Abraham Lincoln

A book is never a solitary endeavor. Particularly this one.

For much of my writing career, one of my dearest friends (and former editor), Lonnie Hull DuPont, often served as the first reader for the initial chapters of my books. Lonnie was my biggest cheerleader and champion of my writing. We met at a writer's conference years ago after fourteen male editors had rejected my non-fiction book, *Thanks for the Mammogram*, because they—or their higher-ups—were uncomfortable with the idea of b-b-breast cancer and humor.

Lonnie, who had a great sense of humor and the best laugh of anyone I've known, loved my book proposal and sample chapters, but suggested I write a few more chapters before she pitched it to the editorial board at her publishing house to ensure I could continue the humor throughout. That was the beginning of a wonderful editorial relationship and a beautiful friendship that lasted nearly twenty-five years. Sadly, I lost my beloved, irrepressible friend to a rare cancer much sooner than any of us expected while writing *The Alphabet Sleuths*.

I had told Lonnie my latest idea and sent her the first paragraphs of the first draft (which later changed drastically), and she said, "I like Claire already. Good job!" That was the last feedback my longtime friend and mentor gave me. As Lonnie's health began to decline on the other side of the country, I wrote like the wind, hearing her voice in my head, spurring me on. I wound up finishing the first draft of this book the day my dearest friend died, which I found fitting.

Then, I fell apart.

Lonnie died ten days after my beloved Aunt Sharon, who had been in my life since my Wisconsin childhood and had become almost a second mom to me. Sharon was one of the most joyous women I've ever known. Like Lonnie, she also had a delightful laugh and a fabulous sense of fun. So. Much. Fun. We laughed like crazy whenever Sharon came to California to visit. And now, these two joy-filled women—the women who meant the most to me in the world (after the death of my mom), the ones who brought such love and laughter and encouragement to my life—were both gone. Within days of one another.

I was bereft. How could I go on without them?

How could I write without Lonnie's encouragement, cheerleading, and stellar editorial feedback? As I grieved these devastating losses, I lost my confidence and my writing mojo.

Thankfully, others stepped into the breach.

Huge thanks to my dear friend Cheryl Harris, who read chapters as fast as I wrote them and asked for more. Thank you, Cheryl, for loving my Alphabet Girls and for laughing along with them. You're the best. I owe you a drink.

Thanks also to writer friends Edith Maxwell, Grace Topping, Jennifer Morita, Penny Manson, and Kim Orendor, who kindly read early chapters and gave me constructive feedback and suggestions. A special shout-out to Grace for going above and beyond and rereading my reworked first chapter multiple times. Thanks, Grace. You're a peach. Thanks as well to longtime friend Hannah Gleisser, who read the reworked first two chapters when I begged her to and lived to tell about it.

A tip of the baseball bat to Kim Orendor for the Dodgers suggestions and vetting the sports stuff for this non-sporty woman. Any fouls are my own.

A special thanks to James L'Etoile for answering my police-and-gun-related questions and vetting those scenes while in the midst of his own deadlines. Any mistakes are mine.

Props to pals Jane Firebaugh, Dave Meurer, and Sandy Munro, who graciously read the entire book, cover to cover, in an early iteration and gave me the brutally honest feedback

I needed. *The Alphabet Sleuths* is now the book I wanted it to be, thanks to their helpful comments. I owe you.

A special shout-out to Laura Kujubu and Jennifer Morita, who read early chapters to ensure the character of Atsuko was true to her Asian American heritage. Thanks, guys. (And Jennifer, I'm thrilled that your fabulous mystery debut, *Ghosts of Waikiki*, is now in bookstores!)

A massive debt of gratitude to my dear friend, Catriona McPherson, who, at the eleventh hour, when she was in Scotland and I was a grieving, neurotic mess, generously read the first reworked (again-and-again) ten pages and pinpointed the difficulties I was having clearly and succinctly. The moment I received Catriona's insightful comments, I thought, *Ah, of course*, and fixed the problems. Thanks to her, I got my writing mojo back. Catriona, I owe you a great dinner—cooked by Michael, of course.

Thanks to my fabulous agent, Vicky Weber at CMA, and to Rachel Slatter at Severn House for falling in love with my Alphabet Sleuths. I'm delighted to be a part of the Severn House family—with added thanks to Sara, Tina, and Katherine. Special props to Jet Purdie for the great cover.

As always, my heartfelt gratitude to my Renaissance man Michael, my partner-in-life, for listening as I read countless scenes aloud and heard what didn't work. (Important tip for novice writers: always read your work aloud before turning it in.) Thanks also for laughing out loud at the funny bits. How lucky am I to have you in my corner? Thanks, too, for loving to cook and keeping me well fed. Shut the door.

Note to readers: I wrote the Barbie-loving Barbara long before the *Barbie* movie juggernaut arrived.

[illegible] The *Alphabet* [illegible] is now the book it is, and it [illegible] thanks to their helpful comments. I love you.

A [illegible] shout-out to [illegible] and [illegible] [illegible] early chapters to ensure the character of [illegible] was true to her [illegible] American heritage. Thanks, [illegible]. And [illegible] I'm thrilled that your fabulous mystery [illegible], *Ghosts of* [illegible], is now in bookstores!

A massive debt of gratitude to my dear friend, [illegible] McPherson, who, at the eleventh hour, when she was in [illegible] and I was [illegible] [illegible] and [illegible] pages and then [illegible] difficulties I was having clearly and succinctly. The moment I received [illegible] thoughtful comments, I thought, [illegible] and fixed the problem. Thanks to her, I got my writing [illegible] back. [illegible] I owe you a [illegible]

Thanks to my [illegible] agents, [illegible] at [illegible] and to [illegible] at Severn House for falling in love with my Alphabet [illegible]. I'm delighted to be a part of the Severn House family [illegible] thanks [illegible] Special [illegible] the [illegible]

As always, my heartfelt gratitude to my [illegible] my partner-in-life, for [illegible] [illegible] and [illegible] He always reads my work [illegible] before [illegible] Thanks [illegible] and [illegible] Thanks [illegible] [illegible] Stuart [illegible]

[illegible]

[illegible]